and they had a great fall

and they had a great fall

A NOVEL

SHELBY SAVILLE

SHE WRITES PRESS

Published 2025

Printed in the United States of America

Print ISBN: 978-1-64742-846-4
E-ISBN: 978-1-64742-847-1
Library of Congress Control Number: 2024923089

For information, address:
She Writes Press
1569 Solano Ave #546
Berkeley, CA 94707

Interior design and typeset by Katherine Lloyd, The DESK

She Writes Press is a division of SparkPoint Studio, LLC.

chapter one

Jake Laurent forgot how to be afraid. It was the one thing his director wanted from him, and he couldn't convey even this most basic emotion. He tried to channel the dread pooling in his stomach into his performance, but even that wasn't working. He inhaled deliberately to slow his heart palpitations as his mind raced. This was the big one—the most commercial film he had ever done. The one that would catapult him to megastardom. The one with Garren Christensen, an Oscar-winning director. The one he was screwing up.

"Jake, you're up," called the assistant director motioning toward the cameras. Jake took another deep breath to stamp down the panic rising in his throat and reminded himself this was the last scene of the day. Garren just needed him to run up a steep hill and look afraid. *This should be easy*, he thought to himself. *Why isn't this easy? What the fuck is wrong with me?*

Garren walked over as they were finishing the final camera placements. "We're going to CGI the Hunters in later. I need you to convey the absolute fear that, if caught, these monsters will literally tear you apart. Make sense?"

Jake nodded and cleared his throat. "How many will be chasing me? Are they right behind me, or down the hill a bit?" He looked down the hill to visualize where to look when he turned around. He wished for visual cues or at least other cast members to help his performance. He was just starting to realize how hard it was to act to eventual CGI.

"They're about three feet away," he said. "So, they aren't right on you, but you wouldn't have time to pause when you turn around. Got it? We have to go . . . now."

Jake walked over and took his mark. He tried to summon the Hunters from a deep multiverse, along with the terror they would cause. It still wasn't coming to him—in fact, he couldn't focus on anything but the deafening ringing in his ears. The last few weeks had not been going well. It was clear in rehearsals that he was not giving Garren what he wanted, but he'd hoped it would click when they actually started filming. It didn't.

Garren yelled "Action!" and Jake sprinted up the hill as if his life depended on it. He threw a look over his shoulder to see what was behind him, contorted his face attempting to communicate sheer terror, and then finished his run. Garren yelled "Cut!" and Jake walked back down the hill.

"Hey," Garren started, "your run was perfect." Then he paused. Jake had seen that face before. Garren was displeased.

Jake looked at him and furrowed his eyebrows. "But. . . ."

"When you turn your head around, you need to look terrified. You looked . . . bored. At best, you are giving me annoyed."

Jake could hear the frustration in his tone. He'd been hearing it for days. He let out a sigh and nodded. He understood the directions but didn't understand how he was expressing "bored."

"Stupid face," he muttered as he walked over to his mark to start again.

Eleven takes later, his legs were burning, and he wished for this night to be over.

"Dammit. Reset and try again," he heard Garren yell. Jake could hear murmurs from the crew. One hundred people were working late just because he couldn't get a fucking glance right.

He took his time walking down the hill, stalling. Jake was beginning to think Garren was going to punish him and make him run up that hill ten more times, even if he nailed the next take.

"Sorry, sorry," he said, putting his hands up to indicate that he did *not* want Garren to give him any notes.

"Listen," Garren said, the tension evident in his voice, "we're going to do a take where you don't turn around. It's late, we're running into overtime, and I need to get this crew off the clock. We'll try to work it out in editing."

Jake felt his hands shake with nervous energy and exhaustion at the same time. He felt small for the first time since he'd stepped onto his first movie set at a mere fifteen years old. Performing was the one thing that came easily to him, but not on this film.

At least this was the last take, and he could go back to his trailer, clean up, and go to his temporary apartment. Alone. He took his mark and waited for Garren to call, "Action." For the thirteenth time, he sprinted up the hill, this time without looking behind him. About two-thirds of the way up, his legs gave out and his knees buckled. He let out a loud grunt and somehow kept moving forward, scrambling rather than running. At the top of the hill, he hung his head.

I can't even get this right, Jake thought to himself. *I almost fucking fell.* He turned around to face the tired, overworked crew and the director who just wanted a good, seven-second scene from his lead actor.

Garren, however, was all smiles and gave Jake a thumbs-up as he ran up the hill. Jake met him halfway. "Yes Jake," he said. "That's what I wanted. You embodied the fear with that fall and grunt, and that desperate scramble to get away. Really nice way to play the scene."

Jake just gave him a weak smile and a quick head nod. He didn't have the heart to tell him it was an accident.

He felt Garren's hand grip his arm, pulling him to the side before they reached the crew. Jake reluctantly turned to face the man he was desperate to impress. Garren spoke first. "This is what I need, Jake. You are the lead and the entire film rides on the audience believing in you. When I watch you through the lens, I can see you're holding back and it's not working."

Garren's eyes were fixed on Jake, and he couldn't look away. He let out a sigh. "Yes, I know I'm not connecting the way I want," he said. "I'm trying to figure it out. Maybe I'm having trouble acting to nothing. I think the heavy CGI is tripping me up." He put his hand up quickly to dismiss the comment before he let on the extent of his inexperience. "Actually, no, that's no excuse . . . I will figure this out. I'm sorry. . . ." Jake hung his head and slowly shook it side to side, trying to come up with an explanation of what was going on in his mind, and why he couldn't translate it to the character. He wasn't used to being a disappointment.

"Jake," Garren started. His tone softened. "Go back to the book, the source material. Get connected to your character. Take a minute to understand Tom and what makes him tick. It boils down to a simple arc of an unexpected hero."

Jake gave him a slight nod of understanding but didn't speak. Garren returned to his commanding tone. "After we finish out this week, I'm giving you a few days off. We are moving things around and shooting material that will not require your presence."

Jake raised his eyebrows. "I'm that bad? You're shooting around me?" He knew he wasn't feeling it but was he *that* terrible? He believed the next day or scene would be the one where he'd find his groove. He could feel panic rising back up in his throat. He swallowed hard to keep from vomiting.

There was an uncomfortable pause before Garren responded. "I thought starting with your scenes first would give the CGI artists enough time. But we're moving at a snail's pace, and we'll run out of budget if we keep this up. I need to get this film on track in less than a week—before the other principles arrive. If we don't get on schedule, I'll be forced to make another plan."

Jake opened his mouth to ask him what he meant by *another plan*, but before he could get any words out, Garren was pulled away by the assistant director. He watched Garren and the AD walk away. Crew swirled around him as he walked back to his trailer. Despite being surrounded by people, he'd never felt more alone. He yanked open the door, stormed inside, threw his phone on the table, and collapsed into a chair. He was officially freaking out as his mind raced through potential scenarios. He knew in his gut what *another plan* could mean. *What if he fires me*, was a question on repeat in his mind.

He glanced down at the table and his eyes landed on a magazine with his picture on the cover. He scoffed when he read the text just below his smiling face. "An up-and-comer leading the future generation of entertainment." He picked up the magazine and threw it across the room. It made a satisfying clang as it hit the trash can. *If they could only see me now*, he thought. *This is the most important film of my career, and I'm completely fucking it up.*

When Kat Green opened her eyes, she was disoriented at the darkness of her bedroom. *Why is my alarm going off?* she wondered. *It's too dark for morning.* She tried to refocus her brain to orient herself. Her eyes landed on her phone, which was now illuminating the room like a flash of lightning. It wasn't her alarm. She grabbed the phone off the nightstand and her heart raced. *Middle of the night phone calls are never good.* As she swiped to answer, she saw Jake's name lighting up her screen. That realization did little to calm her nerves. Kat answered, sleep heavy in her voice. She barely said "hello" before Jake's voice burst on the call.

"Hey. Shit, you were sleeping, I didn't think about the time. I'm an ass. Of course you are asleep. I didn't wake Becca did I? What time is it anyway?"

"Whoa . . . can you slow down, Jake?" She asked him, rubbing her eyes as if she could forcefully eliminate the slumber fogging her thoughts.

He began again, at the same speed, without taking a breath. "I needed to call you. I know it's been a while and I'm sorry. I feel like you're ignoring me. But . . . I think I just needed to hear a familiar . . . no, not just that, I needed to hear *your* voice. I know I'm not making much sense . . . Damn, I don't make sense to *myself.* I'm not okay. I mean, I *am* okay, like not in trouble. I'm just struggling here in this goddamn city, on this goddamn movie, with this goddamn director. Well it's not the director, he's great. I'm not . . . I suck . . . I'm not sure why I called . . . well, yes, I *do* know. I guess I'm hoping and asking . . . can you come here? I need something . . . *someone*, I think . . . I need *you*."

Kat leaned back against the pillows. She had trouble processing how sad and small he sounded. Although she recognized his voice, this didn't sound like Jake. The Jake she knew was confident—sometimes maddingly so—charming, and full of life. She'd once called him the human equivalent of Friday.

"Jake," she started, speaking in a whisper so as to not wake her daughter, Becca, who slept next to her. She adjusted the covers as she sat up and rubbed Becca's back when she stirred. She marveled at how such a small human could take up so much space in a king-size bed.

She tried to refocus her tired brain. "You're asking me to come see you? Where? Are you back in New York?" *He must be in New York if he's asking me to come see him*. Her brain couldn't keep up with him. She had no idea what city he was living in at the moment.

"Right. That would help. I'm shooting in Denmark. In Copenhagen. I've been here for a few weeks. I passed the

PathMobile office last week and thought of you. You haven't left my mind since."

For a moment it was silent. When he finally spoke again, his voice was low and quiet. "Kat, I miss you. I wish you were here. I want you to be here. With me."

"You want me to fly thousands of miles to Denmark?" she asked, suddenly getting clear on what he was asking her. She almost laughed but the fragility in his voice stopped her. It was clear he was dead serious. "What's happened? Are you okay?"

"Honestly, I don't know if I *am* okay," he said. "All I know is I need you. I feel . . . I need you."

Hearing the phrase "I need you" surprised her and she sucked in a sharp breath. By his own admission, he never "needed" anyone. And neither did she. She'd always felt comfort in the want and desire she felt with Jake, but him throwing need on her was brand new. She felt unsettled in the pit of her stomach, but she tempered her unrest by reminding herself that she was talking to Jake. By now, she should be used to his flair for the dramatic—it frequently manifested itself in a barely controlled panic. In the past, it humored and charmed her; in the middle of the night, it unnerved—even irritated—her.

"I don't see how . . . Jake, it's a lot to ask. Insane . . . even for you. And last time—" she started, apprehensive about his ask. The last time they'd tried to meet up, she'd rearranged her entire schedule to return early from a business trip while Jake was on a rare visit back to New York. She'd landed only to find out he'd already left the city. She'd never felt so stupid.

"I know. I said I was sorry," he interrupted. "I hate that we still aren't talking. This is different, Kat. I wouldn't have called if I wasn't serious."

"The timing. . . ." she said, beginning to process what he was asking. "Becca starts kindergarten in two weeks, and PathMobile is finalizing the virtual assistant launch. This is a big launch and

I'm in charge. Everyone is watching . . . including our COO, who's looking to recommend his replacement to the board when he retires, and—"

"Wait. Kat. Is that another promotion? Are they considering you?" Jake asked, jumping in, sounding more like the Jake she knew. "That's incredible. Damn." He paused. "I get it. It's too much to ask. I'm an idiot. I just feel so lost here and. . . ."

"Jake, I can't figure this out at 4:15 in the morning. Give me tomorrow—I mean today, to think about it." She didn't like to operate on the spur of the moment and this request made her mind race. She couldn't believe she was actually considering it. *Why am I considering this*, she chastised herself. *This is not possible and definitely not a good idea*. She most certainly would not be running to Denmark to reignite a casual affair that started during the pandemic lockdown and ended silently due to time, distance, and, frankly, Jake's inability to prioritize anything above his own schedule.

Once they hung up with a promise to connect later in the day, she knew she wasn't going back to sleep. She scooped up Becca and carried her back to her own bed. At five years and ten months old, she was getting almost too heavy for Kat to carry. *She's getting too old to keep sneaking into my bed*, Kat mused. She took great care not to wake her as she covered her with her favorite unicorn blanket.

She padded through the dark to the living room and flopped down on the couch. The silence in her apartment was deafening. She had gotten used to being alone at night since the day her husband, Ben, had taken his final breath. It had just been her and Becca from that day forward. Becca filled her life in ways that gave her a specific kind of parental joy, but at night, the silence persisted.

She had lived in silence at night for four years until she'd met Jake, the only son of her next-door neighbors. He'd been home for a rare, extended period of time when the entire world locked down due to a global pandemic. Once they'd met, their relationship moved unexpectedly fast. He was so different than her. He was impulsive and impatient and lived his life out in the open; she found solace in control and privacy. Beyond the contrast in their approach to the world, there were nearly eight years of age separating them. His twenty-five-year-old expectations lived in stark contrast with her thirty-three-year-old perspective. When Jake had gone back on location a year ago, she'd lived again in the silence.

Kat hugged her knees to her chest, took a deep breath, and realized her face was wet with tears. His call *had* rattled her. On top of her frayed nerves, she was tired of hearing a roaring silence and feeling alone. She hadn't let herself think about how much she missed the energy Jake had brought into her life. Until tonight.

He was asking her to go to him. What did that mean to him? What did it mean to *her? Jake means complication and messiness*, she thought to herself. To say Jake was complex didn't begin to describe him. It wasn't just that *he* was complicated; his *life* was complicated.

Why did he call me? Why now? What are we? When he'd left, they had agreed not to put a definition on what they were to each other. To define it would be to put it in a box, full of expectations neither of them could sustain. Kat's only priorities were her daughter and career. She did not have room for the complication of a relationship—especially with someone with a life and schedule as unpredictable as Jake's. She refused to confuse Becca, who was already growing up without her father. Kat wouldn't have her daughter define her life by father figures who left her. In turn, Jake admittedly was not prepared to add consistency to a fully formed life such as Kat's. So, they kept just far enough away so as to never acknowledge anything other than the moment they were in. Him calling tonight and "needing her" was decidedly different.

She looked out the window at the city lights and let an exasperated sigh. She was annoyed at her inability to stop obsessing about his phone call. Why was she even still thinking about this? *It didn't make rational sense, and there was no way to figure out how to swing a trip right now, of all times. It was unfair of him to ask*, she concluded as her irritation became tinged with anger. When her phone alarm blared again, she pushed the call out of her mind. She would text him later in the day to let him down as easy as possible.

chapter two

Kat opened her closet, pulled out running clothes, and prepared to start another normal Tuesday. Since Ben's death, she'd gotten very good at singularly balancing the logistics of their household with the unrelenting demands of her job.

Kat had skillfully optimized her morning routine down to the minute:

> 6:15: Wake up Becca, help her get dressed, and feed her a healthy breakfast (usually Greek yogurt and berries).
>
> 6:45: Uber to Becca's Montessori preschool two miles away (the best on the Upper West Side).
>
> 7:15: Drop Becca off and run home, detouring through the winding paths of Central Park. This was an efficient way to both fit exercise into the mornings and catch up on the latest industry podcast. Today's selection was an interview on CNBC featuring the CEO of PathMobile.
>
> 7:35: Shower, first coffee of the day, a banana and an organic granola bar.
>
> 8:15: Walk to the office, pick up a second coffee.

Having perfectly executed the morning, Kat continued her walk to the office. She went to resume the CNBC podcast from her run, but instead, she found herself scrolling through her library on Spotify. She clicked on the playlist titled "Kake." She couldn't remember the last time she'd listened to music, much less *that* playlist, which during lockdown, had been on perpetual repeat.

She let out a small laugh as she remembered Jake creating it during the pandemic. Just as the title blended their two names, the content combined his music taste (hip-hop with a side of R&B) with hers (unapologetically pop). Each song was a different style, but all fun, playful, and sexy—a perfect amalgamation of their time together during quarantine. The memories lifted her steps, and she walked into the office with a larger-than-normal smile on her face.

She was usually at her desk before 8:30, and today was no exception. She scrolled through her emails and took a sip of her oat milk latte with one-third of a packet of raw sugar.

An internal IM popped up, its window covering part of her email. It was from William, the current COO of PathMobile. *Looks like you're in the office. Swing down.*

She picked up her coffee, laptop, and phone and walked a few offices down, opening his glass door when he waved her in. "Good morning, Will," she said, sitting in the chair across the desk from him. She opened her laptop in preparation for the impromptu meeting.

"Morning," he replied, looking up from his computer. "How's the launch of the PVA going?"

PVA was the internal name for the Path Virtual Assistant, a product launch she had led for the past six months. She knew the project and timelines inside out and pulled up the project plan that was live on her laptop.

"It's going according to plan. We're preparing the website for pre-orders in just under eight weeks, November first. Teaser marketing will start one week prior. We'll be in stores and online by Thanksgiving. Our television spots are flighted mid-November through December, with a spike on Black Friday." She rattled the details off with confidence. "Current US sales projections are 24 million units this year, 25 percent of which are projected to be pre-orders, with the rest during the holiday surge."

"Wonderful," he said. "As long as we stay on this timing, this is going to be the biggest launch Path has ever had. And your leadership has been exceptional. You know I'm retiring after this launch?"

"And it will be a sad day for all of us," she said with a smile. She liked Will and would genuinely miss his mentorship. She was not surprised as he had informed everyone that he would move to part-time status at the end of the year and fully retire before the end of Q2.

He returned her smile. "My wife won't be sad. Nor will my pickleball game." He closed his computer and looked at her. "I need to give the board options for my successor at the next meeting. I'm putting your name down for consideration."

This was always the plan. Will had put her in the product position as a fast track to a potential COO role, but now, hearing it out loud, she swelled with pride. If this happened, she would be the first woman to hold a C-suite position at their company.

She deserved this promotion. She had spent the last year doing anything needed to make sure that every device, every app, and every accessory they launched was flawless. It had required her to work nearly fifteen hours a day, including weekends, often logging time into the wee hours after Becca went to sleep.

All those hours would finally pay off. Not only in elevated title, but the new salary would allow her to stop worrying about her and Becca's future. Good schools were not cheap in Manhattan, and she would finally have an assurance that she could give Becca the best. This was hers to lose. The last hurdle was getting the nod from the board.

"How many options will you give them?" she prodded. She figured there would be more than one and had already hypothesized who she was competing against. She worked harder than most at her level, but high-profile C-level positions were not necessarily given to those who worked the hardest, or even those with the most talent. Reputation and relationships were driving factors, too.

Will laughed. "You're the first to ask that question. You always know your numbers, Kat. Three. I have to give them at least three. If *I* could choose, it would be you."

"Thank you," she said. "So, what do you think will sway the board one way or another?" She appreciated Will's vote of confidence, but she knew the board didn't know her as well and would evaluate her differently.

"There's a big thing in your favor, and two things against you," he started. "The big thing in your favor is the PVA launch. It's as high-profile as it gets, and we're at the tail end. If it hits the projected units on time, it'll show the board your ability to run a tight, profitable organization."

Kat nodded. "And what are the two things against me?"

"One is experience. You are one of the best product leaders we've ever had. Your ability to align departments and put them on a simultaneous plan toward a singular end goal is unmatched. But you are still very young. The two other candidates have many years on you," Will said.

Kat went to protest—at thirty-three, she wasn't that young. Plus, her age shouldn't be an issue if her skills are exceptional—but Will cut her off. "That's just reality, Kat. You *are* young. Also, you have far less global experience than others they will be considering."

Kat nodded. Although she had some global experience, Will was right, she was primarily focused on the US market.

"Frankly, I'm kicking myself. I should've had you oversee one of the global early-launch markets. Seeing how smooth the US is going, you could have easily done the US alongside a regional market like Ireland or Denmark," he mused. "It would have set you up well for the board nomination."

Kat looked up at the ceiling for a second and took a deep breath. She would never call herself spontaneous, but this might be her only chance to prove to Will that she would do whatever it took to get the COO nomination.

She blew out her breath and asked, "What if I went now? I saw the timelines for Denmark in our last global call. Aren't they the first market going live with pre-orders? I can assist in their pre-launch, monitor impact of their regional marketing tactics, and optimize the US launch." Although Path's corporate headquarters were in New York, the company had been founded in Denmark, and Kat impressed herself at her own quick thinking. She would get the most credit for visiting that office.

He chuckled. "You're always on your toes. That's not a half-bad idea." Will hesitated and then spoke, "You would have to go immediately. Is that feasible?"

"There are a few things I have to coordinate, but it should be possible," she said, thinking of Becca. She couldn't commit on the spot and the pressure of being a working mother loomed over her. She wanted to prove she could pivot at a moment's notice, though, even when it meant unplanned travel. She'd been counseled more than once to be more spontaneous and less rigid—mostly by male counterparts without the sole responsibility of a young child at home.

"Kat, I love the idea, but I can't look like I am playing favorites and sending you out of the blue," Will mused.

"You don't have to be the one to send me. I'll go on my own. Logistically, this works out perfectly. I've been planning a trip to Copenhagen to see a friend right after our November launch. I can just move the trip up a month. You wouldn't have to get travel approved. It's already booked." She cringed at her uncharacteristic white lie. She hated lying about as much as she hated being spontaneous. "All you're doing is approving for me to work remotely from the Copenhagen office."

She paused and watched Will's face process her proposal. "Please Will," she said, "let me do this. It's a good idea, and it gives me a chance to prove to the board that I have more dedication than anyone."

"Okay Kat. I'll approve your request to work remotely. Ten days. I need you back here focused solely on the US before October first. I'll call Poul, the Denmark regional president, and let him know you're coming. By the way, he's a personal friend of our founder, so Poul is a good person to impress. You keep focused, use the global early launch to make the US even more successful, and your case will be practically flawless to the board." He stood up, indicating the meeting was over.

Kat walked back toward her office, picking up her pace when she got out of Will's view. *Shit.* She needed to work fast. Although this wasn't the first time she had to arrange last-minute travel, it unnerved her all the same. Her first call was to Linda, Kat's mother-in-law . . . or ex-mother-in-law. What do you call your mother-in-law after your husband dies? She still didn't know and had never brought herself to Google the answer. Becca's grandmother—that's what she called Linda.

"Hi Kat!" she answered cheerfully. Linda sounded out of breath and Kat could hear dogs barking in the background.

"Sorry to bother you so early," Kat started.

"No worries. I am out in the garden pulling weeds. Easier to do it in the morning while the ground is wet. It's beautiful today, how's the city?"

Kat had little time for small talk and spared no time asking Linda if she could take Becca to upstate New York while Kat went out of town.

"Of course. We love having Becca here. . . . she's starting to remind me so much of Ben." Linda stopped talking, and Kat heard the hitch in her voice. Kat remained silent. She couldn't do this . . . she couldn't talk about Ben . . . not right now. After a moment, Linda continued, "You've been traveling a lot for work, Kat. I don't know how you keep it up."

"It's part of the job. I'm working toward a promotion next quarter," Kat said, internally cringing when she calculated the amount of time Becca had spent with Ben's parents in the last six months. "It will mean increased international travel."

"*More* travel?" Linda asked and Kat's shoulders tensed. She held back her anger at the need to justify herself to a woman she barely knew. They would be forever connected through death, but their relationship since Ben's death was through Becca. They were little more than acquaintances. She was closer to many colleagues than her own mother-in-*something*.

"With this promotion, I can finally pay you back for the apartment," she said, keeping her voice steady. "I know I ask a lot; I can hire help if this is too much." She was steeped in guilt over the burden she put on Ben's parents. She was a constant reminder of the son they'd lost, and it ate away at her.

"Kat, stop," Linda interrupted. "I've told you before, please don't worry about paying us back and no, you don't need to hire help. We are always here when you need us," her voice was devoid of the earlier cheerfulness. "Text me your flight time, and I will come get Becca for as long as you need."

Kat was relieved when she could hit "end" on the call with Linda. She pushed it to the back of her mind as she went to her last stop. Emily Meyer, President of Product, was Kat's second-in-command. Emily would need to take a larger role with the on-the-ground US teams while Kat worked out of Denmark for ten days. Kat had no doubt Emily could handle the role. Emily knew the job and did it with the same precise efficiency as

Kat. *This will be a good challenge for her*, she thought. Emily was just waiting for the day when she would have Kat's position, and instead of a competitive relationship, they made a good team.

"Great idea to see an early-launch market," Emily said off-hand. "Things are fine here. We don't even need you." She winked at her, teasing. "I'm guessing this has to do with you being named COO next quarter?" Emily was fishing, but Kat didn't bite. If Kat became COO, she would recommend Emily for a promotion into Kat's job. A lot was riding on the launch, for both of them.

Kat kept them focused on the task at hand. "Let's go through the status of each departmental workstream today at 1:30 so we're both in the loop. I'm worried about the design and marketing departments. They say they're on track, but I saw an email last night about a delayed video creative. Marketing is notorious for missing our deadlines," she said as she left Emily's office.

As Kat walked down the row to her office, it finally hit her. She was indeed going to Copenhagen. *This is the best decision for my career and for Becca*, she convinced herself. That shiny brass ring was right in front of her, and she was grabbing on with all her might.

As she settled in to review the marketing plan, she was interrupted by her text chime. She glanced down to see Jake's number pop up on her screen. She stifled a smile as she swiped open her phone to reply. *Going to Copenhagen has nothing to do with Jake*, she thought as she typed confirmation that she was coming. *It's not about hearing his voice last night . . . and most certainly not about how much I've missed him.* Her heart raced and she set her phone face down on her desk. She buried her head in her hands and whispered to herself, "What the hell am I doing?"

chapter three

Under seventy-two hours later, Kat woke with a start as the plane touched down in Copenhagen. She stretched her legs, took in a deep breath, and ran her fingers through the tangles that had formed in the back of her hair. The eight-hour-and-fifteen-minute flight from New York to Copenhagen had been a special form of drudgery, especially stuck in the middle seat of row 27.

As the plane taxied to the gate, she switched her phone off Airplane Mode. She wasn't surprised to see texts from Jake. Five, to be exact.

J: Hi!

J: Glad you got on the plane okay. Not sure if you have your phone on? Probably not. Sleeping? Doubt it if you're in coach (why didn't you let me book the flight? I would have put you in first class . . . duh).

J: Anyway . . . I wish you would let me pick you up (really). I have good disguises. It's better here than in the US. Less paparazzi fuckers.

J: Shit. I'm going to be late. We have night scenes to shoot tonight. You get in at 7? I'll be home around 9. My keypad entry is 7302. Text me if you didn't write down my address.

J: Can't wait to see you. Might be closer to 10. Not sure.

She let out a laugh at his flurry of texts. He was a lot to take in all at once: brilliant, manic, confident, and unsure, all rolled up in one person. She wouldn't deny how excited she was to be in the same orbit as Jake, even for just ten short days. After a year of dwindling texts, video chats, phone calls, and any other way of staying connected without actually connecting, she didn't know how she would feel when she was in the same room as him. Until he'd called, they hadn't had any contact in over four months. During the flight, she couldn't stop wondering why Jake was so troubled, and, after all this time, why hers was the number he dialed.

She walked at a brisk pace through the Copenhagen airport and barely looked at her phone as she shot off a quick text to Jake.

K: Just off the plane. No rush. Do what you need to get done. See you at your place later.

Next, she texted Linda, letting her know she'd arrived safely. She reconfirmed Becca's bedtime. The grandparents indulged Becca far more than Kat did, and Linda let Becca stay up way too late. She could at least remind Linda of the rules and ask her to try to keep Becca on schedule. She glanced at her watch once she was through customs and immigration: 7:35 p.m. She gave herself an internal high five for how fast she could navigate an airport.

She'd prearranged a car to take her to Jake's temporary apartment. Kat handled all her own logistics for her peace of mind, because although Jake had the best intentions, his schedule was not his own. It didn't take her long to locate the driver holding up an iPad with her name on it.

He looked surprised. "You were fast!" he said, eyeing her single carry-on suitcase. "Welcome to Copenhagen. Do you need to grab your bags?"

She shook her head. "No, I always carry on. This is it." She didn't trust the airlines enough to ever check a bag. Too risky.

The twenty-minute ride from the airport to Jake's apartment gave her enough time to call Becca. As FaceTime connected, she could overhear Becca's sweet voice negotiating with Linda to hold the device by herself.

"Hi, Momma!" she said, her face peering into the camera.

Kat waved to Becca with her free hand. "Hi Sweetheart!" she said. "Are you having so much fun at Grandma and Grandpa's?"

Becca nodded with the unbridled enthusiasm of a five-year-old. "We had lunch. It was fun do!"

Kat looked into the phone, scrunching up her nose. "What?" she asked. She heard Linda giggling and saying "fondue" in the background.

"Oh, fondooo," Becca said, correcting herself. "We ate with fairy forks. I want to use them for every meal," she said, referring to the fondue skewers. She held one up so close to the camera it took up the entire screen. "This is my favorite. The purple one." Kat was not surprised. A meal consisting of cheese and bread would appeal to any almost six-year-old, especially her imaginative, sweet girl, who turned skewers into fairy utensils.

Kat felt a twinge of guilt that she was gone. She knew it was entirely self-inflicted, but the twinge was there. It settled Kat to hear her voice and know that Becca was bubbly and happy and any angst about them being apart was solely felt by the mom and not the child. "So, honey, what are you going to do the rest of the day? I mean, the fairy forks sound amazing, not sure your day could get any better," she teased.

"Mini golf!" Becca exclaimed. "Oh, goodbye Momma, Daisy needs me." And with that, she thrust the phone to Linda and ran after their dog.

Kat spoke to Linda for a minute and reminded her of the chemical-free sunscreen in Becca's suitcase. The fall sun could be harsh, and Kat didn't take any chances. Hitting "end" on her phone, she tucked it in the pocket of her light jacket.

As she rode through the city center, Kat leaned her head back on the soft, leather seats as she gazed out the window. This was not her first time in Copenhagen; she had visited as a stop on her honeymoon with Ben almost seven years ago. Kat had insisted on seeing Copenhagen to visit the birthplace of PathMobile, a company she had just joined and where she wanted to build her career. Nostalgia crept in as she once again saw the vibrant city, the colorful buildings, and the steady stream of bicycles that flowed through the streets.

It was a beautiful autumn evening, and the air had a crispness as the cooler weather of fall was beginning to peek around the corner. The city felt alive and seemed to infuse its inhabitants with its own vibrancy. She was struck by how it directly contrasted with New York City, which was chaotic, tough, and sometimes soul-sucking, giving credence to the idea that "if you can make it there, you can make it anywhere," as if a city was something to be survived. She was taken by how Copenhagen looked clean and sparkling, so different from the raw landscape of Manhattan. The copper spires and cobblestone streets appealed to her in a way that metal and asphalt never had. Kat had wondered if being in Copenhagen on her honeymoon had made her romanticize the city, but even today, she felt the same magic.

The car pulled up to the address Jake had texted her, a bright yellow, three-story building near the Nyhavn canal. It was connected to other buildings, green and blue, and looked like a façade of a movie set. It looked like the kind of place Jake would choose—creative, offbeat, in the thick of the action, but with zero pretension.

She tipped the driver, walked into the building, and realized it was a walk-up with no elevator. She threw on her backpack, picked up her single roller bag, and started climbing the stairs. By the time she got to Jake's floor, she was thankful she'd packed light. She found 3F at the end of the hall, typed the code in the keypad, and turned the heavy handle to open the door.

She flipped on the lights, and the first thing she noticed was the classic Danish architecture—clean lines, functional, and bright. There was a small kitchen that opened to the living room, which was painted with a bright geometric pattern. In any other place, it might look garish, but here, it added an artistic charm. She rolled her suitcase down the hall and saw the open door to his bedroom, with triangular ceilings mimicking the roofline. Large skylights poured moonlight over his unmade bed.

She let out a sigh and looked around. What she saw gave her an insight into Jake's life at the moment. His apartment was a disaster. It wasn't just the disarray, but despite living there for three weeks, it was clear that he hadn't moved in. A suitcase bursting with clothes sat in the corner of the en-suite bathroom, a mountainous pile of sneakers resided near his closet, take-out containers filled his trash, and books were scattered across the kitchen table. Actually, books and drawings covered most of the tables. She chuckled to herself. It screamed Jake, bursting with light, color, and chaos.

Jake stole a glance at his phone for the tenth time that day. He told himself it was to check the time, but it was really to see if Kat had texted him again. He read her last text: "No rush . . . see you at your place. . . ." Kat had a way of making it clear that she didn't really need him—or anyone, for that matter. Didn't need him to pick her up, didn't need him to tell her how to get to his place, didn't even need him to be there when she arrived in a foreign country. If it were Jake, he would've had a whole team to help him. *Not Kat. She seems to always have everything under control*, he thought.

He still couldn't figure out how to move through the world with her kind of calm rationality. He felt an overwhelming sense of life coming at him, and it simultaneously terrified and thrilled him.

But today, nothing thrilled him, and he wanted it to be over. They were finishing a list of over-the-shoulder and long-range shots, none of which required any acting. It only required him to stand still or hit a mark, like a prop. He believed Garren was punishing him for his shitty work these past few weeks by making him stay this late and do these shots. A stand-in would do this grunt work, but they had changed the schedule and his stand-in was not available until the following week. Jake's stomach dropped and his anxiety heightened as he thought about the new shooting schedule.

Garren finally called "cut" for the last time that night. Some of the crew clapped. No one liked the tedious process of pickup and bridging shots, and they'd been at it for hours. Garren called out to say goodbye and that one of the production assistants would send a new schedule in a day or so. He sounded light, but Jake knew enough about filmmaking to know a schedule change was always a big deal.

Shit. It was late. Much later than he'd predicted. Kat was at his apartment, probably pissed. He had asked her to come but hadn't expected her to actually get on a plane and show up. But she had. And for her first night ever in Copenhagen, he'd made her hang out in his messy apartment. Alone. While he was in the middle of the worst job of his life.

Kat looked at the time on her phone. After taking a quick shower and unpacking her things, it was already 11:15. Jake was later than she'd expected. With Jake not home, she was relieved to get some time to concentrate on work. She had a crushing amount of email piled up from the hours she was in flight.

She set her laptop on the kitchen counter and laid eyes on a small bag sitting by the far edge. She pulled off a note with her name on it, written in Jake's unmistakable scrawl:

Kat,

I remembered you like black licorice (which, btw, I think tastes like day-old coffee grounds left in the trash). It's a big deal in Denmark. The store said it was called "zoute drop" and it's salted black licorice (which, btw, sounds worse . . . like you found aforementioned coffee grounds and accidentally spilled salt on them), but . . . regardless . . . enjoy. See you soon.

—Jake

She laughed as she read his note. She could hear his voice giving her a hard time for her love of the often scorned, bitter candy. Kat pulled out a cellophane bag tied with a silver ribbon, opened it, and popped one of the deliciously salty, bitter nibs in her mouth. She took her time chewing the sticky candy, delighting in the extra sharp flavor.

She settled in and opened her laptop. She was ready to wind down, and work was the best way she knew how. She was not embarrassed to admit, while other people might unwind and relax with a book or movie, she enjoyed a good spreadsheet. Numbers were absolute. She understood them. Analyzing numbers to find efficiencies, patterns, and opportunities was her own form of meditation.

It was barely 5:00 p.m. New York time, but since it was a Friday, Kat didn't want to keep the team for long. They worked through the unit projection spreadsheet from the sales team, and eventually the only person left on the line was Emily.

Kat opened a bottle of wine she had bought at a shop on the corner and poured herself a glass. When she'd first arrived at Jake's apartment, she'd realized that not only was it a mess, but the only things in the fridge were some condiments and milk, and the pantry only contained various protein powder and bars. She assumed he must be doing some physical transformation for this film. It made her curious about the movie being filmed and the role he was playing. After taking stock, she rushed down to Kihoskh, a wine and convenience store on the corner, before they closed for the evening. This was her routine whenever she was traveling, and this would be no different. She took a sip, forgetting she was on video.

"Ahhh, that looks good!" said Emily still typing. "Oh wait, what time is it there?"

"It's 11:22 p.m. here. Late. But I haven't adjusted to the time change. It usually takes me at least forty-eight to seventy-two hours before I feel normal." She leaned back in her chair. "Emily, it's Friday. Get out of there. Enjoy your weekend."

"Yes, I'm leaving soon. Hey, looking at your background, where are you staying?" Emily asked. The question was innocuous, and Kat answered jumped in with a quick answer. "A temporary apartment. It's right off the canal. It's nice." She left out the detail of exactly whose apartment it was.

Emily stopped typing and looked into her screen. "Nice. And when do you meet the Denmark team? Will you see them this weekend?" Kat knew Emily was just making friendly conversation, but the questions were beginning to unnerve her.

"I'll see them on Monday. I'm visiting one of my friends this weekend. They're working in Copenhagen as well," Kat said, trying to keep her tone light and casual. She didn't want to completely lie to Emily, who she counted as one of her few friends, but she also didn't want to cause more questions.

"Interesting coincidence," said Emily, raising her eyebrows.

Kat cut her off before she could say more. "Yes. I was going to come in November, post-launch, but I moved it up to observe the Denmark pre-order period. It made it easy to say yes at the last minute. I can work, but I can also see my friend while they're still here."

"Interesting pronoun, too, Kat," Emily said with a wink. "Want to tell me about this 'they' mystery person?"

Kat laughed and shook her head. "Go home, Emily. Have a good weekend." She and Emily were friends, but Kat was still the boss. She never knew how much of herself to reveal and always erred on the side of not sharing at all.

Once the call ended, Kat worked on her final emails and refilled her wine glass. She was just about to text Jake and see if he was okay—he was rarely on time, but this was late, even for him—when she heard the keypad beep. Her stupid stomach fluttered, realizing he had arrived.

chapter four

Jake burst into the room with a flourish, and Kat's face erupted in a smile. Video chats and phone calls over the past year had made it easy to forget how she felt when he was mere feet from her. *He is so damn beautiful,* she thought. She silently cursed her body as she felt an instant attraction.

He was nearly a head taller than her five-foot-four frame and had a mop of dark, almost black hair that had a personality of its own. She remembered how his curls could at one moment be perfectly coiled around his face and another minute be facing the sky, which just added to his unpredictable charm. His eyes were a shocking light gray with a hint of green. They had a coolness and depth that unsettled her when he fixed his gaze on her. His nose was lightly speckled with freckles so faint they didn't show up on screen. In person, his face looked eternally sun kissed.

His features were sharp and angular; in certain perspectives, he almost had a hint of unattractiveness, but on screen, it was captivating. When you saw him through a camera, you could get lost in him, which is one of the reasons he was crowned the "it boy" of the moment. When he came on the big screen, she felt as if his presence altered the very air of the theater.

As he walked toward her, Kat could not take her eyes off him.

Jake breathed out a sigh of relief when Kat smiled as he walked through the door. He'd admonished himself the entire way home for not being there when she arrived. He couldn't keep from picturing her look of disappointment.

Seeing her smile, he realized his anxiety was unnecessary. Once again, his worry and stress were self-created. It was common for him to navigate stories and scenarios in his head, none of which were based in reality. His mom used to beg him to "stay in the real world, *ma belle conteuse*"—"my beautiful storyteller," she liked to call him. Living life with every emotion always just under his skin, ready to burst to the surface at any minute, was useful to a working actor, but confusing and brutal to a teenager. Jake believed if he had not found acting early in his teens, he may not have survived the conflict constantly raging inside him.

He all but ran over to the kitchen where Kat was sitting and threw his arms around her before she could even snap her laptop closed. She slid off the stool and fell into his hug, almost knocking him over. Jake laughed a real laugh for the first time in weeks, already feeling the consuming heaviness lighten. He engulfed her, wrapping one arm around her waist and another over her shoulder. He knew how their bodies fit together. He felt her body relax into his. He held her a beat longer and gave her one tight final squeeze before releasing her.

He hadn't realized until that moment how much he'd missed her. After a year of nonstop work on different sets in foreign locations, he was used to feeling out of place. But at this moment, he felt the familiarity of home: Kat, his family, New York, the rush of the city, all of it. And it felt good.

She stood in front of him in jeans, a light blue sweater, and bare feet. He let his eyes trail across her body. She was fit, but still soft and curvy in all the places that mattered. He'd loved the feel of her when they'd embraced; he'd forgotten how comforting her body felt against his. Her dark blond hair was still slightly damp, strands falling around her face, which was devoid of makeup. He was drawn to her natural look. He lived in a world of beauty, but much of it manufactured.

Having her here, right in front of him, heightened every one of his senses. He drew her into one more embrace just to make sure she was real. He drew in a breath as they broke apart once again. She smelled of the soap he had in the shower, and he felt a wave of comfort because, in that moment, she smelled like him.

Her large, piercing green eyes crinkled at the edges as she smiled at him. Her eyes were one of his favorite things about her. They were open windows into her mind: fiery when she was debating a point, commanding when she was working, and twinkling whenever Becca was around. When she looked at him, Jake felt as if her eyes gazed into his soul. He couldn't believe he'd stayed away from those eyes for so long.

"I can't believe you're standing here," he said, taking a step back. "Hope your flight was okay. I'm so sorry about tonight. We were shooting bridging scenes and pickups, and they take forever. It was the most boring twelve hours of my life. You're not mad, are you? I mean, I couldn't really help it."

He was rambling. He chastised himself, because he couldn't get his thoughts together like a normal person. He often felt like too many synapses fired in his brain all at once and there was no controlling the onslaught of thoughts that came at him all. damn. day.

She waved away his comments and pulled a second glass off the dish rack. He wondered where she'd found a dish rack . . . or wine glasses, for that matter. Clearly she already knew her way around his apartment better than he did.

"You look like you need a drink. I started without you," she said, and flashed him a smile that lit up her entire face.

He grinned at her. He'd painted her with a serious brush in his memories. Always in control. He'd forgotten the playful, fun side to her. He hadn't known what to expect since they'd had zero communication for months.

The past year had certainly not built upon their relationship. *If anything, it should have fractured it*, Jake thought. But here she was. She'd shown up when he'd asked. He had done nothing in the past year that would warrant her coming to him. *She should have said no*, he thought wryly, *she should have told me to fuck off.* But instead, there she was, filling up his wine glass.

Cabernet. His favorite, a welcome indulgence after the day he'd had. He took a long sip, swallowed, and felt the warmth of red wine run down his throat. He turned the bottle, looked at the label, and said, "Oh, wow. This brings back memories." He gave her a mischievous grin as he set the bottle back down.

The wine flooded his body with a distinct, sensory memory of the start of their friendship, forged in the beginning of the pandemic. He'd left his current rental flat in London and had flown home to shelter in place with his parents. He hadn't lived full-time under their roof since he was seventeen, so being quarantined with them in his twenties was jarring. Gone was his freedom and entire sense of independent livelihood. Jake remembered that period as a time of crushing isolation, trapped in a bubble that quickly became depleted of air. He'd been holding his breath, trying to make sense of an uncertain future.

He'd met Kat when she'd hosted dinner for his family. The two families were an agreed upon "pod" so his parents could continue to help Kat with Becca. Because Jake was rarely home before lockdown, he'd not met Kat until that night. When she was there, he felt like there was more oxygen in their tiny bubble. She was the deep breath he needed, and their friendship came quick.

On Friday nights, it became their routine to share a bottle of cab as soon as Kat's Zoom meetings had ended and Becca was in bed. That particular night they were lounging on the floor, balcony door open, listening to the eerily silent New York City.

They'd passed the time by looking through scripts that Roger, Jake's agent, had sent over. Productions had installed safety protocols, and he was desperate to get back to work. They had tried to stay quiet and not wake Becca, but their laughter over the absurd projects had been free flowing. Jake remembered the exact moment he'd decided to shatter their friendship. He'd been warm and happy from too much wine, and the only thing he'd wanted at that moment was to kiss her. He'd stopped laughing, leaned forward, and put his hand on her cheek.

Catching and holding her gaze, Jake had whispered, "Can I kiss you?" With lips only inches away from her, his youthful boldness had bordered on arrogance.

"No," she'd said, and pulled back, breaking the momentary connection.

"No?" he'd asked, incredulous, the mood momentarily broken. Honestly, no woman had ever told him no. At least, not since he'd been fifteen years old and had finally lost his virginity with Nikki Allen. One thing he'd gotten used to with burgeoning celebrity was that no one ever said no to him.

Kat had looked straight in his eyes and whispered, "Because you're too young for me. And I'm too broken for you." Jake had fixed her with an intense stare. He was disarmed by the vulnerability in her response; he'd never wanted anyone more than at that moment.

Again, he'd leaned toward her, whispering, "I'm not that young, Kat. And I like things that are broken." He gestured to a book on the shelf behind her. "In fact, I have a weird fetish with Humpty Dumpty." He'd smirked, and she'd let out a laugh.

"Damn you," she'd whispered, and had crashed her lips into his as if she were angry to be kissing him. She'd nearly knocked him backward, but once he'd processed what was happening, he had put one hand back on her cheek and one on the back of her neck to slow the kiss down. He had wanted to savor the feeling of their lips pressed together, clinging to the one thing that made him feel alive again.

Kat watched Jake and could see he was remembering their first night together during the pandemic. His eyes lingered on her, waiting for her commentary. She furrowed her brow at him and spoke, "It's also *my* favorite wine. By the way, it was my favorite before *and* after the Humpty Dumpty incident," she said, smirking at him.

"Oh, is *that* what we're calling it now?" he asked, taking another sip and returning her smirk. His eyes were sparkling. He looked happy, and she started to wonder what had made him call her, near dawn, sounding so desperate and lost. Now, sitting here, they were bantering like they still lived next door to each other.

"Speaking of eggs, are you hungry? Did you eat yet?" she asked. "Unless you're tired. Oh shit, it's 12:30 a.m. Man, jet lag feels so weird." She was so tired that it had seeped into her entire being, and she could no longer discern the difference between levels of exhaustion. He looked drained when she really examined him—she could see it in his body language and the dark shadows under his eyes. She had never seen him look so depleted.

"I don't sleep much these days. I do need a shower though," he said, running his fingers through his hair. "I *am* hungry. Starving. I didn't eat much on set today. Sorry. There's no food in this apartment. I thought I would get back here much earlier, and we would go out." He glanced at his watch. "Not sure who delivers this late."

"Well. You're lucky I'm here," she said, her voice light. She reached into his refrigerator and pulled out some eggs and cheese. "I picked these up down the street at Kihoskh. I got here and realized you had nothing, and my crushed pretzels from the plane weren't going to cut it. How about breakfast for dinner?"

"What? You don't want a protein shake for dinner?" he asked, gesturing to the empty cabinet. "And it's technically time for breakfast." He pointed to the clock on the microwave. "Officially morning," he said over his shoulder as he walked toward the bathroom to take a shower.

Kat watched him walk into the other room and felt a familiar flutter in the pit of her stomach. She tried hard to ignore it, but the feeling of his hands running through her hair, his breath on her neck, came rushing back. She'd forgotten the pull of his natural charm and how quickly he captivated her.

She *had* been angry months ago when he'd disregarded their plans to meet in New York. But more than angry, she was disappointed. The hurt was deep, and she realized that although her brain agreed to harbor no expectations, her heart certainly had them. She hadn't talked to him in months, not because his leaving warranted silence, but because it was the only way she could protect herself.

She wanted—*needed*—to protect herself and wouldn't let anyone break her any further. Ben's death had broken her in ways she couldn't have imagined. Of course, it broke her heart to lose the first real love of her life and the father of her child. That pain, she'd anticipated. But his death had also stolen her ability to see unpredictable possibilities in life.

She now understood how unexpected mortality can come

for you, and it altered her entire approach to living. She couldn't leave anything to chance, because she owed it to Becca to bring stability and safety to the forefront of their lives. If she was honest with herself, she couldn't remember the last time she allowed herself to take a risk, even if it was for her own happiness.

Actually, she did remember. It was the night she'd first crashed her lips into Jake's, yearning to feel alive again. And she *had* felt alive. Until he'd left.

He hadn't left *her*; he'd left the country for his career, which often took him across the globe for months or years at a time. He wasn't someone who could bring stability into her life. For that reason, she believed that she could desire him, but she needed to keep her walls up so that he didn't distract her from the real reason she was in Copenhagen.

Yes, she thought, *I can keep my distance. After all, I'm really just here for work.* She would spend the next ten days getting global experience, gain extra points at work, help Jake through whatever mental demons had driven him to call her the other night, and maybe squeeze in a little fun. She most certainly would not allow herself to fall into him. Not again.

Jake emerged from the bedroom with wet hair, wearing only a pair of soft bamboo shorts. He felt more awake after the shower, and his stomach growled. He walked up behind her as Kat put their breakfast-dinner on two plates. Leaning over her shoulder, he saw her constructing an egg-and-cheese sandwich on a bagel. "Whoa. You didn't!" he exclaimed. "Are those Liberty Bagels?" She'd packed his favorite bagels, and he felt a rush of affection toward her for remembering.

"Yes! From JFK though. They have a kiosk at the airport now. They're not as good as the actual bagel shop, but I figured it was better than nothing." She shrugged.

"You are a legend," he said, picking up both plates and moving to the table. "Seriously, thank you. This makes me happier than you know." Taking a bite, he was transported straight back to New York.

He missed home. He'd returned to the city only once in the past year, to attend his grandmother's funeral. The visit had been fraught with sadness and conflict. He and his parents had fought about how long he had been gone, and they'd all but accused him of abandoning the entire family, including his grandmother, who passed before he could say a proper goodbye. The guilt had eaten away at him until it had transformed into anger, and he'd lashed out.

That fight was why he'd left early, despite asking Kat to come home from San Francisco to see him while he'd been in town. She believed it had been a schedule mix-up, but he'd left the city in a destructive mix of anger and frustration. Afterward, Kat ignored his texts and calls for months, reminding him how unforgiving she was when she was angry.

Tears pricked his eyes, and he fought them back. God, he was a fucking mess. It was egg and cheese on a bagel, and he was ready to cry like a damn baby. He was caught off guard by his own reaction and how fast it washed over him. It was his absolute favorite comfort food in the world and the first thing he ate whenever he was back in the city. She'd remembered, and despite the shitty way the past year had gone, she was here, with an egg-and-cheese. Fuck. He was in trouble if he was already feeling this emotional. He always had a propensity for strong emotion, but he'd tried to bury everything the past year. Bury it all in work, drugs, and sex, all the while convincing himself he was doing just fine.

He gritted his teeth and sucked in a breath through his nose while the tears threatened to fall past his eyelids. He rolled his eyes upward to keep the drops from falling, reconstructing his emotional dam. He jumped up from his chair, grabbed his backpack from the floor near the table, pulled out his G Pen, and loaded a new cannabis oil cartridge. He needed something to tamp down the manic anxiety he could feel just below the surface.

Plopping back down on his chair, Jake slowly inhaled the calming vapors as Kat watched him. *She must think I'm crazy*, he thought, suddenly flustered by his own conflicting feelings about her sitting across from him. He was simultaneously elated and humbled, while also feeling nervous and agitated. She wasn't going to let him off easy, and he could see the mix of expectation and concern on her face as her eyes studied him.

"Jake," she started, "what's going on with you?" Her tone was soft and considered, and he began to fall apart at the concern in her voice and the unconditional acceptance he saw in her eyes.

He pressed the heel of his hand into his eye, knowing the tears were finally going to fall. He didn't know if it was the wine, the food, or her. But he was close to spiraling into a familiar darkness—one where he often struggled and scrambled to find the light. He didn't want to drag her with him, but he couldn't stand to go there alone. Again.

She didn't speak. Didn't try to break the tension. Didn't try to lighten the mood. He appreciated that she was giving him space. He knew they wouldn't move from the table until he started talking. Kat wasn't his therapist—he'd had plenty of those—but she was someone he trusted with this side of him. That is why he'd asked her to come. No, almost begged her to come. He cringed internally when he thought about that phone call. It was not his proudest moment. He'd smoked a lot of weed, and instead of calming him down, it had skyrocketed his anxiety. The only person he believed would answer the call was her. He'd never expected her to say yes, but she had, and now she was here, sitting in front of him, asking him to show his broken self to the only person he trusted to pick up the pieces.

He inhaled and started talking. "What's going on with me? I wish I fucking knew what is wrong with me. For one, this film. This is my big one. I feel like everyone is watching me, seeing if I'm good enough to carry this big of a film." He shook his head. He was aware of his fast rambling, but he couldn't organize his thoughts. "And right now, Kat, I'm just not good. The one thing I know I'm good at is acting. It's the only thing I'm naturally great at"—he paused to take a drink—"and right now, I go to set every day and I'm just fucking it up. Take after take after take." He leaned back in his chair, balancing precariously on the back legs.

He felt a dam burst inside him and it all tumbled out: the disconnection from the role, the disappointment of the director, the frustration of the crew, the general sense that he was letting everyone around him down. And he didn't know how to fix it. Garren had asked him what his process was and what he needed. The issue was that he didn't know his process. He just *was*. He just did it. He knew when it was right. And he knew when it was wrong. And right now, it was very wrong.

"I can't pinpoint what's wrong, but I feel outside myself, like I'm watching myself in a movie. A bad, straight-to-streaming, like *free* streaming, shit-bag movie. My own life is a bad film on repeat," he said, laughing at his own dramatic characterization of his situation.

But he didn't find anything funny. He was confused, and it was finally hitting him how scared he really was. "I mean, this is the largest film I've ever done. And it's mine. I'm the lead." His voice dropped to a whisper. "What if I'm only built for small indie films? What if I can't carry this big of a film? What if I am not what everyone wants me to be . . . expects me to be. . . ."

There. He said it out loud. The thing he was most afraid of. His heart raced, and he could barely control his panic as he heard his own voice admit his failing. There were artistic and monetary expectations of him. Expectations to rise up to the level of blockbuster stardom, and he was beginning to believe he was going to be a huge disappointment. And, given the nature of being a celebrity, it would be a very public disappointment.

Kat was quiet. Jake stopped talking and wished she would say something. She finally spoke, "I know you *think* you have no process, but there have to be ways you've connected to films before. What's different this time?"

He appreciated her pointed question, even though he didn't have the answer. Jake shrugged his shoulders. He closed his eyes and shook his head from side to side. "I. Do. Not. Know." He rubbed his eyes with his long, slender fingers.

Kat reached out, took his hands, and looked at him with such intensity that he wanted to look away, but he was caught in her gaze. "Jake. I see you and I know how much work you put into every role you take on. I have never heard you this stressed about the size of a film. Maybe focus more on the role and the character and less on the scale of the film? I don't have answers, but I know we can figure this out."

He squeezed her hand, comforted by the "we" in her sentence. It was hard for him to admit that he needed someone to help sort out what was going on in his head. He gave her a half smile and said, "One thing that makes me happy is that you're here, Kat. I feel crazy for asking you to come like two thousand miles because my confidence is shaken. Who does that?"

She gestured toward him and said, "You do. And it was more like three thousand, eight hundred sixty-four, but who's counting?"

He let out a full laugh. *Yes*, he thought, *she's right*. He was the kind of person impulsive enough to ask her to come over three thousand miles. He rubbed his eyes and let out a yawn. He looked at the time. "Kat. It's 2:30 a.m. I'm beat. Are you tired?" The weed made him sleepy, and his entire body felt heavy.

She gave his hand a squeeze and yawned. "Dying. I feel like I'm dying. I need to sleep. Like two hours ago."

Her candor made him laugh. He realized he'd been talking nonstop for almost a full hour. "Thanks for listening, by the way," he said, leaning forward. "But let's get to bed." Jake nodded toward the bedroom behind them.

Kat stood up and put their plates in the sink. "So, sleeping. How do you want to do this? I just assumed you had a two-bedroom, but. . . ." She gestured toward the single bedroom door on the other side of the apartment.

"I have a king. Plenty of space." When Kat raised her eyebrows at him, he smirked. "Get your mind out of the gutter. It's just a bed and there's plenty of room. I'm too tall for that couch, and I'm certainly not going to ask you to come three thousand, eight hundred sixty-four miles just to sleep in a hotel or on some shitty couch in a temporary rental."

Jake had called because he'd needed and wanted her presence. He didn't want her to think he'd called her all the way to Denmark for a hookup. It was more than that—how much more, he hadn't really processed—but he'd let her take the lead on anything physical during her stay. He didn't know if time and distance had created too much space for them to reignite what they'd had. All he knew was at his lowest point, the only person he'd wanted was her, and that meant something.

"My mind is far from the gutter," Kat grumbled. "I just hope you don't snore or kick in your sleep. I already live with a pint-sized bed hog." Jake chuckled in response as they walked into the bedroom. He went over to the side he usually slept on, sat down, and gestured to the bathroom. "You go first."

After a moment Kat called out from behind the bathroom door. "You have more beauty products in here than I use in an entire year."

He laughed. "If your face was photographed every day of your life, you would have a lot too. This million-dollar face needs to stay young." He took out his contacts, and as he put drops in his eyes he continued, "I think I saw my first laugh line yesterday."

Kat swung open the bathroom door. "Ahh . . . now I know why you *really* called me." She teased. Jake rolled his eyes at her. She walked past him wearing a loose tank top and frayed pajama shorts. Despite his resolve, Jake's body reminded him of their physical history. He had a strong desire to touch her, draw her into him, but he wanted to give her space, not to mention he was dead tired. He pulled back the covers on the other side of the bed and patted the pillow. "No snoring, at least, I think," he said, "and I won't hog unless you do."

After she climbed in, Jake went to brush his teeth. When he came back, Kat was already fast asleep.

chapter five

Kat opened her eyes and squinted at the light beaming through the skylight. She sat up and scanned the room to reorient herself. Yesterday was nothing if not surreal, with a very long flight followed by hours of conversation with a man she had barely seen in over a year. When she'd crashed into his bed, she'd been so disoriented she'd felt like she was having an out-of-body experience, both from the drain of very little sleep and the intensity of Jake. She could feel his anxiety—it vibrated off him like a flickering lightbulb about to blow. It was a higher intensity than she expected. She'd seen his constant undercurrent of unrest during the pandemic, but this was something else. Fear? *Maybe it* is *fear . . . maybe more*, she thought.

She got out of bed and walked into the kitchen to find Jake sitting at the table reading over his script, coffee in hand. He was wearing glasses, and Kat cocked her head as she looked at him. She didn't realize he wore glasses. This was the first morning they'd spent together. In all their times together, Jake had never spent the night. She couldn't imagine letting him in the same bed she'd shared with Ben. The same bed Becca snuck into nearly every night. For a minute, she registered how much she didn't know about him. How much they didn't know about each other.

When Jake saw her, he jumped up and began pulling levers and pushing buttons on his Breville. She was humored that he had no real food in the apartment but managed to have the fanciest coffee machine she'd ever seen. "Latte?" he asked, which was her favorite morning coffee. She was surprised he remembered, because she rarely drank them at home. Unlike him, she did not make fancy coffee at home, preferring her quick, efficient Keurig.

"Usually, but not today," she said. "Can that fancy machine make an Americano with two shots of espresso?" She needed a jolt this morning. The jet lag plus the wine last night were making her brain fuzzy.

He chuckled. "Damn. You mean business." He put a cup under the coffee spout.

She pulled her phone off the charger and checked her text messages. Two were from Emily. On a Saturday, this couldn't be good. Checking the time, she did some quick math. She'd slept late, and it was past 11:00 a.m. in Copenhagen. That would be about 5:00 a.m. in New York. Emily was always up early. She texted Emily to let her know she was available to talk and then popped in her AirPods.

Emily called right away. Her perpetually perky voice burst on the call as soon as Kat swiped to answer. "Hey, sorry, this will be fast." she said. "I didn't know if this warranted calling you, but I thought you'd want to know just in case. Oh, and good morning!"

Jake walked over to Kat and handed her the cup of coffee. "Hey, I made sure I had oat milk and that sugar you like." He handed her a small carton, container of sugar, and a spoon.

She nodded silently poured the milk in her cup. If she wasn't on the phone, she probably would've hugged him. Given how few supplies were in the apartment, it occurred to her most of his "food" had been purchased for her. She grabbed the cup and took a sip, thankful for the caffeine about to course through her veins. She put her fingers on her lips, motioning for him to be quiet. She was not on mute and knew that Emily had heard. She turned around to look out the window.

Emily interjected, "Hey! I heard that. Who was that?" When Kat didn't say anything, Emily insisted, "Oh, is that mystery pronoun?"

Kat feigned ignorance. "Oh, I didn't know what you were asking. It's the barista. I'm picking up coffee."

Emily let out a loud laugh. "Oh, okay . . . right . . . you aren't going to tell me. That's fine."

"So, Emily, what's up?" Kat asked, refocusing her. Emily brought Kat up to speed regarding an issue that could throw a wrench into their launch plans. The stickers they used to seal the individual boxes that held the devices were faulty, and boxes were popping open during shipping.

The PVA was a premium technology device, and they couldn't have boxes popping open at will. At the minimum, it would look cheap; at the max, the device could fall out and be damaged in transit. It wasn't an insurmountable issue, but one that had a level of urgency that warranted a live conversation, even on a Saturday. They had to avoid any delays that would affect the launch date, which was already promised to the board. Emily was right to call her.

Kat grabbed her laptop and sat down at the kitchen counter. She opened it and started reviewing a document Emily had sent her with shipment dates and units. "Are they all faulty or just a percentage?" she asked, her voice sounding as stressed as she was starting to feel.

"It looks like about fifty-three percent of the boxes are sealed with the new stickers, which are not consistently sticking," Emily said. "We have confirmed the manufacturing lines for the devices produced last month used the old stickers, for the most part. I'm still confirming, but I think those should be fine."

"Okay, I need you to get the number of units with the functioning sticker solidified by Monday. I'll figure out the projected orders in the pre-launch markets so we can understand how many units they'll need. If we have enough available units, they will still make their shipping dates and have enough in-store inventory at launch."

"I'm waiting on shipment dates for a new group of stickers with the proper sealant. If they get here in under a week, we won't really have to make a noticeable adjustment to any of our launch plans, right?" Emily asked. Kat could hear the nervousness in her voice.

"Maybe. Right now, this will require a minor adjustment, but let's start mapping alternative scenarios in case this goes south. Find out how locked the marketing dollars are in case we need to adjust the start date. Worst-case scenario, we might have to shorten the window for pre-orders prior to launch to still make the Black Friday push," Kat said, eager to get ahead of this potential issue. She had enough experience to know that a launch could indeed be undone by a tiny sticker.

She hit end on the call and sighed. She needed to call Will immediately, to get ahead of this. This was not the Saturday she'd planned in her mind. She only wanted to drink some much-needed coffee, have breakfast, and talk to Jake. Instead, she was spending yet another weekend stressing about work.

While she and Will were in the middle of an intense discussion about worst-case scenarios and impacts to forecasts and budgets, Jake set down another coffee and a plate in front of her. It was half of a bagel and scrambled eggs, made with the leftover supplies from the night before. He rubbed her shoulder and handed her a fork. Kat couldn't remember a time anyone made her breakfast, or any meal, and she mouthed "thank-you."

When the situation had been dissected and every possibility considered, Kat took out her AirPods and put her phone to the side. She noticed Jake watching her.

"That seemed intense," he said. "You okay?"

"I think so," she replied. "This launch just has to be perfect, and now it might get derailed by bad adhesive on a small sticker . . . but there isn't much more to do until we get more information. On Monday, we'll—"

He cut her off. "I'm sure you'll handle it. I asked if *you* were okay. That sounded like a pretty stressful start to a Saturday."

She nodded to show him she was just fine, but tears pricked her eyes. She stood up and pretended to need something out of the fridge so he couldn't see her. It had been a long time since anyone, including herself, had asked if she was okay.

Jake was a curious observer when Kat was at work. He didn't know what the hell she was ever talking about, but she slipped into a character of her own—one in full control, cool, calculating, and always efficient. He'd watched her during his lazy pandemic days, when he would lie on her couch and listen to her virtual meetings.

He'd studied her as if she was a film character. He'd been fascinated by the formality of the language used by her and her team—phrases like "parallel path," "on the same page," and "distributed workforce" intrigued him. He would roll the phrases around his tongue, having only a vague idea of what they really meant. Part of the reason he could inhabit different characters was his absolute love of studying people.

Today, however, she seemed more stressed than he had ever seen her. She insisted she was fine and in control, but he could feel her unease. She made it clear she didn't want to talk about it, but he tucked away a mental note to ask her about it later. He wished he had her skill to weather a crisis with calm action.

"Hey, what's your call time today?" Kat asked, looking up from her laptop. He was not surprised that she had moved on to thinking about his logistics for the day.

Her innocent question made him look down at his cup and

hesitate before answering. He had not yet mentioned his forced break. Even though it was only a few days, film shoots had tight schedules and, as the lead, having time off was measured in hours, not days. He knew it was bad when Garren changed the entire schedule.

"None," he said, "I have a few days off while they shoot around me. I'm so terrible that they're not going to waste another inch of film on my half-assed acting." He continued to stare into his cup, face burning.

"Is that what the director said?" she asked, and he could hear a hint of skepticism. She closed her laptop and set it aside, her sole focus on him. He looked at her wide eyes and wished he hadn't said anything.

"Not exactly those words," he admitted, "but that *is* what they're doing. The other principal actors come in a few days, and we should be further along in the schedule, so they're making up time with shots that don't require my presence. I need to use this time to get my shit together. *That*, he did say."

Jake didn't really know what would happen if he came back and still didn't deliver. They were too far along to replace him . . . weren't they? His heart raced at the thought of being fired. He was imagining the Twitter chatter and how people would delight in his failure. Industry reporters and the keyboard trolls would tear him apart without a second thought. It would derail his career in a way he couldn't allow himself to consider.

Jake avoided her eyes, set down his coffee, and scratched the back of his head. He watched Kat stand up, put her plate in the sink, turn around, and disappear behind him. She put her hands on his bare shoulders, pressed her fingers into his muscles, and began to lightly rub. At least he didn't have to face her.

"Taking a few days to regroup? Actually . . . that sounds like a good idea," she said, pushing her thumb just under his shoulder blade. "Take it for face value. A needed break. Don't make this more than it is." Her voice was soft and calm. Jake leaned into her touch.

"Hmm," he said, letting his head roll forward while he took a few deep breaths. That was the spot that always gave him trouble and she knew exactly how to release it. He'd forgotten how she'd learned his body during those pandemic days. His brain lingered on the memories of the long summer nights on her balcony, where her touch had been the balm he'd needed to make it through another week. She pressed her thumb into the knot with a firm, focused touch. It felt good; almost painful.

"God, I'm just . . . I don't know. I feel like it's me against the entire world right now," he whispered, almost to himself. It wasn't just the fear of being fired. He felt disconnected with everyone and everything around him. He groaned as she finally broke through the knot and felt relief in his shoulder. *She's the only one that can do that*, he thought. He rolled his arm forward, enjoying the newly released muscle. She moved down to his lower back. He leaned forward, resting his head on his arms to give her better access. He sucked in a sharp breath when her fingers found another tight muscle.

Her voice broke the silence. "Just breathe into it, Jake. All of it." She went down to a whisper. "Get out of your head. Stop thinking so hard and worrying about what might happen. Just let yourself be."

He felt her hands lift off his back. They traveled to his head and as her hands ran through his hair, he felt himself harden between his legs. He adjusted his position to try to hide how his body was responding to her touch. He hadn't realized how starved he was for gentleness. In the past year, he had plenty of physical contact, but none as giving and kind as this.

For the second time in less than twenty-four hours, tears came to his eyes. He kept his head down, exposing the back of his neck, and let a few tears fall. The care she took was almost too much. She stopped what she was doing and whispered in his ear. "You may be against the world right now, but I promise, the world is *not* against you."

He nodded his head. He listened to her words, but it didn't quell the constant unrest that had settled into his being. She gave his shoulders a squeeze and then he felt her lips on the side of his neck, kissing him. It was soft, and her lips lingered. Jake was transported to a time when sensual, stolen kisses had been commonplace between them. Last night, he'd decided that he would take her lead on anything physical, lest she think he called her all the way to Copenhagen for sex. That was definitively not why he'd called, but he wouldn't deny that it had been on his mind since she'd arrived. He hoped she was trying to reignite the intimacy they'd once had. Jake rolled his head back toward her, wanting her to kiss him again, eliminating the separation time and distance had created.

She jarred him out of the moment when she clapped his shoulders. "I'm getting in the shower," she announced. "And then we're moving you into this apartment." Before he could turn around, she disappeared into the bedroom.

Kat admonished herself as she stepped into the shower. *I can't believe I kissed him . . . like that*, she thought. She reminded herself of the barrier she needed to keep between them. Kissing him was not the plan. *But I want to kiss him again.* She rolled her eyes at herself. She wasn't used to being this scattered in her thoughts. She'd only been trying to end the massage and lighten his mood. But instead of a quick peck, she'd lingered longer than she'd meant to, and it had been softer and more sensual than she'd planned. She'd looked at his face when he'd rolled his head back. His lips had been parted, and his eyes half closed. She'd been dangerously close to kissing those perfect and expectant lips. Her body couldn't deny that she wanted him.

Her rational brain took over and she resolved to reinstate the boundaries they'd had—at least on their emotions. She'd seen his tears and knew she was only an inch deep into the darkness inside him. He had called her because he wasn't okay, and she needed to be careful with his emotions. And hers. He had a way of making her lose focus, and she was already feeling her brain scramble when she was around him.

She pushed her rational brain to the side. They couldn't be together for any length of time before the invisible boundary was shattered, bringing their bodies together. The "Humpty Dumpty" incident had ended with her on the floor, a script under her back, and Jake pressed against her, his arms holding her tight and their bodies working with a sense of urgency, as if either of them might pull away at any moment. The escape, the high, and the release had been addictive and like addicts, once they'd indulged in that drug, there was no turning back.

It was only sex—raw and unfiltered. Sometimes, an intense power struggle, a synchronized dance of control. Other times, it had been pure fun, both taking pleasure in watching the other person come apart. It was an unspoken agreement that they had no expectations of the other person. She believed they were both running from their own demons and the high had allowed them to break free, even for just a moment, from the invisible chains they'd put on themselves.

Her chains were ones of unrelenting responsibility, driven by the need to be successful in her career so she could take care of Becca. She understood Jake's chains were the expectations from directors, producers, the press, the fans, and everyone who believed they owned a piece of him.

She sighed to herself. It *had* been over a year since they had been together . . . could it be that she had imagined his response? In the past year, there had been very little connection between them, and recently Jake had been with a constant string of women, all documented in the media. Each one more beautiful than the next. Before he'd called, Kat figured their relationship had fizzled to nothing and she'd been content to let him go, not because she'd wanted to, but for her own self-preservation. She'd come to believe their time together although intense and meaningful to Kat, had been a casual fling to Jake. It was entirely possible that he'd moved on and the intensity of Kat's desires were now wholly one-sided.

After she'd showered and changed, Kat walked out of the bedroom and found Jake unpacking his suitcase. She wasn't going to dwell on the moment they'd had just thirty minutes earlier, and clearly, neither was he. She resigned herself to the reality that the kiss meant more to her, anyway. After all, he was the one who'd stayed away for an entire year. She vowed to herself that, moving forward, he would need to make the next move.

"This won't take long. I never bring much with me," he gestured around the sparse apartment.

At the risk of sounding lecture-y, Kat responded, "I think you'll feel more settled, maybe more committed to this film, if you move in. You look like you could pack up and leave at a moment's notice."

Jake tossed a pair of socks in a drawer and shot her a resigned look. She decided not to push him any further.

As they worked, Kat was planning the rest of the day in her head. She couldn't help it—she was wired for constant anticipation.

"Are you really free all day?" she asked.

"Yep. Hey, based on this morning, do you need to go into the office today?" he asked. "I understand if you do."

"No," she said. "There's not much more I can do today. But I do have a few ideas for sightseeing in Copenhagen."

Jake thought about what they might encounter when they ventured out in public. He was worried about her comfort in public with him. He couldn't imagine she had any understanding of what his life was really like. A lot had changed in the two years since the pandemic had started and back then, they'd been in a bubble, away from the world. Their stolen moments had been a complete secret, kept even from those close to them. He needed her to understand the public realities of being with him.

"Kat. We should talk about this," he started. "I get recognized on the street much more often than a year ago. I need you to be prepared."

Kat was quick to respond. "I thought about this a lot on the flight here, because I do want to hang out with you, and I don't want to hide the entire time," she said. "But what I really have to avoid is anything that would identify me as more than an acquaintance. Jake, your stans are really attached to you and obsessed with everything you do. I don't want to be a part of their chatter if I can help it."

He nodded in agreement. He knew that some of his loyal fans were very . . . how could he put it? Stalker-ish. He never worried about getting kidnapped or going missing, because his stans would find him in a split second. Hell, every time he wore a new shirt, it was less than eight hours before the brand and a link to buy would be posted. They relished every tiny detail of his life. If they thought he was dating someone, they would stop at nothing to know everything about her.

She continued, "I need to be as anonymous as possible. Mostly for Becca. If I'm identified, it inevitably leads to her. I keep imagining your fans approaching her on the street and that gives me the chills. I would never want anything we do to impact her safety."

"Kat, oh God, of course," he interjected, horrified at the thought.

"And the other reason I don't want to be identified—or if I am, it *must* be just as acquaintances—is for my career. This is a bad time to look like I'm running around Copenhagen on vacation . . . with a celebrity no less. I *am* here because of the PVA launch, after all. A project that as of this morning, might not be going so smoothly."

"Ahh. . . ." Jake said, giving her a knowing look. "That makes sense. Do they think you're only here for work? Like, would you get in trouble if you're in *any* photos with me? Because we'll show up, at least on social media. It's inevitable."

"I did tell my boss I was going to visit a friend while I was here, so I didn't lie. And I'm not here on the company dime, so a few friendly photos shouldn't cause an issue. If this launch tanks and I appear distracted, it *will* cause an issue. I will definitely lose the COO spot. I don't think it's inevitable that we will be photographed." she said with defiance. "I believe if we follow a few simple rules, we'll be okay."

She is nothing if not a systematic thinker, he thought. "Rules?" Jake said, raising an eyebrow. "This should be interesting. Tell me your rules." He tried not to smile as Kat began to speak in a serious tone.

"Rule number one: we shouldn't touch in public. Don't put your arm around me, grab my arm, etc. You are a touchy-feely person, but if you don't touch me in public and there won't be any photos that could be misconstrued. We don't look like a couple, so there won't be a problem.

"Rule number two: we need to be careful not to walk or stand super close. People don't want me in the picture anyway. If we aren't close, I won't even show up. Problem solved, easy.

"Rule number three: we need to be careful going in and out of the apartment building. Whenever we can, we should try to separate. Just to make it less obvious that I'm staying here. I don't think anyone is going to stake out your apartment to see if I go in and out, but they will if we're seen together repeatedly." She finally paused to take a breath.

"Are you done?" he asked, "I mean, I was thinking I should be careful to not look directly at you, either. Kinda like a solar eclipse." He was teasing, but he could feel his shoulders tighten as the stress crept into his body. He understood her reasons, but he didn't like her rules. He didn't want to live a stilted existence out in public. And as someone who had lived in the public eye for nearly ten years, he knew these rules wouldn't work for long. He worried about what would happen when they were photographed together. Because they would be, and for someone who lived with emotions on the surface, it would be hard to pretend she was just a casual acquaintance. But he would try, for her.

Jake reached over and shook Kat's hand as if it were a business transaction. "Deal," he said. "We'll hang out, but never be in the same space or look each other in the eye. Sounds like a blast."

Kat went into the bedroom to put on some mascara and changed her outfit now that the apartment was in better shape. She wanted to be more presentable, knowing that there was a chance any of their interactions could be immortalized via social media. It made her uncomfortable, but she figured her rules—even the ones Jake mocked—would prevent too many photos from being taken, and most importantly, help them steer clear of any internet chatter that would involve her.

After she had pulled on a pair of jeans, T-shirt, sweater, and a pair of bright white trainers, she looked in the mirror. She wanted to look casual and put together without appearing as if she was trying too hard. Although, she *was* trying . . . and this felt . . . hard. Looking at herself now, the woman that stared back at her looked more youthful than she felt. She always considered herself an old thirty-three-year-old. She already had a child and the big job. Her life had accelerated in a way that made her feel older than her years.

Pulling her hair into a top knot, she turned to see Jake walk out of the bathroom dressed in a pair of ripped jeans, a concert T-shirt, and a black hoodie. Jake looked like he didn't try, but somehow, was also on the cutting edge of fashion. He had a distinct street style that looked both casual and put together at the same time. It registered in her mind how very young he appeared.

The actual age discrepancy between them was eight years, but if you didn't know that fact, you would assume the age gap was even larger. If the roles had been reversed, and she were a man, it wouldn't raise eyebrows. But, in this instance, looking physically like she was at least ten to twelve years older than him made her uncharacteristically self-conscious.

He was running his hands through his wet hair, fresh from the shower. It was all the grooming he needed to do to arrange his curls into a perfect, tousled mop. She shook her head at the unfairness. His hair was part of his look and one thing most people noticed first when they picked him out of a crowd. There was an entire fan-run Instagram devoted to his hair. Like two million other people, Kat followed it.

He picked up his wallet by the door and put it in his pocket. Kat tucked her phone in her back pocket and met him at the door.

"So, where do you want to go?" he asked, stepping into her personal space.

"It's a surprise. Just you wait. I have a plan. You'll see," she said, reaching for the door handle.

She felt him take her hand and before she could react, he pushed her up against the door. His lips met hers in a soft and tentative kiss. It was a repeat of the earlier kiss: sweet, sensual, and lingering for just long enough. But instead of pulling away, he deepened the intensity of the kiss. They kissed until they were both out of breath, and she felt Jake's body against hers. Kat shut off her mind and her body responded to him, running her fingers through his hair as her tongue met his.

When he pulled away and stepped backward, despite herself, she let out a small, almost imperceptible whimper. She wished she didn't want him as much as she did, but that kiss nearly undid her.

He smirked and reached behind her to open the door. "Good," he said, "I just wanted to make sure we were on the same page."

Well, that certainly wasn't her imagination.

chapter six

Jake pulled a ball cap out of his back pocket and pulled it on before they stepped out of the apartment building. He slipped on sunglasses despite the overcast day. While it was easier to move around Copenhagen than New York, he couldn't always escape fans or the occasional paparazzi. He was used to it, but it made things a little more difficult.

He was taking extra precautions today, because he understood Kat's reasons for distancing herself in public. *As long as she doesn't distance herself when we're alone*, he thought, his heart still racing from the kiss at the door. He didn't know how their relationship would change as they navigated a public existence. In the shelter of the pandemic, they'd been quarantined together and could explore each other unencumbered by public scrutiny. He doubted Kat really understood the unwieldy nature of his life at the moment.

He clenched his jaw when he thought about the incessant public focus on his love life. It was hard enough to be taken seriously as a young actor without being linked to every woman in his presence. Every female under thirty he'd been photographed with in the past year had set off a flurry of dating rumors. He wished he got the same immediate reactions to new projects he signed, instead of the obsession over what he wore, where he dined, and who he dated.

He smiled to himself when he thought about being with Kat: they were a secret, kept from the whole world, including those close to them. In a world where everything he did was out in public, it felt special to have something that was just his. Being with her now, he realized how close he'd been to pushing her out of his life.

He thought about the text Kat had sent when he'd hastily left New York before she could arrive. He didn't hear from her until the next day when she'd written: *It's fine. Just because we fuck around sometimes doesn't mean I can have expectations of you. I get it. Enjoy your travels.* At first, he'd read the text at face value because that was what they agreed to during a hushed discussion in the twilight hours before he'd left for a short film in Croatia. They'd made a pact:

1. Stay close.
2. Nothing serious.
3. No expectations.

It had worked for both of them. But he'd soon realized she was clearly upset, a reaction they had yet to discuss.

Kat looked at her phone, noting that the taxi had arrived. As they were walking to the car, she said, "This shouldn't be too hard. Oh, and if anyone asks, I'm just a family friend here on business. I don't even need a name. A nobody. Which is true. As far as your fans and your industry are concerned, I *am* nobody."

He shook his head as he opened the car door. He had very few somebodies left in his life, and she was certainly one of them. He needed her to know, whatever this was between them, it was something to him. "I wish you wouldn't say things like that. You aren't a nobody to me. You know that, right?"

She glanced in his direction and got in the car. Her reaction was so unclear, it made him curious.

Once they were settled in, Jake changed the subject. "Hey, how's Becca? I miss that kiddo." He ran his hand through his hair and adjusted his hat. "She ever figure out how to do a handstand?"

Jake watched Kat's face lit up as it always did when she talked about her daughter. "Yes, she figured out the handstand. And only broke one lamp in the process," Kat said, and both of them laughed. "She turns six in two months and starts kindergarten right after I get home from this trip. Can you believe it?"

Jake shook his head. He thought of Becca as a hilarious four-year-old who loved to play My Little Pony and used the entire living room as a gymnastics playground during the pandemic. He fondly remembered how she'd created stories with her stuffed animals that would rival the dramas of Hollywood.

Kat beamed with every story she relayed to him about Becca. As an almost six-year-old, My Little Pony and friends were no more, replaced by dragons of all kinds. She was a budding athlete, moving from gymnastics to itty-bitty soccer.

Jake promised to kick the ball around with her next time he was in New York. He found himself nostalgic for the endless rounds of hide-and-seek they would play while waiting for Kat to finish a conference call. Becca always hid in the same place: under a blanket on the couch. Jake had relished searching for her until she could no longer contain her giggles. He suppressed a smile as he remembered how their laughter had been so loud that Kat had to step out onto her balcony to finish her calls.

Kat let him know that Jake's dad had taken up playing cards with Becca and, much to Kat's chagrin, he had taught her daughter War, the most inane, never-ending card game ever created. And one that Becca was now obsessed with playing. The thought made him let out a loud laugh as he snuck a look at her phone to see where they were headed. She quickly covered it up.

"Come on, Kat. Where are we going?" he pleaded. As much

as he was enjoying her taking full control of this day, he was not used to surprises and the suspense was getting to him. He spent so much of his life governed by a written production schedule that there was little spontaneity left in his world.

"It's just around this corner," she said, pointing up the street. When they got to the corner, he saw a big sign out the window that said Tivoli Gardens. The taxi pulled over and they got out of the car.

He wrinkled his nose as the disappointment hit him. He didn't want to spend his little free time in some sort of garden. At least he was outside and not in the bubble of trailers, rental apartments, limos, and planes. *It's been awhile since I have been out in the real world*, he mused to himself. "I didn't take you as a botanical garden type of girl," he said aloud.

Kat pulled out her phone, scanned the electronic tickets, and stepped just past the ticket booth.

"Jesus, Jake," she said, "You've been here how many weeks and you don't know what Tivoli Gardens is?"

He took a second to look around, and he realized that it was an amusement park. He flashed her a grin. "Oh, thank God. Roller coasters are much more interesting than rose bushes." Well, she didn't seem to worry too much about being out in public. *She picked a damn amusement park to be our first outing!* The thought made him laugh, and he better understood why she had been so adamant about her rules.

As they walked under the archway and into the grounds, she chided him. "You, my friend, need to have more fun. You've been working nonstop for how long? A year? How many days off have you had? Like, real days off?"

He tried to count in his head. There weren't many, and he couldn't remember the last time he had a full day off. He spent most of his downtime in a trailer on set, an airline club, or a hotel conference room. The longest stretch of time off he'd had was for his grandmother's funeral, and that visit had been a disaster. Kat was right. He hadn't had a break in a very long time.

It wasn't for the lack of trying. He'd talked to Roger, his agent, six months ago about taking a small hiatus but was cautioned against it. "Strike while the iron is hot," Roger had said, referring to the number of offers coming Jake's way. He'd urged him to keep working and stay visible, lest he fall off the radar of top directors and producers. Jake knew it was a real concern, but he still felt a weariness beyond physical exhaustion. He couldn't answer Kat's question, so he stayed silent.

"You've made my case," she said. "So, for the next few days, you're going to just let loose a bit. Have fun, relax, stop overthinking everything, and most importantly, hang out with *me*," she said, smiling, but her tone was adamant. She sounded serious about their fun and the juxtaposition brought a smirk to his lips. He tried keeping a serious face.

"Okay, fun, relaxation . . . hanging out with you . . . no thinking. I can do that," he said. "From what I saw this morning, I'll ask you the same question: when did you last take any time off and just have fun? Hmm, Kit Kat?" Jake's tone betrayed his amusement. He could see that she was not pleased he'd turned the tables on the conversation.

"Touché," she said and put up her hands in surrender. "And never call me Kit Kat." She shot him a look before continuing. "Okay . . . back to you. Really. I was thinking about it in the shower today. I think you need to stop thinking so much and go back to body awareness. You once told me the best acting wasn't what you said in the script, but what you said with your body language. Do you remember? You said body language was true acting. Anyone could read words on a page. I think you need to go back to that. Just be physical again and figure out the physicality of your character."

He was struck that she remembered. He had forgotten about

their conversation, though it came back to him now. They'd been on her balcony, hanging in two lounge chairs, enjoying the cool air that came into the city at night. Jake had brought over some weed and, uncharacteristically, Kat had taken a hit—careful not to get too high in case Becca needed anything, but enough to make her open and relaxed.

She'd wanted to know every element of his creative process and even then, he'd had trouble putting it fully into words. But he did know physicality was key to moving the character off the page and into his mind and body. It was the most in-depth anyone had ever talked to him about his craft, beyond the perceived glitz of show business. She was the first person who tried to understand the work he put into every role. Remembering that night, talking until the sun peeked over the skyscrapers, he believed that she might be the only one who really respected his work.

"Right. I remember. I was very smart once." He wondered to himself what had happened along the way to make him forget. He'd started questioning himself so much he couldn't remember how to harness his own creativity.

"Shut up," she said, breaking him out of his thoughts. "Don't be down on yourself. Have fun. Take care of your body. Keep your space in order. Declutter your world, and your mind will come along. How can you play a character on a page until you understand how they move through the world?"

He knew she was right, and it gave him a clarity he hadn't experienced for a long time. Except . . . he tried to stifle a smile. "*This* is what you thought about in the shower? I'm a little disappointed."

Kat gave him a look he interpreted as amusement mixed with annoyance. "Hey. Now it's *your* turn to get your mind out of the gutter."

"Oh, so you're admitting that your mind *was* in the gutter

last night?" he teased. As much as he appreciated her ideas and thoughts, he enjoyed teasing her even more.

She rolled her eyes, "You are ridiculous." She paused. "Stop deflecting, I'm serious. Stay off the weed too, for just a little while."

Everything else made sense, but not that request. He put his hands up and started to protest when Kat quickly interrupted him. "Please. Just try. You can't be present and physically aware if you're clouded and running from yourself." She spoke as if she could see right into his brain.

Running from yourself played over in his mind for a minute. He was unsettled at how well she could read him and was aware that he was running from something. Not just something. Himself.

Before he could answer, he was approached by a nervous fan. He glanced at his watch. It'd only taken ten and a half minutes for him to be spotted. He obliged with a selfie and made the obligatory chitchat with a stranger. As usual, once a fan spotted him, a group gathered, each person wanting to immortalize the meeting. He still found it curious that people really cared who he was, much less went out of their way to get a picture with him. He heard over and over from fellow actors that he would one day resent the interruption and he hoped that would never be true. As they grouped around him with excited chatter, he lost sight of Kat.

Kat stepped aside and watched Jake with his fans from afar. She admired his ability to give every one of them their moment. His patience was unwavering, and he took his time to make sure they were happy. *That's why his fans love him so much*, she thought. He was very real and accessible, letting them each have a piece of him. *Does he give too much away to other people*, she wondered, and she felt anxious as she thought about what that would mean as his career accelerated.

It was clear Jake would be a while, so she stepped away and strolled through part of Tivoli by herself. Even though it had been nearly seven years, being back in Copenhagen and now seeing Tivoli again made her melancholy. She felt a heaviness in her entire being and she found herself taking deep breaths to calm her mind. In her everyday life, she was good at keeping thoughts of Ben out of her mind. It was easier to compartmentalize him to the past. A bad dream. But here? He was everywhere. They'd only spent two days here, enough time to do the key tourist sites and for Kat to take a picture at the entrance of the building where PathMobile was founded.

Tivoli was one of the places both Kat and Ben had loved the most. It'd been early summer, and the grounds had been a mosaic of beautifully colored petals. Today, with the fall leaves floating gently down the man-made canal that ran through the grounds, it was a more subdued landscape. Kat stood by the two-person dragon boats as they floated through the leaves. Watching the boats, she could almost see Ben sitting across from her as they weaved their way through the waterway—two lovers talking about the seemingly infinite ideas for their future.

The naivete of those young newlyweds was a gut punch. All the plans they made that day, giddy with anticipation for the future—neither of them knew the cancer had already taken hold of Ben's body. They believed they had unlimited time to build their life together, but less than two years later, he was gone. She let a tear fall as she indulged in her disappointment. She would only allow this brief interlude, for fear she might never find her way out of the black hole of sadness, which always felt just beneath the surface. She never allowed herself more than a moment to step into her grief, lest it take full control. She didn't have time for grief, and Kat deemed it a useless emotion. After wiping her eyes and taking a few breaths, she turned back toward the entrance where she'd left Jake.

By the time she walked over, only a few moms were left, telling Jake how much their daughters loved him. Kat walked over and handed him a box of popcorn and a bottle of water. She had purchased her own as well.

"Yes!" he exclaimed. "I'm starving." He opened the box and shoved a handful of popcorn into his mouth.

One of the moms blurted, "See, he does eat!" Jake gave her a questioning look, so she loudly declared, "You're just so skinny in person. Tiny body, big head. Like a lollipop!" She reached over and pinched his hip. Kat couldn't believe she touched him, and she opened her mouth to protest. He didn't say anything but took a sidestep out of the woman's reach and flashed her his signature smile. With a mouthful, he mumbled, "Lucky genetics." They laughed, took one more group photo and walked away.

"That was rude," Kat said. "People just say or do anything to you, don't they?"

Jake shrugged. "I guess I'm used to it," he said, looking around the grounds. "Ready? I want to get on some rides."

"Yes!" she said. "I want to hit the Demon, the Star Flyer, Vertigo and, if we can, I *love* bumper cars."

Tivoli was truly a historic treasure, dating back to the 1800s. It was an amusement park with beautiful gardens and shimmering ponds. She had never experienced a place like it anywhere else in the world.

"It's beautiful here," he mused, taking it all in. "I'm in your hands." He tilted his popcorn toward her. She held up her own box.

"Rule number four: no sharing food. Puts us too close. Easy photo op," she said. She would create as many rules as it took to keep her off social media, horrified at the idea of one of Jake's stans lamenting about a new woman in his life. She'd seen it happen with every girl he'd had dinner with, dated, or dared to drunkenly kiss at a party. They were ruthless toward every woman who came near "their darling Jake."

It disturbed her to think about how attached complete strangers were to even the tiniest aspect of his life. Becca came to mind and worry seeped into her mind. At a minimum, she pictured complete strangers coming up to Becca on the streets to say hi, as if they knew her. That on its own was dangerous. When her brain went to worst-case scenarios, her heart raced.

Jake's voice brought her out of her hypotheticals. "Rule number five," he said, "rule number four only applies to food that comes from vintage amusement parks." He smirked at her.

"You laugh, but you'll be happy that I think about these things. I'm so hungry. I was going to bring you a *rød pølse*. They're the best here. I can already see the memes of you eating a giant, red hot dog," she said, gesturing toward a stand displaying foot-long hot dogs—a Copenhagen staple, they were delicious and, indeed, dyed a bright red.

Jake threw his head back, laughed, and took a step behind her. "Lead the way." He touched the small of her back as they navigated through a narrow sidewalk. She stiffened and glanced over at him. "I know, I know," he said. "Rule number one: no touching. Sorry. It's tough not to touch you," he said with a wink. She shook her head and gave him an exaggerated glare. "Hey, Kat. You're the one who decided our first public outing should be an amusement park."

"Well. It's the end of the season, and they're closing in just a few hours, so I figured this would be the best time to go," she reasoned. "But you're right, I'm really testing my rules with this decision. I just wanted you to have fun. I feel like an idiot." She said, heat creeping up her neck. He was right—she'd thrown them right into the thick of things. Navigating the public with him was new for her and even though she wanted to control it with her rules, she didn't really understand how he navigated such a public life.

Jake pulled out his phone and was preoccupied for a minute, so Kat looked up a map of the park to navigate them to the rides.

They walked in silence and at a slight distance. Her text message alert buzzed in her back pocket, and she pulled out her phone.

J: Hi. I have something to tell you, but I'm trying to do what you asked.

J: So I thought you would appreciate it if I texted you instead of what I want to do.

J: I want to whisper it in your ear.

J: I'm happy you brought me here.

J: I'm even happier to be here with you.

Kat didn't know how to react. She admired Jake's ability to just blurt out what he was thinking. She felt like he was almost compelled to do it, as if keeping it in would make him explode. His earnestness and honesty were so much a part of him and were so in contrast to her instinct to gain control by holding back. The sweetness of the moment disarmed her. She couldn't make herself look at him and instead just stared at her phone.

J: You don't have to respond.

J: I just wanted you to know.

As they wound through Tivoli, Jake realized Kat was right. He had not had fun in a long time. He'd blown off steam occasionally over the past eighteen months, but that usually meant losing himself in his work, doing a whole lot of drugs, or finding someone to share his bed. He hadn't had this kind of pure, silly fun for as long as he could remember. They jumped from roller coaster to roller coaster, even riding the Rutschebanen, a wooden rollercoaster from the early 1900s. They skipped the drop rides, but Kat insisted they ride the weird Danish kiddie rides.

Following Kat's rules, they did not sit together, which made Jake roll his eyes every single time she took the seat behind him. Instead, Jake had fun with his fans, who were delighted to share a roller coaster ride with their favorite celebrity. He enjoyed the game of sliding in next to a single rider and waiting to see the look on their face when they realized who was next to them. Or bumping someone in a bumper car and seeing the initial reaction: "Who just hit me?" He would smile at them and wait for the scream of delight. He knew there would be shared videos and photos over the next few days on his fan accounts. His PR team would be delighted. He really did owe them something positive after the last few months.

Kat seemed very happy to let the fans be front and center while she assumed the role of photographer, making sure the angles were good for both Jake and his young fans. She also pointed out a few shy girls holding back, clearly wanting to meet him. He took extra care to engage them in conversation. He overheard a group of young girls ask Kat who she was, and she always read from the same script: "Oh, I'm a friend of Jake's parents. Visiting here on business and checking in on their favorite son."

After they had ridden everything he could stomach and the evening was winding down, they stood across from the Pantomime Theatre. It was a gorgeous open-air stage facing a lush, grassy courtyard. On the stage was a glimmering blue, aqua, and green backdrop, reminiscent of a peacock. With its distinctly Chinese design, it should have looked out of place against the vintage aesthetic, but the eclectic design fit in perfectly. Tivoli Gardens was full of wonder, fantasy, and beauty. It was as if you could step through the gates and be immersed in a different time, a different world—one that was free of anything not built with the express purpose of enchantment. It was a world Jake wanted to live in. One without worry or ugliness.

He studied the outdoor theater, overwhelmed by its stunning

design and the way his soul connected to the empty stage. The plaque nearby gave a construction date of 1874. He was humbled by the decades of productions, actors, and performers who had stood on that stage and given all of themselves to their audience. He felt a kinship to those ghosts and could feel their presence.

He didn't know how to be anything other than an actor. He only knew how to perform with all his emotions on the surface, allowing the audience to feel him through the screen. He was beginning to understand how he could lose a bit of himself each time he embodied the spirit of someone else. He wanted to use his performance to push people out of the numbness of life. It was his reason for being, but he didn't know how to do it without fracturing his own psyche in the process.

"This place is pure magic," he whispered, almost to himself.

"I love it here," Kat said, spinning around slowly. An easy smile came to his lips as he watched her take in all of Tivoli. As the lights started to flicker on, it became a beguiling place. He took a minute to take in the playful ambience of the twinkling lights and vintage buildings. The entire vibe was inviting, and he felt a comfort in the growing quiet. The park was nearly closed, and crowds were dissipating. Only a few screams of laughter remained in the distance.

He watched her, the shimmering lights dancing in her eyes. They weren't standing too close (rule number two), but he could feel her wonderment as he watched her spin with open arms, looking as if she was trying to embrace the magic and history all around them. She stopped spinning and looked over at him. Her face was full of awe, and he thought he saw a hint of sadness. *This place overwhelms her, too*, he thought. Her sparkling eyes and her cheeks, red from the cool September air, made him want to kiss her right there, but he was forced to practice a restraint unfamiliar to him.

They locked eyes for a moment before she snapped them

both out of their Tivoli-induced trance. "I'm so hungry!" she blurted. "Popcorn is not a meal. I found a sushi place near here. Please let's have a proper dinner!"

His stomach was growling, and he was beginning to get a headache. As much as he loved it here, he loved the idea of sushi even more. He nodded his head and gestured toward the exit before following behind her. Once again, she decided their next move. Another choice he didn't have to make. Spending time in her presence, where he didn't need to think of anything, made his mind feel clear and open for the first time in weeks.

Kat enjoyed leading Jake around Copenhagen, and she could see he was finally relaxing. She was giving him the gift of relinquishing control so he could get out of his head. If he could just enjoy, just be, she thought he might snap out of the dark space he inhabited inside his mind. She was acutely aware that everyone in his life needed something from him. She wanted to be the one person that didn't take from him and just let him be. To her, he wasn't a star or an object. He was just a human, and she wanted him to be him.

When they arrived at the sushi place, Kat was relieved to see it wasn't crowded. The hostess did a double take when they walked in. Kat stood off to the side while the hostess took photos and a short video with Jake. She pinched the bridge of her nose, trying to stop the pounding in her head. She just wanted to sit down, but he was determined to let his fan have her moment.

The hostess leaned over and whispered, "Mr. Laurent, I don't want you to get interrupted constantly during your dinner. We have a table in the corner, partially blocked by that pillar. It's not the best table, but you can be hidden. Do you want that?"

Jake did an exaggerated nod. "Thank you, that would be wonderful."

She winked at him and led them to their seats. Kat saw the

hostess slip Jake her card with her name and number "in case you need someone to show you around town."

Kat felt anger bubble up in the back of her throat. Even though she declared that she needed to be a nobody, it still stung to actually be one. *It's best if people don't notice me*, she reminded herself. Still, she would at least prefer women not flirt with him right in front of her. The hostess probably thought she worked for Jake. As she followed behind the two of them, she felt her irritability come to the surface.

Once they sat, she blurted, "You think she's cute?" Kat tried to sound light, but her tone betrayed her jealousy.

Jake looked at her, pausing for a moment. "No, Kat," he said shaking his head and holding her in his gaze. A slow smile came to his lips. "But I think you're cute."

His answer hung in the air and momentarily silenced her.

She knew part of her jealousy was her stomach talking, and the other, her ego. "Sorry. I'm hangry. Forgive me for anything else I say in the next ten minutes."

He laughed and replied, "Me too. If I don't get food soon, I might have one of those tantrums that show up on Twitter."

At that moment, the waiter arrived, and they placed a very large order, without even looking at a menu. Jake looked at him with a serious face and said, "We're so hungry, we might disappear. Like just dry up right here. Wither away."

He was being dramatic, and the waiter was clearly charmed—so much so, he walked straight to the kitchen and returned with edamame and shrimp shumai. He winked as he set down the food. "This is on me. I can't have you dying on my shift," he said.

Jake replied, "You're my hero." The waiter beamed as he walked away.

Kat took a few bites of food and sipped on some sake that Jake had ordered. She felt warmth flush her cheeks. It was the perfect drink after an evening outside in the fall air. She leaned back in her seat and returned his smile. "Did you have a good day?" she asked. At Tivoli she was reminded of his language of physicality, and she could see his relaxation. She adored seeing him at ease, with her and with himself.

"The best day," he said, returning her smile. "Thank you again. That was amazing. You were right. I did need to let loose for a sec. I hope *you* had a little fun too." He raised his sake cup for a silent toast, and they clinked their small cups together. They both took a sip, and Jake asked, "So, what's next on the itinerary of the best day ever?"

She loved that he put it all in her hands. She was emboldened by their day together, the warmth of the sake, and the look he had in his eyes. Kat held his gaze and gave him a sly smile. They were going to finish what they started. She lowered her voice and said, "Next activity? We go back to your apartment and fuck until dawn."

chapter seven

Jake choked on his sake. He wanted to grab Kat's hand and bolt out of the restaurant. Before he could reply, the waiter reached over them to set down their sushi. Jake coughed into his napkin.

"You okay, sir?" asked the waiter as he refilled their sake cups.

Jake nodded and said, "Yes, yes. I'm good," then flashed him a smile. "Hey, we're in somewhat of a hurry, so can I give you this now?" Jake asked, fishing his credit card out of his wallet. He wanted to expedite this dinner as quickly as possible. He was surprised by Kat's boldness, but not surprised at all. In all her rationality, she was always clear on what she wanted.

"Sure thing, Mr. Laurent," the waiter said, and walked away to run Jake's card.

"What's your hurry? Maybe I want dessert." She picked up a sushi roll and popped it in her mouth. He watched her deliberate chewing. "Mmm. This is delicious, you should try some," she said in a cheery voice.

He leaned over and whispered, "Kat. If I could, I would bend you over this table right now." His heart raced. He was charged up and her comment threw him right over the edge. He felt like he was vibrating. He often felt this way when he was anxious, excited . . . really, any emotion. It was the kind of reaction he'd spent years in therapy learning to control.

"Rule number six," she started, pointing her chopstick in his direction. "no sex in public." She looked dead serious except for the smirk on her lips. She was teasing him, and it was having the desired effect. He wanted her and she was going to make him wait.

"Fuck your rules," he growled. He reached over with his chopsticks and snatched a piece of a dragon roll. His nostrils flared as he refereed the dueling desire and frustration wreaking havoc on his thoughts. Kat laughed and pushed the plate of sushi close to Jake. *How is she still sitting there like we're having a normal dinner?* Seeing her unaffected made him crazy, but it made him want her more. It was a power play, and he was turned on by her control.

The waiter returned with his card and set it in front of him. He leaned over and whispered, "I'm not supposed to do this, but can I have a quick photo? My fourteen-year-old niece is a huge fan."

"Of course!" Jake said. "Crouch down here so your boss can't see." He gestured to the other side of his chair. Jake was relieved he didn't have to stand up. Rule number seven was probably "no hard-ons in public." He could only imagine the Insta comments *that* would generate.

Eventually, the waiter left them alone, and Jake looked at the table. They had made a pretty good dent in what they'd ordered. Once Kat had declared their next activity, he'd wanted to skip the meal, but it felt good to eat real food.

Part of his image was his slender frame, and he was pressured to keep it that way. It allowed him to play younger characters, which was part of why he got so many offers—his young look, coupled with experience, made him desirable to directors. His team counseled him to stay small and young-looking for as long as possible. He didn't often get to enjoy a full meal, existing mostly on protein shakes that offered all the appropriate nutrients and calories, but none of the joy. Watching his weight was his least favorite part of his job.

Kat was fiddling with her phone. "My taxi is two minutes away. I'm going to head out."

He tossed his napkin on the table. "Great. Let's go," he said. He couldn't wait to get her alone and a car sounded like a great place to start.

"Call your own. I'm not walking into your apartment building with you," she said, standing up. "It's a good idea for us to leave the restaurant separately, too."

Frustration jolted into his body, but he wasn't going to challenge her. He put his hands up. "Yes, rule number three." He opened his phone and ordered a car. It was only five minutes away. He would be right behind her.

He watched her walk out and thought about the difference twenty-four hours had made. He had been a ball of stress—fucking up a movie, angry, and *hard to handle*, as he had heard the assistant director say. He'd laughed more since Kat had arrived than he had in several months. She was a safe place—not always easy, but always safe. He understood the reasons they didn't discuss or define what they were to each other. At twenty-five, he told himself, he didn't want the stifling expectations or responsibilities that come with relationships.

But he *had* called her. When his world seemed dark, he'd called her. Although he'd yet to make complete sense of it, he knew she was someone he wanted in his life. What he wanted, what he could sustain, and what she would give him were questions he couldn't answer. At the moment, he didn't want to figure it out. He just wanted to be with her. "No thinking," she'd told him.

His phone buzzed with an alert, letting him know the car had arrived. On the way out, he obliged a few tables with quick photos when they asked.

It was a short ride to his apartment, and he flew out of the car and into the building. As he bolted up the stairs, his phone rang. He pulled out his phone to hit ignore when he saw Roger's name pop up on the screen. Damn. He'd agreed to a call today to discuss an upcoming film where he was under contract. Swearing under his breath, he answered.

"Hey, Roger," he said, out of breath from running up the first two flights of stairs.

"Jake! How the heck are ya?" Roger asked, dispensing the obligatory pleasantries.

"I'm okay," he said. "Sorry, I'm hoping this can be fast, I'm kinda in the middle of something." He typed his code into the keypad and opened the door. Kat was on the other side of the room, looking out the large window. She turned, and Jake mouthed "sorry" while motioning to the phone at his ear.

Roger let him know the start date of his next project was moving earlier and might overlap with his current project. He needed to know if *Zero Code* was on schedule so he could confirm Jake's arrival date in Prague with the producers.

"No, we're a bit behind," Jake said, sighing. "Also, I was planning on having at least a month off after this. We talked about this, Roger."

Roger ignored his comment about time off, instead questioned why they were running behind. There was no way to skirt the fact that they were behind because of his performance. He figured Roger already knew. "I'm having trouble connecting to the part . . . I don't know . . . it's just not coming."

Jake held the phone away from his ear as Roger started his lecture.

"Your reputation is one of the key reasons you've moved to offer only, Jake. You're still young and don't forget, the only thing consistent about directors is that they hate risk. If I tell the studio the film can't start because you are having issues, it will snowball. You have to fix this. Shit. We have to control this. You are too new to studio-driven films to have a reputation for being difficult, or worse, costing the studio money."

"I kno—" he tried to interject, but Roger barely took a breath as he spoke.

"Jake, this could be bad. You should've told me right away. You have to get back on that set and show them what you can do. You're better than this." Roger continued, his voice getting louder. Jake often remarked that he lectured him more than Jake's own father. Today would be no different.

"I get it," he said, not hiding the irritation in his voice. "I screwed up. Reminding me of it isn't helping." All the worst-case scenarios only made him spiral further into his own self-loathing. This was the exact opposite of getting out of his head.

He paced the room, feeling a quiet panic building. He tried to calm the shake in his voice when he felt both of Kat's hands on his shoulders, forcing him to stop pacing. She faced him, concern evident on her face. He tried to turn away, shrug off her hands, but she held him with a firm grip. She leaned up, and he felt a soft, slow kiss on his neck. She was silent as she gently licked the ear that wasn't pressed up against the phone and brought her hands up the back of his shirt.

His head rolled back, he took a deep breath, and slowly let it out. He let his anxiety dissipate and flow through his breath. As Kat had counseled him earlier in the morning, he just breathed into it. This was more than desire. He understood it now. She was bringing him back to his body and away from the pressures he was creating in his mind. He wanted to hang up the phone, but Roger was working through schedules to do follow-up calls, including one to their PR team. He kept the phone on, but he was barely listening.

Kat didn't stop at his neck. She slipped her hands past his waistband and took him in her hand, slowly moving up and down with a gentle promise of what was to come. Jake bit his bottom lip to stop from groaning. He closed his eyes and let her make him feel good. He opened his eyes with the intention of putting his forehead on hers, but instead, she kneeled, slid his pants down, and took him in her mouth. There was no hesitation, only a light touch in every spot that sent electricity right through him.

"Goddammit," slipped out of his mouth. She was killing him. He had to get off this call.

"What?" Roger said, confused.

Jake pulled the phone away from his ear and shouted, "Roger, text me the times. I'm hanging up now." He hit end on the call and threw his phone on the chair.

Jake let out a groan that was nearly a growl. Feeling Kat's mouth on him almost made him come undone the instant she'd touched him. She took full control, allowing him to turn off his mind and just be in the moment. So many women he'd slept with needed constant assurances and wanted him to initiate every move. He never knew if they were in it for him or because he was good for their own career or social following. He quickly learned that his rising star status also meant more people wanted to use him for their own good. But not Kat. Never her.

He ran his fingers through her hair and caressed her neck. He pulled her back and sank down to his knees so he could devour her lips. He went in for a deep, strong kiss, feverish and breathless as their hands became reacquainted with each other's bodies. His movements were frantic as he tore at her clothes, pulling his own T-shirt over his head. Once they were rid of their clothes, he slowed down and took his time kissing her soft breasts. He knew every move, had explored every spot, and knew every way to touch her to make her whimper. They lay down on the floor, and Jake settled his body on top of hers. He loved the feel of her body under his.

The last woman he had been with flashed in his mind. She'd been some sort of model—Victoria's Secret, maybe? He honestly couldn't remember. He had been able to see every rib and hip bone, just like himself. When they laid together, it had felt like bone on bone. He'd been so weirded out by the feeling that he never saw her again.

He felt Kat's fingers brush his back and run all the way up to his neck. She playfully pulled his hair and crushed his lips with a hungry kiss. *Oh, she wants it a little rough?* He gave her a devilish smile before he nipped her shoulder. She let out a small giggle, and he felt her breath quicken. He moved back to her mouth and pushed his body even closer to hers. He was so lost in their kisses that he barely heard her say his name.

"Jake? Jake?" she breathed.

"What? What?" he asked. It came out almost as a moan. His mind was hazy with desire, his brain synapses were slow to fire.

"Condom? We need a condom," she said as she bit his earlobe.

"Yes. Shit. Yes," he said. God, he'd almost forgotten. She'd made him crazy and foggy. They were very close. He had never gotten this close without a condom. He got up and grabbed his pants a few feet away on the floor. He'd stashed one in the side pocket.

Kat raised her eyebrows. "You had a condom in your pocket? The whole day?"

"Well, rule number six had not been established yet," he said shrugging his shoulders as he flashed her a smile. She let out a loud laugh.

He moved to the couch, sat down, and carefully rolled on the condom. He was planning to join her back on the floor, but as soon as he was done, Kat climbed in his lap. He almost came as she straddled him, her aggressiveness affecting him down to his core. Her lips kissed just under his ear. "Did you know you have a freckle right here?" she breathed. "It's one of my favorite spots to do this . . ." she said, and Jake felt shivers up his spine as her tongue tickled his neck.

It was all he could do to hold back, but his body was entranced by her control. Once she lowered herself onto him, he felt her let out a long, low breath.

"Jake, why does this feel so good?" she whispered in his ear. She pressed her lips to his, and his mouth parted as their tongues met.

"Are you really asking me to answer that?" Jake breathed. He couldn't believe she was talking. He was barely able to form a complete sentence. He put his hands on her hips, and she began to move, her eyes locked with his. She found a steady rhythm, her movements building momentum. He threw his head back and gazed at the ceiling. "Fuuuuck," he said with a grimace as he tried not to end the moment too early.

She was right: this felt amazing, even perfect. It was the high of sex, but also the high of being with someone where it felt effortless. He loved how their bodies came together: he was all hard angles, cut, nearly sharp, whereas she was curvy and soft. She was his shelter, softness and release in a world that felt too hard.

Jake buried his face in her shoulder. "Oh God, I'm sorry," he said. "That was fast. This is what happens when you tease me all damn day."

She pushed his head off her shoulder and planted a kiss on his lips. "That was amazing. I needed that. I think we both needed that," she said, sliding off him onto the couch. She lounged back and stretched her legs, laughing out loud.

Jake walked across the room to clean up. "Why are you laughing?!" he asked, the mild panic clear in his voice. He didn't think what they had just done was worthy of laughter, no matter how brief it was.

"Look at the time," she said. "We didn't even make it twenty-four hours. After a year, I thought it might be at least a week or so, or never."

"Never?" he asked. "I can't imagine never." He walked back over and joined her again on the couch. They weren't done.

chapter eight

As Kat rested on top of the bed, she thanked the universe for the gift of Jake. She worked to catch her breath from the many times they had brought their bodies together. Earlier, they had found each other again, right there on the couch. It had been slow, deliberate, as if nothing else mattered other than bringing each other to the brink and then watching each other come apart.

It didn't take them long to realize their desire had not been satisfied, and they kissed their way to the bedroom, not bothering to pull back the covers or even get on top of the bed. Instead, Jake had bent her over the side and taken her from behind. The feeling of his hot breath on her neck and his arm around her waist as he pushed into her had made her come almost immediately. It had been rough, needy sex, trying to quiet a desire that felt endless. Afterward, they'd sprawled on the bed, sticky with each other's sweat, only their breathing could be heard in the room.

"You're trying to break me," she said, resting her hand on his chest. "I'm going to need a minute," she panted and lifted her head to look at him lying there, curls tangled, eyes cloudy, and face flushed. God, he was so fucking beautiful. It overwhelmed her for a moment until she processed the number of endorphins running through her body.

She propped herself up on her elbow and lazily ran her fingers across his chest. She kissed a small tangle of hair. "Hey, I have a question," she started. "Can we talk about something?" His eyes widened, and she realized what he might be thinking. She was not going to talk about *them*. They never did, and she wasn't going to start tonight. "Don't worry, it's about your film. Can I ask you a few things?"

He chuckled. "I didn't think that was where you were going," he said, rolling to his side to face her. He ran his fingers along her arm and kissed her shoulder. She loved how he made her feel in that moment, cherished and desired. She forced her brain to come back into focus.

"What's the film about? Can you tell me?" She twirled a finger around a curl by his ear. What she really wanted to do was kiss the curl, his ear, and every inch of his body in front of her, but she forced herself to retreat from the feeling of desire that overwhelmed her. Discussing his film pushed the desire out of her mind.

Jake smiled as he moved away from her. "Of course." He pulled back the covers and crawled into bed. Lying back on his pillows, he stretched out his arm, and motioned for her to join him. She snuggled up to him and her eyes were heavy as she nestled in his arms, her head on his bare chest.

"Have you heard of the multiverse?" he asked, and when she nodded, he continued, talking her through his character (Tom), the scientific plot points (complicated), the love story (good), the dreaded scene where killers chase his character (bad), and the heroic acts Tom must perform across the multiverse (weird). She found herself drifting off to sleep, hearing his voice and his heartbeat as a kind of lullaby.

Kat felt like her eyes had just closed when a bright light flooded her face. In her dream, Jake's hands had been on her, rubbing her shoulder, eventually moving to more of a shake. Her brain came to the conscious realization that Jake was indeed nudging her awake.

"Kat . . . Kat . . . Wake up." His voice had a calm, but insistent tone.

"What?" she asked, looking around with a start. "What's wrong?" Her eyes adjusted to the bright light as she looked at Jake.

"Nothing," he said with a goofy smile on his face. "I figured him out. I couldn't wait to tell you."

"Who? What time is it?" She sat up and rubbed her eyes. He wasn't making any sense and even if he was, her brain wasn't comprehending words.

"Three-thirty a.m. Tom. My character in *Zero Code*," he said, his eyes bright. "I'm starting to figure out what makes him tick." He looked so expectant and so happy that Kat almost forgot that he'd woken her from a dead sleep. On the bed was his laptop, script, and about twenty Post-it notes full of scribbles.

She plucked one off the blanket in front of her and read it out loud, "The world made him fragile, but he turned fear into power." She put it back on the bed and turned to Jake. "Tell me," she said simply.

"I've been thinking about him a lot," he started. "Tom is a guy who's been so bullied, so underestimated his whole life, that he doesn't even know what he's capable of. I think he was strong once and believed in himself, you know, like we all do as kids. But so many people didn't believe in him that he stopped believing in himself. But it's more than just having no confidence. After being beaten down repeatedly, he's turned fragile, close to breaking as a human being. Garren, the director, pictured him as a stoner or a deadbeat, but that's not it. He's not a screwup. He's a broken human, holding on by the thinnest thread."

Jake went on, speaking quickly, barely taking a breath.

"I think that's why I was having trouble with him. I'm too in my own head and not in Tom's head. I had a great childhood and, frankly, adulthood. If anything, I had too many people believing

I was awesome." He laughed. "So, I think I'm going to try a few things.

"You were right about the physicality of the character. I don't think he moves normally; he exudes a sense of wanting to disappear into himself. He wants to hide from life. Because of that, I think he would hunch when he's around other people, make himself seem smaller, less noticeable. I think he doesn't look people directly in the eyes—he just wants to get through life unscathed. I want to try physically shrinking into myself and trying a bit of a stutter. I think that physical change will bring Tom out, especially in the beginning of the movie before he morphs into the hero. Seeing him stand tall and face the horrors that everyone is running from, that's the story. That's the story arc. That physical metamorphosis is the key to the merger of Tom and me."

Kat nestled into the pillow and observed Jake's dissection of a person that only existed on a page. He'd found ways to relate to Tom in order to become him, even for a short while. Watching him mentally climb into another human was both awe-inspiring and frightening. She'd never seen him in action before, but now she could see it, quite literally, all over the bed. She couldn't imagine opening her mind far enough to become another person.

"Jake," she started, "I could never do what you do. Every role is so different. You start over every single time. Even that concept stresses me out. I like everything to be defined and fit in a logical process. I could never just figure it out like you do."

It isn't just about acting, Kat thought. *It is how we see life*. Jake saw the unknown and undefined as a blank canvas, an opportunity. For her, the unknown was something to be feared, managed, or controlled. She wanted to be more like him than she cared to admit.

He looked at her for a beat and then leaned over and kissed her shoulder. "I think you'd be surprised at your ability to drop into the undefined and be okay. Better than okay." He lifted her chin. She closed her eyes and their lips met. She wanted him to linger, but he pulled away and said, "I mean, you came here, didn't you?"

She didn't respond and he didn't elaborate. She wondered if he was right. If she just let go a little bit, would everything really fall apart? He went back to his work—so focused he was nearly in a trance—and she watched him taking notes, making marks in the script, and gathering additional ideas. She lay back down, taking it all in, just watching him until the earliest peek of morning came through the skylight.

chapter nine

Kat crept into the kitchen. Jake had finally managed to fall asleep during the early dawn hours, but her own attempts had been futile. Her body desperately wanted a few more hours of sleep, but her mind was racing, and she knew the only thing to quiet it would be to check her email to see if she had received the unit projections that were unaffected by the adhesive issue.

When she opened her inbox, Emily's email was already waiting. It had arrived yesterday and was still waiting for Kat to add the global unit requirements. Seeing the time stamp of the email gave her a twinge of guilt. She should have checked sooner. Jake was already shaking her focus. *Get it together. You're here for work*, she reminded herself. If she sent it off soon, it would be in Emily's inbox before she woke up.

She was compiling figures from each regional president to calculate the total unit requirements when Jake walked in, wearing only a pair of boxer briefs sitting low on his hips. He stretched his arms up to the ceiling, rolled his shoulder, and rubbed the sleep out of his eyes. His curls were a wild mess, both standing up and in his face at the same time. *How can he be hot and adorable at the same time?* She mused before moving her eyes away from Jake and back to her laptop.

He walked behind her and started to make coffee. Kat couldn't wait to finally get some coffee in her body. On a typical day she would've made herself a cup, but his coffee machine was intimidating. "Thank God you're up," she said. "I work for one of the top technology companies in the world, but I cannot figure out how to use that monstrosity."

He chuckled as he adjusted the dials and the machine started to grind the beans. "I've got ya," he said, his voice soft, barely awake.

As she went back to adjusting the spreadsheet, she felt his lips on her neck from behind. She stopped typing, leaned back in her chair, and rolled her head to one side. She let out a soft moan and closed her eyes. His kiss brought her back to last night and her pulse elevated.

"I wish you would come back to bed," he murmured, planting kisses on her neck with increasing urgency. His voice was low, hoarse, and full of sleep. It was all Kat could do to not follow him back to the bedroom, but she really had to finish this work—at least, that's what her brain told her. She opened her eyes, leaned forward, and moved away from him.

"I can't," she said. "This has to get out in the next hour. I want to get it to Emily before she wakes up." But he was not so easily brushed off.

"Who's Emily?" he whispered and continued to kiss her neck. "She's not invited." His soft tongue licked her ear.

Kat laughed quietly, reached back, and tousled his messy curls. As much as she was enjoying him, she had work to do. "Jake, I'm serious," she said.

He let out a playful growl and nipped her ear.

She couldn't believe she was telling him no. But she needed some space from him, just for a minute. The intensity of last night had been disarming and frankly she didn't know how to process how Jake put every one of her senses on edge.

"Mkay," he mumbled as he grabbed her coffee off the machine to set it down next to her. She expected him to sit across from her or go take a shower, but instead, he pulled up a chair and sat down next to her, his legs touching hers. He wasn't going to give her space. He put his hand under his chin, took a sip of coffee, and peered at her laptop. She watched him read the spreadsheet in front of her. He let out a low whistle.

"That's a lot of money. Is that your budget for the launch?" he asked, looking intently at the screen. She had a moment of pride at the spending she controlled. It was eight figures with a projection of generating ten figures of sales for the company. Assuming her launch plans stayed on track.

"Yes," she said, amused at his sudden interest. "I know, it's boring stuff."

"Not to you," he said, leaning back and putting his arm on the back of her chair. "Talk me through what you're working on. What was the issue yesterday?"

Kat took a beat. He'd never asked her about her work, although he had observed plenty through the pandemic. She pulled up the timeline and total projections for the launch and explained the current issue. She slipped into familiar territory as she detailed why the adhesive could cause a delay or worse, impact the number of units sold. She'd already delivered sales projections to the board and missing those substantially would be unacceptable.

She was going to do everything in her power to keep the launch on track. Her ability to deliver was a key reason she was in the running for COO, and if that came into question, she'd lose to another candidate. She stopped talking when she realized he was staring at her. "What? Am I putting you back to sleep?"

He shook his head. "What does a COO do?" he asked, and Kat could see he was trying to understand her world a little.

"Second to the CEO. The COO does just about everything to make sure the company is profitable. You have to understand and lead just about every department in the company, in any market." Kat once heard it described as the Swiss Army knife of a corporation. She thought that was a good description. "My biggest issue is that I lack global experience. Will, my boss, spends at least a third of his time in our global markets. That's why I'm here."

"Sounds hard. And stressful," he mused. "You love it? You must. You've learned how to do everything."

Kat didn't reply right away. She had never put love and her job in the same sentence. "I've never asked myself if I love my job. I'm good at it. Great at it. But love? I don't think I've ever connected that emotion to my career."

Jake's eyebrows lifted. "Really? I can't imagine working this hard on something I didn't absolutely love," he said, gesturing to her open laptop.

"I'm a single mom, Jake. I don't have the luxury of just doing things I love," she said, with an edge to her voice.

"Bullshit, Kat." He challenged her. "Nowhere does it say you can't do something you love because you have responsibilities."

Kat looked up at him, stricken. "What do you know about it? What responsibilities do you have?" How could he begin to know what it felt like to carry any real responsibilities? She resented his challenge and was not going to back down.

Jake bristled. "That's not fair and you know it. I may not have a child, but I have a lot of people who rely on me. And if I don't deliver, or if I say one wrong thing in the media, poof, my career could be over. It's different, but the responsibility is real." He paused and put his hands up in surrender. "But you're right, I don't really know *your* responsibilities, and I shouldn't have called bullshit on any decision *you* make in *your* life. But, you still haven't answered me. If you don't love it. What drives you?"

"Financial stability. For Becca." Her voice broke, but she wasn't going to let the tears flow. No. Not in front of him. She wouldn't admit to him her true fears. The nights spent awake trying to convince herself she wasn't a failure. If Becca couldn't have a father, she would at least have the best of everything else. The pressure was suffocating and overwhelming. It was true she couldn't assign love to her career, but that didn't mean it wasn't important to her. Her career was a means to an end, not a passion.

"Money's not everything." Jake shrugged.

"Says the person getting paid five million a film," she fired back. She hated his naivete and was reminded of their different lives. Of course he didn't think about money. He had more money before he hit his twenties than many people made in a lifetime.

He didn't reply. She took a deep breath until her voice was even. "It matters, Jake. It matters to me. Schools and apartments in Manhattan are not cheap. And hopefully I will need to think about college. I don't have a fallback for Becca and me. Every choice I make in life affects her. So, yes money is *everything*, and no, I can't just do things I love." She sighed and locked eyes with him. She wanted this conversation to end. "*You* may not think it's inspiring, but it's the reality of the life I live."

Jake put his arm around her chair, pushed her laptop to the center of the table and rested his other arm on the table in front of her. His presence enveloped her without laying a hand on her. He leaned forward, his face close to hers. "Hey . . . I don't want to fight with you. I didn't mean to imply you were wrong for being motivated in that way. I just want to make sure you're happy," he kissed her cheek softly. She felt him rub the back of her neck, but she couldn't look at him. She didn't know if she was happy. She didn't believe her happiness was still part of life's equation.

She moved to the chair across from him. She couldn't have this conversation. This was unproductive, and she was done talking. She pulled her laptop in front of her and put all her focus on getting her adjusted spreadsheet off to Emily. Once she hit send, she closed her laptop and finally took a sip of the latte Jake had made for her. *Just one cup of coffee today*, she thought to herself.

She was jittery enough inside and blamed her emotions on too much caffeine.

Jake remained silent and she felt him watching her. Determined to change the subject, she swiped open her phone and went to Instagram. "Check it out. Your stans were hard at work." She slid her phone over to Jake so he could see the volume of posts and stories from their few hours at Tivoli. The comments were sweet and positive. Kat's rules worked. She only showed up in the background—a glimpse of her hair in one photo, her hand in another. Nothing recognizable. One fan pegged her as his assistant. *A successful outing*, she thought.

"How do I look?" Jake asked without looking down. He gave her a smile, but she could see a hint of weariness flicker in his eyes.

"Hot. And sweet. At the same time. Not sure how you do that, but you do," she said, taking a sip. "Really. No bad photos." It was true. He photographed well, he had just the right head tilt and smile to look good in selfies. She wished she had that skill. She was always looking the wrong way, closing her eyes, or rubbing her nose. If it was an awkward pose, she had it down. He portrayed the perfect mix of cool and approachable.

"Phew," he said with a smile in his voice. He turned the phone face down. He slid it back across the table without looking down. "I don't want to see them. I don't follow my own fans. Fame is destabilizing enough without seeing myself through other people's eyes." He paused and cocked his head. "Wait. Do you?"

She stilled and felt her cheeks flush. She followed about half a dozen fan accounts. She was busted. "Yes," she said, hiding her face with her hands. "Does that weird you out?"

He let out a loud laugh, deep from his belly. "Seriously? I didn't know you were a stan, deep down."

She covered her eyes and hid her face as she started to giggle. "Actually, I'm your biggest stan," she said. "You know that Insta account about your hair? I started one that's even better!" she teased. "It's about your third toe. I call it Jakey Toe. It's very popular."

He was shaking with laughter as he lifted his feet into her lap. "They're all yours," he said. "Worship away!"

She bent her head down to his feet and threw her head back. "Oh, your feet stink!" she yelped, pushing his feet away. As his feet hit the floor, he lurched forward. They were both laughing as their lips met. The laughter turned into the sound of their breath as their lips moved against each other. She ended the kiss, but Jake put his hand on the back of her neck, pulling her forehead against his and locking his eyes with hers. Kat could feel the emotion building. She pulled away and sat back in her chair. She saw a flicker of frustration on his face, but before he could say anything, Jake's stomach audibly growled.

Jake suggested they walk down to the café for some breakfast. He wouldn't let them leave the building separately or do any of the cloak-and-dagger maneuvers from yesterday. It took less than seven minutes to reach the café, situated along the canal. After she'd shown him around the city yesterday, he wanted to show Kat *his* favorite spot. It was one of the few places he'd visit during his brief time in the city. The café was comfortable and charming with rows of pastries in the window. A bell on the door clanged when they walked in. There was a small wooden counter for ordering and a few rustic tables in the back.

It was early and empty. They ordered at the counter. Jake only wanted coffee, but Kat insisted they split a *kanelsnegle*, a Danish cinnamon bun. She also ordered a soft-boiled egg with toast. Once they collected their food, they chose a table in the back corner.

Kat leaned forward in her chair and pointed out the window to a bright orange and blue bird sitting on the window box. "Oh,

I need to get a picture of that bird," she said, grabbing her phone. "Your dad will love it." She tapped her phone to take a picture before it flew away. "Can you believe how much your parents are into bird watching now? Apparently, it's a sport in Central Park. Who knew?"

He hesitated before answering, instead taking a long sip of coffee. She didn't seem to notice and kept talking. "Shoot, I won't text them yet. I told them Becca was upstate while I traveled for work, but I didn't tell them I was coming to see you. Do you think they'll mind? Maybe I should have told them. Did you tell them I was coming? Believe me, I have a lot of guilt about the things I've been doing with their precious only son."

He didn't answer. He didn't know how to answer. He gazed at the back wall and shook his head. Panic spread across her face. "That was supposed to make you laugh. Oh God, I just mentioned us having sex together and talking to your parents in the same sentence. Are you freaked out?"

"No, no," he said without hesitation. "I didn't know about the bird watching." He cleared his throat. "I didn't tell them you were coming. We aren't really talking right now." Jealousy bubbled up in his throat, straining his reply. He didn't think they would get into this conversation right now.

"What? I didn't know," said Kat. "For how long?"

"Months. Not a word in months," he admitted, and felt the shame he'd been working hard to bury. He hated saying it out loud. Given her close relationship with his parents, he was surprised she didn't already know. By now, he assumed Kat knew he was nothing but a disappointment to his family.

Kat had moved next door long after Jake had left to work on a series of projects in Europe and Canada. Over the better part of two years, Jake rarely came home. During that time, his parents developed a fondness for their new neighbors: the husband battling cancer and his pregnant wife.

Once Becca was born, they doted on her unlike anything he'd ever witnessed. They'd bragged to him in nearly every phone call as if she were their actual grandchild. Once Ben died, Jake's mom spent considerable time helping Kat with Becca, a job she took very seriously. From afar, Jake saw this as something his parents had done out of neighborly obligation.

Being home during the pandemic, he'd seen the full depth of their relationship. This was not a relationship held together by obligation or pity; it was a chosen family. The way they took care of *each other* was filled with a visible kindness.

Kat brought groceries home for his parents and picked up his grandmother's medication when the only pharmacy open was fifteen blocks away. She baked snickerdoodle cookies for his dad, which he hoarded, despite insisting he didn't eat sweets. The love and care between them reminded him of his own failings as a son. In his pursuit of his career, he hadn't played the role of dutiful son in years . . . or ever.

"I was dumb, I know. It was my fault." He hesitated. "My mom was upset at how little time I'd been home. She'd asked me to come back a few times, and I couldn't get a break in my schedule—" he stopped yet again. "And then I didn't make it home before Grandma died." He lived with the guilt of not making it in time but was frustrated at the depth of his mom's anger.

He believed his mother wanted him to stick around the Upper West Side for his entire life. She didn't understand the crushing pressure he felt to establish himself in the entertainment industry. If he wasn't overseas, he would need to be in Los Angeles. No matter what, he would spend a considerable amount of time away from New York. Actors had short shelf lives, and he was acutely aware that part of his appeal was his youth. He was consumed with anxiety about missing his window, a fear supported by all those he trusted in the industry. Roger had counseled him to sacrifice now.

"She told me she was embarrassed to have raised such a selfish human being. She was disappointed . . . in me. In who I'd become." His voice shook as they talked. He had been overwhelmed with self-loathing and that did him in. He didn't know how to balance his life with much else and the result came across as, and maybe truly was, selfish. Kat was right this morning. He'd never lived with responsibilities that didn't center around himself.

"And I walked out. Just like that. And then she called, more than once, and I ignored her." He rubbed his face with his hand. He wouldn't let his brain return to the vitriol-fueled comments he had made until his mother had been reduced to a pile of tears. He could still remember her face, shocked and crumbling. He hated himself for that day.

"Kat, I said some terrible things." It felt cathartic to acknowledge the rift between him and his family. He looked at Kat sitting across from him and realized she was the only person he trusted to let in so completely. Being in her presence was like a form of truth serum. He didn't need to play a part with her. He showed her everything, including those parts of him that were ugly and difficult. He drew in his breath and paused for her to comment on the mess he'd made of his entire family.

"I'm really sorry you're going through all this," Kat said, spreading butter on her Rugbrod and taking a bite. She looked at him but did not elaborate.

Jake waited, and when she remained silent, he asked, "Is that it? You have nothing else to say?" His tone bordered on exasperation. "I was expecting a speech, or a lecture, or something." His brain raced as he wondered what she was thinking. She was rarely silent.

"Oh, you want a speech?" she asked, pushing the cinnamon bun toward him. "Take a bite. You need to eat something."

He couldn't believe she was being elusive at a time like this. "You always have an opinion. Let's hear it," he said.

She wiped her mouth and took a drink. He could tell she was weighing her words carefully. She leaned back in her chair. "First off," she started, "I'm not going to get involved. I'll share a few thoughts, but I need you to know, I love all of you too much to pick sides."

Jake nodded, pulled off a piece of the cinnamon bun, and urged her to go on. He noticed her use of "love," and his stomach fluttered. He took a bite of the flaky pastry, his shoulders relaxing as the cinnamon hit his tongue.

"As for your fight, please keep in mind, you were both grieving. You were grieving your grandmother, but she was grieving her own mother. Jake, that's a loss that makes you question your own mortality in a sudden and frightening way."

He saw her tighten her jaw, and she shook her head as if to shake off a thought.

She continued. "Grief does weird things to people. One minute you're pulling people closer, the next minute you're pushing them away. Anything said in a haze of grief needs to have a short shelf life."

She paused for a minute, and Jake realized she was hesitating. He stayed quiet, giving her space to collect her thoughts.

"Also, I will say this just once, and I don't want you to obsess about it. I believe your mom has been grieving the loss of you for a long time. She wanted you to go out in the world and live your own life, but you did it so young and fast. You left and never looked back. I think she's wanted you to include her at least a little bit."

Jake interrupted her. He was gutted. "She told you that?"

"She didn't have to. When she talks about you, Jake, she's so proud. You work so hard, and you are great, like really great. But also—she never admits this—I see the hurt in her eyes when she has to search the internet to know what country you're in. She learns more from your fans' tweets than from you. She wants to be in your life, in a real way. I know for a fact she understands the commitment you need to have to your career, but that doesn't change the fact that she profoundly misses you."

Jake was silent as he took in Kat's words. He knew it was all true. After the fight with his mother, he'd stopped communicating and made her watch him from afar. "I really don't know how to make it right. God, the stuff we said to each other . . . And then I punished her with silence." he winced.

"I can't tell you how to fix it," she said. "I will say, you are a wonderful, passionate, driven human being. You feel everything so deeply . . . it's your superpower. When that's channeled in the right direction, it becomes absolute brilliance. It's what makes you a great actor. When all that feeling is allowed to live in a state of chaos, it becomes combative, even destructive. You got that from somewhere."

She reached over and pulled the cinnamon bun back to her side of the table and took a bite. She swallowed and continued. "You and you mom are so alike it shocks me that neither of you can see it. I'm not surprised at this situation, given both of your electric personalities. I compare it to lightning striking a power line and creating a dramatic but *brief* explosion. Except, in this case, you're letting the sparks burn down the entire house."

As they exited the café, Jake asked if they could walk around the city instead of heading back to the apartment. It was early morning, and the streets were quiet. Even though it was sunny, the air was cool and crisp, and the city glistened. The cobblestone streets were damp with dew that still clung to the cracks, outlining each brick in the patchwork of stone. She was worried she'd pushed him too far. Reflecting on the fracture within his family, she was reminded of the explosive cocktail that was his personality.

They walked along the Nyhavn canal, enjoying some fresh air and silence. Kat mapped Rosenborg Castle on her phone and when she showed Jake, he nodded. She motioned for them to turn down a tiny side street. When they were in the seclusion of the deserted street, Jake moved a bit closer and nudged her shoulder. She furrowed her brow and looked at him. He did it again and grinned. Having spent so little time with him in the past year, she forgot that he often communicated through physical touch, not words. His physicality was a language that was foreign to her, and she wished she was more fluent. She was seeing it here again and tried to decipher his mood.

"What are you thinking?" she finally asked, unable to translate his physical language.

"Thank you for back there . . . at the café. I don't think I realized how much that was eating away at me. I'm a mess," he mused. "I still don't know what I'm going to do, but even being honest with you—no, being honest with myself . . . makes me feel, I don't know . . . less of a mess?"

She felt relieved that their conversation hadn't thrown him into an obsessive tailspin. She'd glimpsed his darkness during quarantine, when he'd felt trapped. "Yeah, you're feeling blocked. I wonder how much this fight has to do with it?" she asked. She knew the answer, but this was his to figure out.

He shrugged his shoulders. "You're probably right. It certainly has been taking up more space than I want to admit. Why are you so smart?" he laughed.

"Meh, it comes with age," she said, winking at him. She knew he hated it when she reminded him that she was older. There were times when there didn't seem to be any age separating them. Jake had indeed had more life experiences than many people at twenty-five, but times like this reminded her how young he really was.

She was acutely aware he'd grown up in a business that required him to act like an adult as a teen, but it had stunted his emotional growth. Living in a bubble, wholly focused on himself as a product, gave him a skewed sense of the world. He lived in his own echo chamber, which made it easy to eschew reality. She had a visceral feeling of being simultaneously drawn to him while wanting to protect him. She wouldn't allow herself to process the full complication of her feelings toward Jake. Pushing her thoughts to the back of her mind, she navigated them through the city.

They turned onto the grounds of Rosenborg Castle and the surrounding park. Similar to Tivoli, the castle was a unique, breathtaking piece of architecture nestled inside the city. She was in love with this place that was home to castles *and* amusement parks, art installations on the street, and beautiful surprises around every corner. Maybe that's why she loved Copenhagen—the separate elements of the city didn't make sense, but they worked as an entire package. Leave it to the Danish to create a city that was the perfect blend of form and function.

They walked the grounds taking in the old, towering trees dotted with fall colors, the royal gardens, and just beyond, a seventeenth-century castle. She looked up at the brick and sandstone architecture and high towers. They looked like they touched the sky, and she blinked her eyes to take a mental picture. *Becca would love to see this someday*, she thought.

It was barely 7:30 a.m. and the city was just starting to wake up. Kat blew on her hands; they were cold in the fall air. Walking in the sun had warmed her, but in the shadow of the castle, she felt the dampness of the atmosphere. The cold radiated off the stone structure and onto the walkway below.

She wanted to go inside until she read the sign saying tours of the castle wouldn't start for another two-and-a-half hours. She sighed and fought back tears, momentarily remembering her trip with Ben. She'd wanted to go into the castle on that visit too, but Ben, tired of sightseeing, wanted to eat lunch instead. She'd tried to convince him to go in, even for a minute, but he'd rolled his eyes and told her he had no interest in a dusty old castle. He'd dug his heels in, and her response had been irrational anger. It'd been their first fight. And he'd won. They hadn't seen the castle that day. And it looked like she wouldn't see it now.

"Hey," Jake said, touching her shoulder. "What's wrong?"

"Nothing," she said curtly, sucking in a breath to fight back tears. "I'm tired . . . and cold . . . and . . . I just really wanted to go in. It's too early. I'm being stupid."

"Hmm . . . you want to go in? Let me see if I can make that happen." Jake gave her a mischievous look, went around her, and pulled on the door. When it didn't open, he searched until he saw another door and started toward it. Kat followed him, confused. "Jake, what are you doing? It doesn't open until ten. I can come back."

The next door didn't open, and Jake kept walking around the stone building. Finally, he found a door that opened and turned to her, laughing. "Or . . . is it open right now?" He held open the door and gestured for her to go inside.

"No, Jake," she said, stepping back. "It isn't open yet. We aren't allowed to go in there." Her heart raced as she pictured security alarms flashing, guards hunting them down, and a discussion with the police about trespassing. She was certain PathMobile would frown upon one of their key executives getting arrested.

Her thoughts were interrupted by the sounds of the metal door closing behind Jake. It let out a jarring *bang* that carried through the air. Kat stared at the closed door. She kicked a rock in front of her. She didn't know what to do with herself. Jake seemed to be gone forever.

The door flew open, and she jumped backward. Jake flashed her a devilish grin. "Kat! Come in! It'll be fine. It's amazing here. You'll want to see it, come inside." He held out his hand.

She stood back, shook her head no, and crossed her arms over her chest. He let out a laugh and, before she could register what he was doing, he picked her up, threw her over his shoulder, and carried her through the door.

She let out a yelp and smacked him on the shoulder. "What are you doing?" She couldn't even process what had just happened.

He didn't say anything. He set her down, gave her a smile, and opened his arms before him, bringing her focus to the grand throne room they were standing in. Her eyes widened. It was a grand space with a gleaming throne at the end of the room. Kat walked across the checkerboard floor and gazed at the rich tapestries that lined the walls. She was struck by the size and the nearly overwhelming mix of colors in front of her.

"This is stunning," Kat said, turning from the tapestry she was studying. "We should go. We can't be in here."

"Kat, it's a public building with the door unlocked. I don't see or hear any alarms. Worst case, security tells us to leave, that's it." Jake reassured her. Kat just wrinkled her nose at him in annoyance.

Jake shot her a smug grin, turned on his heel, and walked into the next room. She followed after him, shaking her head. *I guess we're going to see the castle after all.*

They walked from room to room, taking in the history of the four-hundred-year-old castle. They were all alone, which allowed her to abandon her rules when Jake took her hand, pulled her over, and gave her a small kiss. Their footsteps echoed in the silent castle, and she absorbed the stillness and peacefulness. She couldn't remember the last time her mind felt so quiet and open.

They made their way past a group of lavish portraits. "I'm tired of talking about me, believe it or not. How come I know nothing about your family?" he asked as they climbed up a spiral staircase to the second floor. "Please tell me you're a mess sometimes too. It isn't just me."

She pretended to focus on her footing, so she didn't have to answer right away. In all their time together, her family had never come up. She was not a native New Yorker and because of the quarantine, there hadn't been a circumstance where her family would have entered his mind. In fact, they hadn't talked about *her* much at all. She liked it that way.

"There's not much to tell," she started. "My mom was very young when she had me. She was only eighteen. I didn't know my dad—I don't think he wanted to be involved. They weren't in love or anything." She hoped he would be satisfied with the abbreviated version of her life. It was the most she ever told people. Once people learn you're a widow, they stop asking about your life, past or present.

"Are you two close? You never talk about her," he said.

Kat didn't want to talk about her. She wanted to deflect and go back to discussing the castle, him, or anything not to continue this conversation. As if he could read her mind, he stopped her.

"Hey, what is it? You can tell me."

She wanted him to know. She was ready for him to know. Without knowing it, he was challenging her with questions she hadn't answered in a long time.

"I don't talk about this much. My mom passed away when I was six. A freak aneurysm, I guess." She shrugged. "The end of this story is that I was raised by my grandparents, who passed while I was in college." It was hard for her not to have moments of bitterness when she thought about how many people in her life had left her.

Jake stopped and put his hand on her arm. "God, Kat, that's horrible," he said, looking over at her with sadness in his eyes. "How did I not know any of that?"

"The honest reality is that I don't remember much about my mom and obviously nothing about my dad. My grandparents were wonderful people. I really did have a very happy childhood, so this story is not as tragic as it sounds," she said. "Why we never talked about it? Because I don't ever talk about it unless asked, and you never asked."

Kat watched Jake as he shook his head without saying a word. He moved closer to her and brushed her hand with his, eventually hooking two of their fingers together. It was such a subtle, sweet gesture. This was his physical language, and she appreciated his light connection.

"It just doesn't seem fair," he said. "First your mom and then . . ." his voice trailed off.

She laughed without a hint of humor. "That's the cruelest part of life I've learned: experiencing one tragedy doesn't protect you from another. Nothing about life is fair." She decided to confess her true take on life. "Jake, I think life is just a series of people leaving you until it's your turn to die."

Jake let out a low whistle. "Wow. Kat, that's a hard way to view life," he said.

She took a second to reflect on his statement. Death had shaped every part of her approach to life. And even if he thought it was dark, it was true. Nothing in life was fair and no matter who you were, death was always around the corner.

She finally spoke. "You know when you were a kid, you had no concept of time? I've never felt that way. I've always had a sense of mortality. My grandmother used to remark that I freaked people out because I was obsessed with death. I was always trying to figure out when everyone else would die. I wanted to prepare, to plan, to come up with ways to control . . . I guess . . . *death*. I know it's one of the reasons I'm so risk averse. I crave safety. It's pretty cliché."

She had no idea why she was telling him all of this, only that she hadn't trusted anyone for a long time, not enough to fully reveal the darkness inside of her. She was trying to control and plan the one thing in life that was unpredictable and inevitable.

She thought for a moment. "It's why I'm obsessive about Becca and keeping her in my perfect little controlled kingdom. I don't feel like anything is safe, and I want to make sure nothing happens to her. Honestly, I know I'm too tightly wound about what she watches, her school, what she eats, who she plays with. . . . It's like . . . if I manage her life perfectly, nothing bad will happen to her." Admitting it out loud made Kat's heart race.

"Oh, I remember," he said with a knowing tone. "You'd never let her have extra dessert and no sweets. Which is practically child abuse," he teased. "I used to slip her Tootsie Pops when she would come over. She loves them, especially orange, which I always thought was weird, because no one likes orange."

"Wait, what?" she said incredulously. "That was you? I found a stash of them a few months ago in a drawer. I was so confused as to where she got them. I can't believe they came from you!"

Jake covered his face with both his hands and pretended to hide. His laugh echoed through the hall. "I can't believe she didn't eat them. Don't let her eat them now, they're like two years old!"

She punched him in the arm to try to make him stop laughing, which made him laugh even harder. *Of course!* She should have known it was Jake, who believed in, above all, enjoying life. Sometimes Kat just felt like she sucked the fun out of life. If he was the human equivalent to Friday, she felt like Monday. She convinced herself it was for good reason, but she didn't even know Becca loved Tootsie Pops.

Jake reached over and intertwined one of his hands in hers and gently pulled her close. He leaned forward and whispered in her ear. "I want to know more about you, Kat. I won't always think to ask you everything, okay?"

Nodding, Kat understood he was asking for her to be more open and forthcoming about her life, and although she trusted him, she didn't know if she trusted herself enough to let down much more of her protective armor. Not even for him.

They both heard the footsteps at the same time. Kat looked at Jake with alarm. Jake took her hand as they quickened their steps back down the stairs, retracing their path through the rooms and breaking into a run out the side door. She could hear the footsteps getting louder and a voice call out, "Hey!" right as they pushed the door open to the outside. As they ran out the door, Kat's heart was pounding in her ears, but Jake couldn't seem to control his laughter. He pulled her toward the garden, behind some tall bushes, and doubled over.

"Kat," he said, standing up, breathless. "The look on your face. . . ."

"You could have gotten us in trouble," she said, her voice in a yelling whisper. "What if we had gotten arrested?"

"Kat . . ." he started, "I'm smart enough to keep us from getting arrested . . . especially in a foreign country. I talked to the security guard before I came and got you. He's a fan and said we could have thirty minutes. There *are* a few benefits of hanging out with a celebrity. You're welcome."

She looked at him with wide eyes as her laughter erupted. She whacked him on the shoulder. Repeatedly.

He feigned pain and pulled her over to him. He put his arms around her, and Kat suddenly got the distinct feeling he was about to kiss her. They were fairly hidden, but they were still in a public park. He lived with such abandon, an in-the-moment mentality. Realizing she would need to be the one to protect them, she stepped away from him and looked around. Her eyes landed on them immediately.

"I think those girls over there are taking photos of us."

"Shit," he said under his breath as his shoulders tensed up. "Keep your head down. I'll be right back." He spotted the two girls trying to be discreet but clearly taking a picture of him. He knew all the tricks by now. They were using the most common—the selfie over the shoulder. He jogged over to them. "Hi!" he called out, waving and putting on his biggest smile.

They looked stunned, and he thought for a second they might dash away. "I'm Jake, but you probably know that. What are your names?" he asked. They stuttered and giggled. Once he learned their names, he said, "Hey, want a photo? Like, a good one? Ones taken over your shoulder are never very good. Your friends will say 'oh, is that really him?' and you'll say yes, but when you zoom in, it'll just be a blur of a weird-looking skinny guy with sunglasses and messy hair. Believe me."

The girls laughed. *Of course* they would rather have a real close-up picture.

"Here's the deal," he said, leaning in and whispering as if they were friends and confidants. "That girl over there. She's a friend of my parents, and she gets annoyed when she accidentally shows up in the photos people take of me. Like, she won't hang out with me much because of it. Something about privacy." He rolled his eyes to signal that he would never feel this way. "I played a little trick on her so she's in a bad mood, so can you just not post those? We can do a full-on photo shoot right here, and you can post any of the pictures we take together. Deal?"

They shook his hand to seal the deal. In their world, they had pretty much won the social lottery. They made an elaborate show of deleting the earlier photos and even permanently deleting them from the digital trash. He spent over ten minutes posing with the girls and generally having fun. At least *they* thought so. He was a good actor, after all. He glanced over and saw Kat looking at them. He made the girls wave to her, which made her shake her head, but he did see a small smile.

Once they had their shots, he kissed both girls on the cheek and said his goodbyes. The young girls were beaming as they walked away, chattering excitedly. He couldn't help but smile, feeding off their energy. As weird as it was for him, he understood his power to make people happy.

He jogged back to Kat, and she asked him if they had indeed taken photos.

"Yes, but they deleted 'em. I gave them some better content," he said as his eyes scanned the perimeter of the park and landed on the black car parked on the corner. "I have a car waiting. We should go. It's getting crowded out here."

He pointed to the car across the street and started to walk at a brisk pace. He had an easy time being out in the early mornings, before nine or ten, but it was a beautiful Sunday. He should have been more careful, and he kicked himself for putting them in that position. He had carried her into Rosenborg partially because Kat seemed disappointed it was closed, but also to get them into a private space. The park was getting busy, and Jake knew it was moments before he was spotted. When they ran out of the castle, he got caught up in the moment and was careless.

He didn't want to hide with her, but this wasn't smart. *You know how to protect her*, he thought, *get your head together*. He vowed to be more careful, starting now—which is why he had texted his assistant to send the private car. They needed to stop using taxis and start using the drivers he trusted. He had protections available to him, and he was going to use every single one of them if it meant protecting Kat.

He finally took a breath when they got back to the apartment. "Kat, I think we should stay here the rest of the day, if that's okay. It's Sunday and the weather is beautiful, but I didn't expect it to be *that* crowded. I'm worried about keeping you anonymous if we continue to be so visible," he said, taking off his shoes and putting his phone on the charger.

"Okay by me," she said, looking out the window at the canal below. "This view is gorgeous. Look at all those people down there," she said, pointing to a busy walkway a few floors below. It was full of people enjoying the clear, fall day. The sun made the canal shimmer like a thousand diamonds floating in the middle of the city.

Jake slid his arms around her waist, rested his chin on her shoulder, and looked out the window. “I like this more,” he whispered in her ear, happy to put his arms around her without making sure no one was watching, photographing, or filming. He brought his lips to her neck, covering her with small sensual kisses, resuming what he started earlier this morning.

He felt Kat lean back, resting fully in his arms. She rolled her head back on his shoulder, giving him more access to her soft skin. She let out a small gasp as he lightly sucked the base of her collarbone. He turned her around, brought his lips to hers and kissed her with a hunger that felt insatiable. He took her hand and pulled her toward the bedroom. If they were going to stay in all day, this would do just fine.

chapter ten

Kat tiptoed out of the bedroom after a lazy morning spent with gentle kisses, soft caresses, an eventual release, and a short, luxurious nap. Jake was still asleep, and she didn't want to wake him, so she closed the door to the bedroom before taking up residence on the couch. She checked the clock on her phone to make sure it was a good time to call Becca. She couldn't wait to talk to her. She dialed the FaceTime, and her face lit up when Becca answered with a loud laugh.

"Hi, Momma!" her five-year-old voice yelled with excitement. Kat turned the volume down on her laptop.

"Hi, Baby! I miss you!" she said. "Tell me everything you've been up to."

Becca was having the time of her life and bubbled with happiness. She'd been playing at the lake every day, and yesterday she'd gone horseback riding. Upstate New York was enjoying an unexpected last burst of summer and their September, instead of turning dreary, was filled with sunshine. The chatter of Becca's young mind delighted Kat to no end.

"Mama," Becca asked, "are you having fun? Are you still in the—what did Grandma call it? Oh, the Coping Place?"

Kat started laughing. "I'm in Copenhagen. It's a city in Denmark. I'll show it to you on a map when I get back. Yes, sweetie,

I'm having fun. This city makes me think of your dad. We came here once."

"I want to go there someday," Becca said with a giggle. Her mind worked in such a beautifully simple way. Her dad was just a wonderful idea to her. He was not a real person, but a perfect storybook character.

"You will, my sweet girl, you will," Kat said, and she meant it. They promised to talk the next day and hung up.

Jake walked out of the bedroom, freshly showered, drying his curls with a towel. "Hey, was that Becca?" he asked. "Next time, let me say hello!"

Kat nodded, but she didn't mean it. Although Becca would likely remember Jake, it wasn't about Jake and Becca. Kat was reminded of another reason she needed to keep her relationship with Jake private.

She'd asked Ben's parents to watch Becca so she could travel for work, which was mostly true. She couldn't imagine their feelings if they'd known they were watching their grandchild, the daughter of their deceased son, so her mom could run off to a foreign country to see another man. She felt like she was cheating on Ben's memory, and by default, his entire family.

"Hey, did you leave me any hot water?" Kat asked, changing the subject. "A shower sounds amazing right now."

"It felt almost as good as that nap did," Jake said, stretching his shoulder. "Get in there, I'll order a late lunch."

Jake was right. The shower felt wonderful, and she spent extra time just letting the hot water cascade over her entire body. The past few days had been fun and challenging, overwhelming and exciting, and she felt as alive as she had when Jake had first burst into her life. She felt a twinge of sadness that it couldn't be this way all the time. It had taken his phone call and her work trip to bring them together and even then, it was fleeting.

She was resolved to keep enough of a barrier up to protect

herself from falling for him, but she couldn't deny how he made her feel: desired, not for what she could accomplish, but because of who she was as a woman. He made her feel cared for in a way that had become foreign to her. The reality of their lives not rationally fitting together was unavoidable, but she couldn't help enjoying, even for a little while, living in an orbit that contained Jake. She was resigned to compartmentalize Jake into these ten days, even though they had already slipped into an intimacy far surpassing their months together.

She pulled on soft joggers and her favorite NYU sweatshirt. Her body and mind were sluggish after their earlier activities and minuscule nap. She hadn't registered how hungry she was until she saw lunch on the table. He'd ordered her a turkey sandwich . . . and a beef sandwich . . . and a ham sandwich.

"Take your pick . . . ahh . . . I didn't know what you liked," he said with a sheepish smile. She picked up the turkey sandwich, unwrapped it, and took a bite.

Jake sat back and took a drink of his protein shake. "So, we do need to talk," he started. Kat swallowed and raised her eyebrows. He sounded serious.

"Yes?" she asked with a hint of concern in her voice. She set her sandwich back on the table, leaned back in her chair and crossed her arms.

Jake continued, "I need to tell my publicist about you."

Kat opened her mouth to speak, and Jake reached over and gently uncrossed her arms. "Please let me finish." His voice was quiet, his eyes soft. She closed her mouth and squeezed his hand.

"As much as I like all the rules you put in place—you know I think they're awesome," he started, winking at her, sarcasm evident, "it's naive to think that there won't be any photographs spun into some story. I've learned—the hard way, I might add—that we need to get ahead of it."

"What are you thinking?" she asked. She didn't necessarily

agree, but his tone said this was not up for discussion. He knew his world better than she did. She'd been listening earlier when Jake confessed that fame destabilized him. She couldn't imagine what it was like to have your every move analyzed under a microscope. What it must feel like to have strangers think they know you, deserve a piece of you, just because they saw you on a screen. If it were her, it would've driven her into hiding. It hit her how unfair, even offensive, it was for her to even pretend to know how to manage his public life.

"I have a call with my publicist later today and I'll tell her you're here. You and I are friends, and our families know each other. You have business here and are just visiting." He paused. "I don't know if they'll get any calls or questions, but if we need to release something at any point, they won't be scrambling."

"Do you think that will happen? They might need to release something? I figured we could be in *some* casual photos without it automatically linking me to you, like romantically." Her heart beat faster.

"Yes. I do think it could happen. We were lucky yesterday, and I'm kicking myself for earlier today," he said. "Letting people on my team know helps us. I'm sensitive to your concerns for Becca, and I understand how the wrong optics could derail your career right now." He ceased talking and shook his head back and forth. "Things are different, Kat. I thought it was hard to manage before, but it's escalating," he said. "I can't just hope it won't happen. I want to have a strategy and a team ready if . . . when it does."

She nodded to show she understood. His last movie, which was out in theaters and streaming, was a critical darling. His profile continued to rise publicly, and she had watched the size and fervor of his fandom increase. She was just beginning to see the impact on his everyday life.

"Do you think we should just stay in for the rest of the trip?

I'll be going into the office starting tomorrow, so it might be easier to only be together here, in the apartment," she asked. She felt naive and stupid that she'd decided Tivoli would be a good idea yesterday and somewhere as touristy as Rosenborg today. He was right—they'd been lucky.

"No, Kat. I won't live in hiding. And neither should you, just because we're together. It's pretty easy for me to be out during the fringes of the day: early morning and very late evening. Less people. We should stick to those times if we can," he said. "But we have nothing to hide and, if I include the PR team to manage anything that comes out, we'll be fine."

"You think a PR team is better than my six rules?" she teased.

"Yes." He winked. Jake hesitated and then continued, "Listen, after Lolla, I promised that I wouldn't catch them off guard."

"Ahh," Kat said. The images of Jake drunk and high, at Lollapalooza, a multiday music festival in Chicago, flashed in her mind. She closed her eyes for a second attempting to push the pictures of Jake draped across multiple girls out of her brain. The virtual chatter had been negative and incessant for days. In the pictures that covered every news feed, she'd stared at his hollow eyes, pale skin, and forced smile and had worried he wasn't okay. Although they hadn't spoken for months, she'd broken their silence and called him. He hadn't picked up or ever acknowledged her call.

"How many girls were you with that weekend?" she asked. As soon as the question slipped out of her mouth, she wished she hadn't asked.

He raised his eyebrows. "Do you really want me to answer that?"

"Yes. No. Whatever. Answer if you want," she said, trying to act casual. Ugh. She knew better than to ask, but her curiosity got the better of her.

He cleared his throat. "Four."

"*Four!*" she said, unable to keep the surprise out of her voice. "You were only there for two days! How does that even happen?" She was louder than she meant to be, trying to get her stupid brain to stop doing the math and figuring out the logistics of four women in one weekend.

"Certainly, you don't want me to answer that," he said. "I was only there for thirty-six hours for a press junket. Those things are fucking boring. Lolla was just a diversion." He looked smug, which made her irritation bubble to the surface.

"Jake!" she scowled at him. Unrest settled in her stomach as pictured him using his power as a celebrity to pick up women for his amusement. Because he was *bored*. She hadn't seen him as a womanizer, but he didn't think twice about having sex with four different women in thirty-six hours. She was reminded that she only knew a part of him and this person, this part of him, she did not know.

"Kat, have you ever done molly? You want to have sex with everyone when you do molly," he said. "I've learned it's not a good idea. Me and molly are broken up." He laughed at his own joke. "My PR team was pissed. They had their hands full with the press junket and then I threw that in their lap." He let out a low whistle. "Kept them on their toes, that's for sure."

Kat rolled her eyes at him and didn't say anything. She didn't like this Jake. She couldn't decipher between hurt or anger when tears pricked her eyes. She blinked them back and hoped he didn't see.

"Hey," he said, frowning. "You upset? Sorry, I wasn't thinking. . . ." He reached over to take her hand. "I'm stupid, of course—"

"No, no," she said, pulling her hand out of his grasp. Her voice was strained. "I asked. I shouldn't have. I just feel bad for the girls, that's all. And lately, all the press can call you is a party boy. I just don't know this side of you." She refused to let him know his weekend of debauchery had hurt her.

His face looked stricken, and she saw a flash of anger in his eyes. "This isn't a *side* of me. It was just a weekend where I needed, I don't know . . . an escape? Please don't think I took advantage of them. It was all very consensual. Believe me, they had no problem going to Reddit within two days to tell their story of what it's like to have sex with me," he said. "Frankly, it read like they enjoyed it significantly more than me."

"But still. The power dynamics, Jake . . . they were in your favor," she challenged, locking eyes with him.

"Were they? I was high out of my mind and barely remember anything. In the end, they got a lot more out it than I did," he said, his voice tight.

She didn't reply. Twenty-five, she reminded herself. He was twenty-five. Unlike most twenty-five-year-olds, he hadn't had have college years to party and experiment. These were his years, long overdue, but he had to do it under the microscope of rising fame. Seeing his mental state over these past few days, it was clear he was trying to escape. He'd escaped into the arms of women looking for social currency through an interaction with Jake.

She had concerns about how far he would go to escape. In his industry, drugs were plentiful, not to mention acceptable. His brilliance and creativity came at a price. For as confident as he was, he had told her many times that he didn't believe he fit into the world very well. Maybe that's why she found him magnetic—she saw a flame that burned a little brighter than in the average person. *His unpredictability excites and scares me at the same time*, she finally admitted to herself.

She stood up from the table and began cleaning up her lunch. She was pensive as she concentrated on wrapping the uneaten sandwiches back in their wrappers. She was taking great care to wrap them perfectly. Anything so she didn't have to look at him.

"Kat, I'm sorry. Are you okay?" he asked tentatively.

"Yes, don't be silly," she said, trying to sound light. "I have no right to have an opinion on what you do with your free time." She shrugged her shoulders and hoped she projected casual.

Jake's expression was troubled. "Kat, you have every—" he started.

"Jake, I don't want to discuss this," she interrupted, referring to more than just the discussion about Lolla. She didn't want to admit to him the feelings of jealousy that swirled around her brain no matter how hard she tried to keep it casual. She didn't want to admit how much she hated seeing him with anyone but her. Admitting those feelings would be setting herself up for an emotional fall she didn't believe she'd withstand. No. She wouldn't let him hurt her. She had seven and a half more days, and she would fortify the wall around her heart.

To make it clear she was done talking and make him stop looking at her, she opened her laptop, so it covered her face. She began to read her email. Continuing the conversation with Jake wasn't productive, and she had work to do in order to prepare for her first day in the Copenhagen office.

Jake couldn't believe he was stupid enough to share the details of his weekend in Chicago. He could only imagine how it felt to see him splashed all over Instagram hanging on, kissing multiple women. Until now, he hadn't considered how she would feel about that weekend. *It happened when we weren't even talking*, he rationalized to himself. He vaguely remembered her calling him after that weekend, but he'd been so hungover he'd deleted the voicemail as soon as he heard her voice. He'd been angry she was ignoring him, and hearing her voice, full of concern, made him resent her more. How dare she refuse to speak to him and then assume he wasn't okay, just because he'd let loose for one weekend? Of course, he now realized he *hadn't* been okay. He'd been alone, drunk, and high. When he'd woken up in the hotel room the next morning, he knew he'd made a very public mistake.

He didn't want to dwell on his mistakes. He needed to get his mind in the present and keep himself from making another mistake. One that could affect his career. He had work to do. Jake stretched out on the couch and opened *Zero Code*. He was committed to re-read the book as he prepared to inhabit the character of Tom. Kat had been right—determining Tom's physicality had brought him off the pages of the script in a way that Jake could immerse himself in. Now he wanted to know more about his motivations. Those he could only understand through Tom's internal dialogue, available in the text of the original novel, and he was excited to lose himself in Tom's mind.

The apartment was quiet except for the soft clicking of Kat's typing. Getting a rare moment to read, during a lackadaisical Sunday, he felt a calm wash over him. Calm wrestled with flutters of anxiety every time he remembered Garren's look of disappointment. He successfully declared calm the victor by focusing on the pages before him. Soon he would receive the revised filming schedule, but for now, he would continue to do the work needed to bring forward the best performance he could when he was called back to set.

Kat snapped closed her laptop, breaking the silence. He looked up to find her staring at him. Her eyes were soft, and her face relaxed. He wanted to ask her if she was okay after their earlier conversation, but he decided to let it go. She'd made it clear she was done talking and for now, he was just happy to have her back.

"Whatcha reading?" she asked, putting her chin on her hand. Her hair cascaded loose over her shoulders. Her frayed NYU sweatshirt fell over her left shoulder. He felt the familiar pull in her presence and just wanted her to be physically close to him.

Jake held up the *Zero Code* book so she could see the cover.

He motioned to her and patted the space on the couch in front of him, inviting her to join him. They'd often read together during the pandemic, both finding comfort in each other and the escape of a story that was not their own. She walked over, sat down, and leaned back on his chest, finding the perfect way to lie together on the small couch. He stretched his legs and intertwined them with hers, his sock feet playfully tickling her toes. His arms curved around her and held the book in front of them so they could read it at the same time. When he got to the end of the page, he kissed the top of her head and turned the page. She grabbed his hand.

"I wasn't finished," she whispered. "I don't read as fast as you."

He chuckled and turned the page backward. Instead of waiting for her to finish, Jake read the words aloud. He felt Kat settle into him as he read the beautiful literary prose on each page. It was a deep story, and reading Tom's thoughts aloud was giving him a full human understanding of the man he would portray on screen. He pulled a pencil off the side table and made a note in the margins of the book before continuing.

"Hmm . . . Tom's internal thoughts are funny. I love his sarcasm," Kat observed. Jake agreed. He had forgotten this part of the novel. He was going to give his lines a second look to see if that was a tonality he could bring into his performance. Kat nudged him. "Keep reading. You should do audiobooks by the way. I could listen to your voice for hours," she said. He kissed her cheek and continued reading.

He read to her for the better part of an hour, stopping only to take a note or make a comment, until she let out a long yawn. He looked at her and her eyes were heavy.

"You should take another nap. A real one this time. You look exhausted," he whispered in her ear and closed the novel. He stroked her hair with his free hand and thought about their earlier conversation on death. He was troubled by her stark view on life. He'd been watching the pressure she put on herself and he felt an intense desire to show her a life outside of the shadow of death. It was manifesting in a want to shelter and cocoon her inside his world.

"No, I like this," she said, and let out another yawn. "Well, maybe just an hour." She sat up, stretched, leaned forward, and gave him a quick kiss. "Will you wake me later?" She asked as she stood up and made her way toward the bedroom.

Jake nodded and went back to reading. After two more chapters, he looked at the time and realized it was time to call Cindy, his publicist and the leader of his PR and social teams. *Cindy will know how to keep Kat anonymous*, he thought. He'd relied on her the past year, and she'd yet to let him down. She was a bulldog, who managed situations such as Lolla with an aggressiveness that was swift and effective.

Cindy had been more upset about the women than the drugs. Apparently, drugs made him seem edgy and less young which, oddly, broadened his appeal. Also, there was the matter of the play-by-play reports that made their way to the gossip sites. A version had been live for a short number of hours before she'd been able to squash it. Though nothing truly dies once it hits the internet, she managed to bury it pretty far away. He didn't know how Cindy had done it, but barely anything resurfaced, except a few photos, keeping the social cycle short.

He needed Cindy now more than ever. He understood Kat's reasons for staying anonymous while she was here, and they had seven days to make it through. But what they had yet to discuss was the future of their relationship beyond Copenhagen. They had agreed to keep it casual, without expectations, but Jake had moved past casual.

If he was being honest with himself, he'd moved past casual the moment he'd picked up the phone to call her. He was anxious, confidence shaken, and he'd called *her*, the one person who calmed and centered him like no one else. From the moment she'd arrived, everything had begun to fall back into place. He wanted her in his life—that, he knew for certain. He wanted to believe he would take anything she would give, even if Kat was not able to move beyond a limited, physical relationship, but he knew that wasn't true. He felt uncompromising in his want of her and would not settle for brief and casual.

Jake had a crushing need to tell Kat the depth of his feelings, but he could feel her hesitation. He knew it was fear—it was a risk, *he* was risk. Kat didn't like complication and bringing their lives together would bring difficulties, but those challenges were about logistics and routines. The thought of them not being together felt more difficult.

He connected into the Zoom meeting and Cindy was already waiting.

"Jake! You're on time!" she exclaimed. She had a thick Long Island accent, and it added to her commanding demeanor. Even though technically she worked for him, she kind of scared him. She'd been his publicist since before he'd done anything that would require public relations.

Although Jake had asked for the call, Cindy ran it, walking through her current list of topics. Most were focused on the last film he had completed. It was dropping in two months, and there would be a PR junket that he would need to do the weekend prior to the drop. It was a grueling time to throw in a press junket, and he silently cursed his overwhelming schedule. He could rarely make sense of the logistics of his life. He was glad to have other people figure it out.

Cindy was working out the travel with the PAs on his current film. "We'll figure it out. Your PA emailed us the revised schedule," she said.

Jake raised his eyebrows "Oh, like today? The most current one?" he asked. He couldn't keep all the schedules straight and had not seen that a new one had been released. He checked his email and there it was. There was also a request from Garren for a meeting tomorrow. Jake was feeling clearer on the artistic direction he wanted to take the character. He hoped it was what Garren was looking for from his performance. Jake shot off an email confirming that he would come to set tomorrow at the time requested.

Having Kat here gave him a minute to breathe, but also the discipline and connection he'd been missing. He realized he'd been completely pushing everyone away and moving himself down a spectacular path of self-destruction. Beginning to come back to himself, managing his life and rebuilding relationships—starting with Kat—had allowed him to feel safe and vulnerable enough to become someone else. He was ready to become Tom in an authentic way that would translate through the screen.

Once Cindy was done working through the logistics of the scheduled junkets, she turned to social. "So, you had fun at Tivoli yesterday, huh?" she said, typing on her computer. "The content being posted is fantastic. I couldn't have done it better myself," she said. "It's real cute. We had some TikTok hits too." This was big praise coming from Cindy.

"I'm having fun with the fans in Denmark. They're very sweet," he said. "I figure this will help grow my non-US fan base." He knew Cindy would appreciate the content from Tivoli. He'd had a great day and it showed.

Cindy smiled. "Now that is what I'm talking about!" She always pushed him to be more thoughtful and calculating about his social media exposure. She characterized his social media presence by saying it was lackluster at best, and borderline damaging at its worst. "Next time let me know and we'll schedule a pap walk." He rolled his eyes at her suggestion. *That* he wouldn't be doing any time soon.

Cindy seemed to be at the end of her list when Jake finally

spoke up. "Is your agenda done? Because there's a topic I want to discuss before we hang up."

Cindy raised her eyebrows. He knew she would be surprised since he rarely added anything on their calls. Typically, he suffered through each topic and tried to make them as short as possible. "This will be interesting. What's up?" Cindy asked.

"It's really nothing, but I did promise I wouldn't surprise you." Jake started.

"What did you do . . . and who saw it?" Cindy interrupted.

"No, nothing like that," he said. "I have a friend here with me for the next week or so and I'm guessing we'll be seen together—it feels unavoidable. I just wanted you to know, in case anything gains traction, and you're asked."

"Who is she?" Cindy asked. Of course, she knew that if he was telling her, it had to be a woman.

"Her name is Kat. She's a friend of mine. Friend of my family, my parents to be exact. She's their neighbor back in New York. She's here on business and she's staying with me." Jake spit out rapidly.

"Okay," Cindy started, "friend of the family . . . this is all fine," she paused, and Jake watched her process his words. It was her job to read between the lines. "Staying with you? Like, in your place? For how long?" she asked.

"Just under two weeks," Jake replied, ignoring the knowing look that Cindy was giving him. He could hear her fishing, but he wasn't going to give her more than he had to.

"If you have nothing to hide, we wouldn't be talking. And if she were only there on business, her company would put her up in a hotel. What are you not telling me, Jake?" she mused. "Is she more than a friend? Safe space . . . you need to be honest with me."

Jake cleared his throat and was thoughtful before speaking. "Yes." It was the first time he'd said it out loud. "Yes, Cindy, we are in a relationship . . . or, at least, I'd like to be in a relationship with Kat. We've been careful out in public but today we were just taking a walk, and someone photographed us. We were just hanging in a park. Not a big deal, but you know, even if there's a picture of me touching her arm, it'll become a thing." He paused. "She doesn't want to be identified publicly. Especially right now."

Cindy put on her glasses. "You're being smart. I need to know a little about her." She paused. "Jake, it's good you're telling me. There are a lot of things we can do to keep this from going public."

He couldn't keep the smile off his face as he started talking about Kat. "Her full name is Kat Green. We became friends during the pandemic. She's the head of product for PathMobile, which means she's wicked smart. She runs a team of like two thousand people. She lives in New York. Duh, I told you that already when I mentioned she was my neighbor. She has the most adorable daughter, Becca, who's almost six. . . ."

"Kat, Kat Green," she said typing into her computer. "Found her on LinkedIn. Okay. She's thirty-three, hmm, older woman, interesting choice." Cindy whistled. "Okay . . . look at that CV. That's impressive for only thirty-three. She's well-known in her industry. Wow. She has a lot of press hits on her own." She took her eyes off her second screen and looked back at the Zoom call. "Jake, she's a heavy hitter in her own right. Okay. We need to talk about her child. Is there an ex-husband we need to manage?"

He shook his head. "No, he's not in the picture."

Cindy fixed him with a disbelieving look. "Oh, believe me, honey," she started, "they suddenly come out of the woodwork when their ex starts dating a movie star."

"Cindy, he died, he's dead," Jake said curtly.

"That's great news," Cindy said cheerfully. "Lucky for us."

Jake was speechless and glanced at the bedroom where Kat was still sleeping.

Cindy must have seen his face, because she took her glasses off and looked into the camera. "Jake, I know you think I'm a bitch, but I'm the one who needs to think this way. This is good for you. If he was alive, you become a home wrecker, and she's a slut sleeping around with a much younger man. But since he's dead, you both become a sympathetic couple. Love after loss. I can see the headlines, and they're all positive for you."

"Well, let's not let it come to headlines," he growled, pissed at the court of public opinion, unfair and unforgiving.

"I have to level with you, Jake. This could have more legs than I thought *if* anything happens and *if* someone picks up on it. Not that we can't manage it. We can. This is just juicier than I imagined. I expected her to be a twenty-one-year-old influencer slash model-of-the-day." Cindy winked at him. "This is much more interesting."

She paused. "Have you ever considered doing anything proactively? Like an announcement or even just a well-timed Instagram? Just get it out there? We're trying to get people to take you more seriously, and this could be good for your image. Helping a young widow move on with her life gives you a much more woke and sensitive image than, f-boy actor on the rise."

He winced at her characterization of how he was perceived. He probably deserved it, given his shenanigans over the past year, but he certainly thought he deserved more consideration for his acting abilities. But it seemed his personal life would always overshadow everything.

"No!" Jake said sharply. "We can't. Not right now. Kat is worried about having complete strangers take an interest in Becca. I think that's a fair concern, given some of the boundaries people cross without a second thought." He paused and waited for Cindy to acknowledge his statement. "Also, she *is* here for work and it's not good optics to look like she's here to hang out with me. So, we need to keep her as anonymous as we can. At least for the next seven days."

Cindy sighed. "And then later? Is she prepared to announce something in the future? We can only keep this a secret for so long." Jake knew she was right, but he didn't even know if Kat wanted a relationship past this week. He certainly hoped so, but her hesitation gave him pause.

"I don't know," he said honestly. "We're still figuring things out. Like, between us. And I don't want to try to figure it out with millions of people watching." He stopped to take a breath and finally said, "I just want time, Cindy. We need time. Can you get us some time to be a secret a little bit longer?"

Cindy put up both hands in a show of surrender. "Okay, this is what we are going to do. This is the story if we need it: she's a longtime friend of your parents, and she's your neighbor back home. She's practically family. She's working on a project here in Copenhagen. This was a perfect opportunity to be neighbors again. Purely platonic. Great friends."

Jake nodded into the camera. "That's right. But only if needed. Nothing proactive." He liked it because it was true. True enough.

"It'll be fine," Cindy said, "and I do want to say, I'm happy for you, Jake." It was just about the kindest thing she had ever said to him. She wasn't done. "Word of advice," she said. "Just don't go making out on the street."

"When are you going to forgive me for that?" Jake murmured. She managed to weave it into every conversation.

"Never. Bye, Jake," she said, and signed off.

chapter eleven

Kat opened her eyes as Jake ran his hand up and down her arm to wake her up. She smiled at him and sat up, rubbing the sleep out of her eyes.

"Hey. How long was I out?" she asked.

Jake handed her a cup of coffee he had set on her nightstand. "Kat, it's 5:45 in the morning. You slept all night."

"What?" she asked, looking around and taking in the unmistakable gray of early morning light. "I can't believe I slept that long. Why didn't you wake me?"

Jake shrugged. "You needed it," he said as he pushed a strand of hair out of her face and behind her ear. "You need a break, Kat. You looked so peaceful. I wasn't going to wake you."

She smiled and took a sip of coffee. She did the math: she'd slept for over twelve hours. She couldn't remember the last time she had gotten that much sleep. "I'm going to get in the shower," she said and glanced at the nightstand. "Where's my phone?"

Jake jumped up. "I'll find it."

Kat stretched her arms and got out of bed. She was still in her sweats from the night before. She'd fallen asleep on top of the covers, and it looked like she hadn't moved all night. The jet lag—plus a few late nights and early mornings—had finally caught up to her. She felt rested and no longer had the sluggish feeling she relied on coffee to mask.

"It's on the kitchen table," Jake called from the kitchen. "Dead. I'll put it on the charger in here."

"Okay," she called. She would check her phone after her shower. It was Monday morning in Copenhagen, which meant it was still the middle of the night in the US. She had to admit, not only did it feel good physically to get that much sleep, but it was also nice to ease into the morning without the normal onslaught of emails from work.

After a hot shower and extended time getting ready, Kat walked into the kitchen. She was in her self-imposed work uniform of dark jeans and black suit jacket. Her hair was pulled into a low knot at the base of her neck. She looked professional, but approachable and appropriate for a tech company where the wardrobe tipped more to hoodies and sneakers.

As she grabbed her laptop off the table and unplugged its charger, it hit her how excited she was to finally go inside the PathMobile Copenhagen offices. She'd taken a photo outside the office during her and Ben's honeymoon visit. She felt as giddy now as she did back then. She'd come a long way from the newly graduated MBA student, paying her dues in the PathMobile finance department. Being new to the company, she hadn't gone in but had sent her boss the picture. She'd been proud to see the birthplace of the company where she wanted to build her career. Today, she would finally walk through those doors.

Jake was busy working, his laptop open, notes around him, and the *Zero Code* novel fanned upside down in front of him. It looked like he had found a lot of material that was inspiring him. She even saw some sketches spread out on the table. She leaned down and gave him a small kiss. She couldn't stop smiling. After the last few days with Jake, topped off with an actual full night's sleep, she felt better than she had in a long time. She was going to ask him to catch her up with the *Zero Code* novel when she glanced at her phone on the counter. It was a sea of green text bubbles and missed calls.

Her heart dropped and panic set in as she grabbed it and unlocked her device. She scanned the names to make sure it wasn't about Becca. Finding a smidge of relief that nothing had happened to her, Kat refocused her brain to the messages.

"Shit," she said as her heart raced.

"What?" Jake asked, looking up from his laptop.

"Shit," she said, unable to say words beyond the singular expletive. As she read the chain, Jake leaned over her shoulder to see what had happened.

E: I just got word from the sticker manufacturer. Their estimate for new adhesive is three to four weeks. Minimum.

E. This is a problem. You know we don't have that much of a buffer on the timeline. We won't get enough stock out to retail and we'll be delayed on shipping pre-orders.

E. I looked into pivoting to other manufacturers, but they're quoting me an even longer timeline.

E. Let me know when you're available to talk. We should discuss this tonight.

E. Kat, sorry to keep texting you, but are you there? I know we need to loop in Will ASAP. I thought you might want to tell him.

E. Kat?

E. Okay, I'm just going to loop Will into this situation and start a group chain.

W: Emily, please write all this up and construct a worst-case scenario timeline. Kat, please let us know when you are available so we can talk live. I think it's 8:00 p.m. DMK time, so hoping we can chat tonight.

W: I talked to Poul, CEO of Denmark. You will meet him tomorrow. Instead of going through the Denmark launch plans, he is going to work with you on solutions.

W: Please make this your #1 priority.

W: He will meet you at the office at 8:00 a.m. sharp. I haven't heard from you, but assuming you will be there.

Tears pricked her eyes. She hadn't been available when this had blown up, and Will had had to take over, giving Emily direction and getting in contact with the Denmark office. She slammed her phone down. She'd been MIA and made her boss step in. *Get your head in the game,* she internally berated herself. *This is not a vacation.* She started packing her bag, throwing things in at a rapid pace. She had less than a half hour to get to the PathMobile offices to meet with Poul. A tear fell, and she brushed it away with a shaky hand. "I can't believe this happened," she said to herself. "I fucked up."

"Kat . . ." Jake started, approaching her like a wounded puppy. "You didn't fuck up. You were sleeping. On a Sunday."

She glared at him and zipped up her overstuffed bag. She didn't want him to make her feel better. She wanted the situation to have never happened. She snatched up her phone and shot off a text to Will and Emily with an apology, an explanation, and a confirmation that she would meet with Poul this morning.

"I called a car for you," Jake said. "It's waiting downstairs."

"Thanks," Kat said as she grabbed her bag and ran out the door.

chapter twelve

Her car pulled up to the PathMobile Copenhagen office at 7:58 a.m. It was a midsized regional office housing a sales and marketing team. It was not uncommon to launch products in the Denmark and Ireland offices prior to the US to work out glitches and get initial consumer plus retailer feedback. Kat had interfaced with Poul, the Copenhagen CEO by way of global leadership meetings, but they had only directly spoken a few times. Poul was a favorite of the board and a personal friend of the founder. Until this morning, she was looking forward to getting to spend time with him. Today, however, she was feeling off her game and scattered. Not the impression she wanted to make on someone so important to her future. In a futile attempt to calm her mind, she took a few deep breaths before opening the car door.

Poul was standing just inside the entrance when Kat walked in the building. He greeted her with cool efficiency. She shook his hand and Poul led her straight through the office and into a conference room. She sat down at the vast wooden table and pulled her laptop out of her bag. She expected Poul to sit across from her, but he sat down in the chair next to her and swiveled toward her.

"Will called me last night," Poul started. "Walk me through the issue."

Kat tilted her laptop toward Poul and walked through the issue affecting units that either had not been sealed or were sealed with faulty stickers. She showed Poul the numbers that were currently available for the early-launch global markets and those that would need to be shipped out directly to retail in the US. With the potential three-week delay on the new adhesive, they were still at a deficit. They could either delay the US launch by three weeks, which would certainly mean missing their unit projections and wasting locked marketing dollars, *or* they ran the risk of lengthy shipping delays, resulting in bad consumer sentiment and costing them additional sales.

They both agreed that neither option was a good one, and Poul offered to mobilize the Denmark team to brainstorm solutions. He called a meeting for an hour later and asked Kat to prepare comprehensive briefing documents to get the team started. Leaving Kat to prepare, he rushed out of the conference room.

Jake didn't feel how strongly he was clenching his jaw until Garren said, "Let's try it," and he released the tension. He'd brought his notes and sketches to the meeting with Garren, and they were fanned out across the table.

Garren flipped through a few of the sketches, pulled one out, leaned back, and looked at it closely. He tossed it in the middle of the table. "Jake let's test this. I want to see how you play this version of Tom." He radioed the production crew to set up on the back part of an empty lot, just to see how Jake's interpretation played on screen.

They walked out of the production tent together, heading to where a small crew was setting up with a few handheld cameras, boom mics, and basic lighting. It wasn't meant to be part of the final print—just enough for Garren to decide if he agreed with

Jake's characterization. If so, it could mean some reshoots of earlier scenes, so it was imperative that their visions aligned.

"It looks like the break was good for you," Garren said offhand. "You were busy."

"Yes," Jake said. He *would* elaborate, but he was already getting into Tom's head and scrolling through an iPad to the section of the script they would be testing. The setup didn't take long.

As Jake became Tom, he felt himself slip away, believing for a moment he was a man who just wanted to slide through the world unnoticed and live his life with the sole purpose of dissolving into the background. There was a very physical aspect to how one would move through a world when trying to disappear while still living.

Jake conveyed the complexity of Tom's fear and self-loathing through his physical presence. Of course, eventually, Tom would become the unlikely hero—strong, witty, and commanding—but that would come later. It was critical to the story arc to capture the more nuanced Tom in the beginning of the film. It would add power to the transformation for the audience.

Garren called cut and motioned for Jake to watch the playback on a small screen. Jake studied the video as it replayed. He stayed quiet and stole a glance at Garren. He couldn't read the expression on his face. Garren hit play for a second time.

"What do you think?" Garren asked, his face neutral. "Does this capture what you were envisioning?"

"Yes, mostly," Jake said, pausing to gather his thoughts. "You described this story to me as a simple arc of an unexpected hero. I think it's more universal than that. It's the story of overcoming your darkest, most scarred self . . . a man who breaks out of who he is *told* to be and finally becomes who he *wants* to be."

Garren nodded. "Jake, I'm blown away. This is different than I saw him, but I absolutely love where you're taking him." Garren shook his head slightly. "There's a lot we have to figure out to adjust the direction." He asked one of his assistants to bring them lunch from craft services. He wanted them to watch the previous footage to decide what needed to be reshot. They'd need go through the schedule and pencil in reshoots in the middle of the current production in order to get back on track.

"This won't be easy, but I think we can do it," Garren said, already taking notes. "I'm going to need some long hours. You ready?"

"I'll do whatever it takes," Jake said, ready to work twenty-four hours a day if that's what Garren needed.

By the time Jake made his way back to the apartment, it was past 10:00 p.m. He and Garren had spent eleven hours watching footage, taking notes, and inserting reshoots into the schedule. Jake walked off the set feeling excited by the collaboration that had occurred, a far cry from where they were only days ago.

He had put in the work to better understand Tom, but he'd also clawed out of the dark cave he'd been sliding into. Kat had given him an emotional ladder to climb out. She made him feel safe and centered, which allowed him the strength to become another person. Jake was beginning to understand: *this* was his process. He had to take the character off the page through understanding how they physically moved through the world and what motivated them and their inner thoughts. Alongside the work to know the character, he needed to shore up his own personal psyche to control and withstand the transformation. Kat not only helped remind him of his process, he believed she was part of the process. He wanted . . . needed . . . her in his life.

He walked into the apartment and found Kat pacing in the kitchen, on the phone. He was surprised to see her back at the apartment. He'd texted her to let her know he would be late, and she hadn't replied. He half expected her to still be in the office.

It was clear to Jake that Kat's day had not gone so well. He saw a defeated look in her eyes when he walked into the kitchen to grab a bottle of water. He retreated to the living room to give her space.

Her voice sounded hoarse and tense. He could only hear her side of the discussion, but the frustration was palpable.

"Only five million units . . . It won't affect it. No, I did the calculations three times . . . Me. I take full responsibility. Yes, I should have . . . I know. It won't happen again . . . Yes, I'm aware." Finally, she took out her AirPods and tossed her phone on the counter with a loud sigh.

She walked over to where Jake was on the couch and flopped onto the other side. He watched her put her head back on the couch, blink away tears, and blow out a shuttered breath. He moved closer and turned his body to face her.

"Looks like you had a rough day. I take it the stickers are still an issue?" he asked, placing his hand on her knee.

Kat swiped a single tear out of her eye and took a deep, shaky breath. "No," she said, still looking like tears were going to flow at any moment. "We actually found a solution today. Well, a super smart marketing manager came up with a solution. It'll still delay some shipping, but the customer won't notice."

Kat went on to explain that the marketing team had come up with an idea to create a larger sticker, with a QR code featuring virtual assistant apps, and use that sticker to seal the boxes. It was a tactic the Denmark team had used when they'd launched a previous device. Their manufacturer in India could turn the stickers around within four days. There was enough buffer in the timeline for a four-day bump without changing any sales projections.

Jake watched her intently as she explained the solution, no longer holding back her tears. He reached over and swiped a tear off her cheek.

"Kat, that's great news, isn't it?" he asked. He couldn't keep the confusion out of his voice. Her story was one of triumph, but her tears were those of defeat.

"Yes, it's fantastic," she said, her voice flat. He raised his eyebrows at her until she continued.

"Will, my boss—the current COO—is disappointed. Specifically, in me," she said, and put her hands over her eyes. "Everyone is watching me to see if I have what it takes to be COO. There are people who think they deserve the job. I bet they'll be thrilled if I fail. This wasn't perfect. I screwed up and I feel. . . ."

Jake knew that feeling all too well. He had just crawled his way out of that unsustainable headspace of shaken confidence mixed with a side of self-loathing. He wasn't going to let her sink into that space too.

"How exactly did you screw up?" he asked. He really didn't see this as anything other than thinking on your feet.

"First off, going to sleep without my phone," she started. He opened his mouth to protest, but she put her hand over his and continued. "Jake, I'm here in Denmark to help them with a launch that happens on Wednesday, and I'm in the middle of leading the US launch. Even on a Sunday, I can't go silent."

"That's ridiculous," he fired back at her. He didn't mean to sound edgy, but he felt guilty. "I'm sorry, Kat."

"No, no. Don't apologize. If I were you, I would have let me sleep, too. None of this is your fault. I know it sounds ridiculous, but this is a one-point-two-billion-dollar launch, Jake. So, whether or not it's fair, it's true. It was a bad coincidence that the *one* time I stepped away was when the shit hit the fan," she said with a sigh. "So, that was one thing."

"What's the other?" Jake asked. He knew this promotion was important to her, and he was trying to understand how her world operated. He thought her schedule and inability to step away, even for a minute, seemed unsustainable.

But, when he thought about it, that kind of dedication was

not foreign to him. His work wasn't so different. When he was on a project, it was all-consuming. He understood a nearly 24-7 focus, but the difference was his shooting schedule had a beginning and an end. In a short time, he'd observed Kat's life and to him, it was a constant state of high pressure.

"I didn't put anything in our manufacturer contract that would protect against this," she said. "They decided to change the adhesive, and I should have put a contingency in the contract that required them to alert us." She shook her head. "Will called it a rookie mistake, and that hurt."

Jake pulled her feet into his lap. "I'm sorry, sweetheart. I can imagine that stings," he said.

Her face told him she was playing "rookie mistake" over and over in her mind. He knew, all too well, the anxiety of disappointing someone you admire. Whether it was a corporate COO or a film director, the feeling of inadequacy was the same.

"Kat, try not to beat yourself up. It's solved. And everyone makes mistakes," he said. "You're not omniscient."

"I don't make mistakes," she fired back. "I can't make mistakes."

He looked at her and shook his head. "That's a lot of pressure to put on yourself, Kat. No one can be perfect all the time. Not even you."

When she didn't respond, he just focused on rubbing her feet. He didn't want to make it worse by arguing with her, but he watched the pressure she put on herself and wondered how she didn't break.

She finally spoke. "I'm just glad the situation is fixed, for now. Oww. . . ." She started laughing when he cracked her toes. "That hurts and tickles at the same time."

Jake loved hearing her laugh and seeing her tears stop. "Oh," he said, setting her feet to the side so he could stand up. "Can't believe I forgot. I picked something up on my way to set today."

He pulled a bottle of wine out of his backpack. "Sounds like you could use it." He pulled two glasses out of the cabinet and filled them both.

"Right! How was your first day back?" she asked.

He sat back down on the couch and handed her a glass. "It went better than I could have imagined. Garren loved the direction, and we were able to sketch out reshoots. Really, it felt good. I know when it's right, and it's finally right." He took a sip of wine and relaxed into the warm feeling.

"Jake, that's wonderful," she said, raising her glass to his and then taking a drink. "This is good. This isn't our normal cab, what is it?" she asked, taking another sip before pulling the bottle off the table to look at the label.

"We needed a new wine," he started. "It's a cabernet and merlot together. I thought a blend would be appropriate," he said, and gave her a wink. He really did want to create a new memory for them—one that symbolized a time they were together, facing the real world, instead of in the temporary bubble of the pandemic. These past few days had not just been about sex for Jake. It had been a comfort; an intimacy and friendship he hadn't realize how much he'd missed.

"Jake," she said softly. "That's incredibly sweet."

He was emboldened by her response, and he couldn't hold it in any longer. He moved closer and took both of her hands in his.

"Kat," he started, "I want to talk about this. Us." He stopped as he watched her face drop, and her eyes fill with tears yet again. "I want—"

She shook her head, "No, we can't. I can't," she said. "You have the worst timing, Jake."

He searched her face and all he saw was sadness. He put his hand on her cheek.. "You don't have to say anything. I needed you, and you came. I just really feel like I have to tell you—"

Before he could say another word, Kat's fingers were on his

lips. “Shh . . . please don’t,” she said. “Not tonight. No more talking.”

Jake sighed with disappointment but didn’t push her. They’d promised to keep it simple and easy, and that’s what he thought he’d wanted. He’d convinced himself that he wanted to be free, unencumbered and without anyone’s expectations, but that was before she was here. She came to him, and they instantly fit together as if they had never been apart. It felt easy and it felt right. That was worth something, and he needed to know if she felt the same. If he was a stronger person, he would have pushed further, but Kat pulled him toward her on the couch and his brain went fuzzy.

chapter thirteen

The alarm on Jake's phone blared and the sun seemed to be beaming straight into his eyes. His back and neck hurt, making him aware that he was still on the couch, blanket askew, his naked body intertwined with Kat's. God, that couch was not comfortable for sleeping, much less with two people. He didn't know why they hadn't just gone to bed. He let out a groan as he tried to reach down to turn off his phone. Kat moved out of the way and untwined her legs from his. She grumbled at him to turn off his phone as she stretched.

He untangled their bodies, but kept his arms wrapped around her. Kat tried to sit up, and Jake tightened his grip. He felt her relax back into him. "Good morning," she said, her voice soft and sleepy.

He ran his fingers down the side of her face and kissed each one of her cheeks. "Are you feeling better this morning?" he asked. She nodded but did not speak.

He gazed at her face, awash in the morning sun. It was brand new for them to wake up together morning after morning, and he liked it. He was unsure and emotional about what was going on between them. Unlike Kat, he couldn't rationalize everything; he lived in an emotional state that, right now, was tearing him in half.

He paused before murmuring, "This is nice." He was treading lightly, lest she pull away.

"Mmm," she said.

He kissed her behind her ear, tracing his finger over her collarbone. "I could get used to this," he whispered, testing the waters. He wanted to see if she, too, felt the desire to go beyond the escape and the simple.

"Don't. I leave in five days," she said untangling her arms from his and sitting up.

"And what if I want it for longer than five days?" he asked her, his tone more challenging than he intended.

"What does that even mean, Jake? I can't stay here. You can't pick up and come back to New York. Stop saying impossible things. You'll just end up disappointed," she countered, her attention focused on her phone as she scrolled through her email.

The rejection went straight to his core. He sprung up, pulled on his shorts, and walked into the kitchen to make coffee. He gripped the dials tightly, overcoming the sudden urge to smash the coffee cup on the floor. He felt a familiar vibration that came when he was angry. He took a deep breath to calm down.

"Hey," she called from the living room, looking up from her phone. "Why are you up so early? What's your call time?"

She was acting like their first interaction hadn't even happened, like everything was normal. Jake's first instinct was to ignore her, get dressed, and walk out—a passive aggressive set of actions to show his anger. But he was trying to work through it and temper himself. *Don't let the sparks burn down the house*, he reminded himself, thinking of their earlier conversation. "I have to see my trainer today," he said, his voice tight. He offered up no other details.

Kat walked in, having slipped on a T-shirt, and reached around him for a glass to fill with water. She took a drink. "Nice. I'm jealous. I'm becoming a blob. Too much wine."

"Work out, then," he said without emotion and took a drink of coffee. "It would be good for you."

She looked at him for a beat and took another drink. She didn't say anything. She was looking at him with a curious expression but did not engage. He studied her face. She looked amused, which pissed him off further. He wanted to ask her if she even noticed how much she'd hurt him. He couldn't meet her eyes for more than a second. They stood in a momentary standoff as he stared into his coffee.

"What gym do you go to? Can I come?" she asked in cheery voice that made the hair on the back of his neck prickle. She was playing a game he couldn't decipher.

"Private trainer, on set," he said. "I can't go to a normal gym." He paused. "I figured you'd have to get to the office."

"Not at 5:30 in the morning, and as long as I have my phone with me, I'll be fine. But it's up to you. I understand if you don't want me there," she said.

She was goading him; he was sure of it. Jake tried not to react, but his jaw tightened as he texted his trainer, Erik, to let him know he wouldn't be alone.

His mood lightened as soon as the car drove onto the set. It was one of the only environments where he felt at peace. Where he really fit in the world. For a few weeks now, he'd met with Erik at a facility set up by the production. Jake had a few fight scenes and needed to look strong on camera. Or at least strong enough. He was naturally thin and often struggled to put on muscle, so he needed to work at it if he wanted to look like someone who could fight off demons from a multiverse.

Erik was not only an effective trainer but also discreet—no tweets or tell-all blogs about the celebrities he trained. Although Jake didn't always like the constrictive bubble of a movie production, it did offer him protection that he was coming to understand he needed.

They entered the makeshift studio and Erik was set up and waiting for them. Although the studio wasn't big, it was efficient, with a the right pieces of cardio equipment and extensive weights. Jake said a quick hello and introduced Kat.

Erik shook Kat's hand. He motioned for Jake to warm up on the treadmill. "I'm going to chat with Kat a bit," he said. "You know what you need, Jake. Get to work, my man." He gave Jake a fist bump.

Jake watched Erik lead Kat over to the corner of the room. Kat was talking in a very animated fashion, and he could see Erik looking her up and down. *Likely assessing her skill and fitness level*, the rational side of his brain told him. *Or more*, the emotional side told him. They seemed to be talking a lot longer than necessary. He kept his eyes fixed on them in the mirror as he started to jog on the treadmill. Erik gave her a high five and a pat on the back and pointed over to the treadmill. *Don't think*, he told himself as he started to jog faster.

He should let it go, but he knew he wouldn't. Kat stepped up on the treadmill next to him. "He's hot, huh?" he asked in a breathless voice as he ran. He knew he was being an asshole, but it felt good. His voice was tighter than he wanted it to be, and he let the anger of this morning flood back into his mind. He sounded as pissed as he felt.

Kat looked at him and furrowed her brow. "Yes. He's totally my type. My age too," she fired back, equally as tight. She cocked her head and gave him a smile that he could tell was meant to challenge him. He had no idea how they had gone from this morning to now, but the vibe was decidedly icy.

"Great," he said.

"Great," she returned. He had never seen her back down from a fight with him and this was no exception.

She turned on her treadmill, matched his speed, and then bumped it up just enough to exceed him. He could tell that she was trying to piss him off. *Good*, he thought. He wanted to fight. He matched her speed, she bumped hers up, and he matched hers again. This continued, neither of them backing down until Erik came over to get them started. *Thank God*, Jake thought, as he slowed down his treadmill and tried not to puke. He wasn't the best runner, probably because he enjoyed smoking too much. Kat looked unaffected as she tightened her ponytail. She shot him a look, cool and confident, and it was almost more than he could take.

Erik started Jake on some agility training for his upcoming fight scene. He had some of the choreography in front of him so he could work on muscles needed to master specific moves. Jake had done this workout before, so Erik left him to work through the sequence.

As Jake worked, he had full view of Erik showing Kat a circuit he'd set up for her. As he demoed each move, he had her try it, all the while touching every muscle she was working. She had him demo a few moves more than once, looking Jake's way. They were flirting, and Jake was vibrating with jealousy and hurt. It didn't help that Erik was taller and more muscular than him. He looked over at them again. *Is he giving Kat a fucking degree in physiology?* Jake fumed to himself. Finally, Erik left Kat's side and came back over to check on Jake.

As he and Jake worked on the moves together, Erik lowered his voice and asked, "Your friend, Kat, how long is she in town?" he asked.

Jake shot him a look and said, "Not long, why?"

Erik hesitated. "She said you two were just friends, so I was going to ask if she was single before I made a fool of myself and offered to show her around."

Jake winced hearing that she'd categorized them as just friends. Of course, it was irrational that she would say anything to his on-set trainer, of all people, about their relationship, but it stung all the same. Jake looked him straight in the eye with unwavering eye contact. "Don't. Just don't." He wished it didn't come out as strained and angry as it did, but he was never good at hiding emotion.

"Got it. Hey, sorry, I didn't know." Erik said lifting his hands in surrender. They went back to focusing on the training session.

When the session was over, Jake walked out with Kat, but they weren't speaking. He didn't dare break the silence.

Kat was vibrating with frustration as they walked. They'd promised. They'd promised to keep it light and never add expectations into their relationship. He was breaking that promise. She needed to cut him off this morning before it got too serious. She too felt a rush of endorphins when they were together, but she knew it was because the body naturally responds to touch—it was a scientific fact. She was leaving soon. No matter how she felt, she needed to be strong. Jake was the emotional one; she was the realistic one. Form and function. That's what they were.

They walked back to his trailer, an unspoken tension between them. She wanted to ask him about the set, about his work. This was the first time she'd ever been on a movie set, but she wasn't going to break the silence between them. He was being ridiculous, and she wasn't going to indulge him.

When Jake opened the door, she finally spoke, but only to announce that she was getting in his shower first. She'd brought a bag with a change of clothes so she could go straight to the PathMobile Copenhagen office. She had a full afternoon and wouldn't be hanging on set all day. She had things to do and wanted to remind him that she had a life outside of the world of Jake—a life she would return to in less than a week.

He gestured toward his shower as he sat down to take off his sneakers.

After a tough workout and a frustrating morning, the water felt delicious, and she indulged in it running down her body. She covered her face with her hands and wiped the water out of her eyes as if that was enough to eliminate the feelings fighting to the surface: feelings of longing when she was not with Jake and feelings of love and protection when she was. She told herself she could keep herself from falling in love with him. She could keep it light and fun. She could keep walls in place to protect her heart.

She turned the dial hotter, and steam began to rise around her. *Damn him*, she thought. This was complicated enough without him destroying the boundary she had so skillfully put in place.

She heard the door to the shower open. She turned and saw Jake standing there, naked. Without saying a word, he stepped into the shower and his lips crashed into hers. His kiss was not gentle.

"Are you thinking of him? Do you want him? Why?" he asked, his voice gravelly and tinged with anger. Their eyes locked and she was unable to look away. She could see right into him. His desire. His confusion. How much she'd hurt him.

All of his emotions coursed through her entire body—his combination of anger and longing. It was over. Her invisible boundary crumbled around her, and she wanted him to barge right in.

"No," she breathed, pressing herself to him. Her heart finally took over, and her rational defenses became useless. She broke his gaze by pressing her lips just below his ear. She drew away and whispered, "You have to know . . . I came all this way for *you*." The water cascaded over both of them as they pressed their foreheads together. Jake moved his head side to side, his eyes closed, and Kat could see the anguish on his face.

He spun her around, pressed into her back, and devoured her

neck. "I don't know why . . . You won't. . . ." His voice trailed off into a pained whisper. "Can't you feel what's happening between us? I can. It's real, Kat. This is real."

She felt her legs would buckle, not just from desire, but from the weight of his emotions and the vulnerability that he was laying at her feet.

"Jake, I can't . . . it's . . . I can't. . . ." She almost couldn't speak as his touch cleared her of all rational thought. "It's all too much," she panted, reaching back and running her hands over his wet hair.

He grabbed her wrists and pushed them above her head and onto the wall. His boldness and aggression were new to her, and it turned her on to have him take full control.

"Too much? I'm too much?" He pushed himself into her, making her gasp. "Is this all you want from me?" His voice was a growl in her ear. "We . . . we are more than this."

Kat might have crumbled if Jake was not holding on so tightly. He began to move, slamming into her with a dangerous blend of passion and anger. Kat pulled her hands free and put them against the wall to keep her balance. She couldn't help herself from moaning as she was taken by his physical possession of her. She wanted to let him take all of her, which scared and excited her more than she could admit.

Jake slowed down and became gentle in his movements, running his hands over her body. He murmured, "Dammit, Kat, stop pushing me away."

Kat let out a sob and cried out as they came together. She reached back to put her hand on his body, and he pushed away from her.

Before she could turn around, she heard the door slam closed. He'd left the shower without saying another word. She slammed her hand into the dial to shut off the water. She felt a cold void surrounding her. She wanted his arms around her; she wanted to feel any part of his body close to hers. Her tears came, and they came fast. She cried at her inability to give him what he really desired. He wanted it all and she didn't trust herself to give herself over to anyone. Not even him. She curbed her tears and got dressed in the bathroom, unable to face him.

When she walked out, he was already dressed. Before she could speak, he walked over and wrapped his arms around her. She didn't know if he could see her red eyes or if he noticed the remnants of her tears, but she needed to be held. By him. The roller coaster of emotions she was on was giving her mental whiplash. She rested her head on his chest, allowing the rhythm of his heartbeat to calm her.

"Kat . . . I'm sorry . . . that was—" he started. She held on tighter and cut him off before he could say any more. "For the record, I do feel. . . ." she said in a whisper, her voice breaking. She couldn't finish the sentence. He didn't reply, but simply tightened his hold on her. She felt him sigh. He loosened his grip and said, "Stop being scared of this . . . of us . . . Kat, I've got you," he whispered.

Their phones pinged at the same time, unwelcome intruders in the quiet of his trailer. Kat's was giving her a thirty-minute notification before her meeting at the PathMobile offices, and Jake was due in hair and makeup. They were out of time.

As they walked out of the trailer, Jake drew Kat to him, and she looked around to see if anyone was watching. Seeing her concern, he whispered, "This is a closed set." She rested her head on his shoulder, her face buried in his neck. "You sure you're okay?" he asked.

Kat turned to him and nodded. She brought her lips to his, as if they could, in fact, linger there. It was her way of showing him that she felt it too.

"Please keep kissing me like that," he murmured. "I just want to be like this, with you," he sighed. "I can't believe you have to leave."

Kat didn't know if he meant right then or in a few days, but regardless, it reminded her that she would be leaving and couldn't give Jake the one thing he wanted—more time.

They heard a throat clear. A young woman—Kat guessed a production assistant—was standing a few feet away. "So sorry Jake, but they're waiting for you."

Kat walked into the PathMobile offices a few minutes before her meeting started. It was the first day the DK website would go live and allow consumers to pre-order the PVA. The office was buzzing with energy.

She passed Poul on the way to the conference room. "T-minus one hour until we go live," he said, passing her. "See you in there, five minutes."

She walked into the conference room, and nearly the entire Danish team had crammed inside. They greeted her as if she was one of the team. After yesterday's long work session and resolution, she felt like they had worked together for years. Before Poul came in to talk to the team about the pre-orders, the marketing team gave her a quick update on the stickers. Everything was going as planned, which allowed Kat to take a breath and just focus on the excitement of the day.

When Poul arrived, they took him through the logistics of the day and the forecasted number of pre-orders they would receive in the next week. Kat admired the efficiency and cohesion of the team.

It was go time for launch, and Poul pulled up the website on the large screen and announced the pre-orders were live. Clapping filled the air, and Kat could feel the pride emanating from everyone in the room.

"Kat, you ready?" Poul asked, gesturing to a large box on the opposite side of the room. She smiled and nodded. "Please do the honors, Poul," she said. She'd had some early devices sent to the Copenhagen office as a gift to the team. Poul handed them out to a very happy crew.

After the excitement died down, everyone dispersed to their workstations. Kat settled herself in an empty office so she could join calls in the US for the remainder of the day. She thanked Poul for including her in the excitement of the day, and he replied with a smile, "*Mit sted er dit sted.*" He translated for her: "My place is your place. Kat, we are very happy you are here." He closed the door and left her alone.

Kat snuck in a FaceTime call to Becca, to show her the view outside the window, which faced the Børsen, Copenhagen's historic stock exchange. She knew Becca wouldn't care about a stock exchange but would love the "dragon spire" on top of the imposing red brick building. She pointed her phone at the spire and zoomed in.

"Momma, is that built by real dragons?" Becca exclaimed. Kat had the urge to explain that dragons were not real, but she stopped herself.

Instead of bringing her to reality, Kat replied, "Maybe. I don't know, but I do think it would take a very tall dragon to make that high of a spire." Becca squealed and proceeded to guess what color the dragon would be (purple), what their name would be (Julie), and why they built the spire (to harness lightning power). They were both in giggles, and Kat was in awe of how Becca's imagination allowed her to explore all possibilities with abandon. *When did I lose that skill?* She wondered if she'd ever had it.

The next time she looked at the clock, it was after 4:00 p.m. She often lost herself while working. She walked out of the office in search of food, but Poul announced a celebratory happy hour and insisted Kat join. She retreated back into her office to pack her things.

She followed the team down the street to a lively café aptly named Café Wilder. Noise spilled out of the open windows. The energy inside was infectious. They yelled "hi" in unison to the bartender, and he motioned to the oversized booth marked reserved in the back. Kat slid into the middle of the booth and the team filled in around her. For a brief moment, she allowed herself to pretend she was simply a member of the team. She tried to follow the chatter as they fluidly moved between Danish and English.

She envied other countries for their culture of travel, having a different country right next door. She found her global counterparts had distinct knowledge not just of different languages, but they also knew how to read and adjust to a culture that was not their own. She was hoping to one day give her daughter a view beyond the Upper West Side.

The pints were pushed around the table, and the team pummeled her with questions about the New York headquarters. Was there really a basketball court (yes), ale on tap in the office (yes) and company yacht (no), and then they moved on to her. Was she enjoying her visit (yes, second trip, loved the city), did she have kids (Becca), and what was it like living in New York City (chaotic and wonderful at the same time). In return, she had many questions for them. Once they had exhausted all the obligatory get-to-know-you questions, Kat sat back and listened to the banter of the team.

One of the youngest members was scrolling through her phone when she blurted, "OMG everyone. Listen to this." She read out loud. "Jake Laurent is in Copenhagen, starting this week, shooting his new movie, *Zero Code*. He will be on location for the next six weeks," she said, her face animated with every word.

Kat knocked over her pint, causing the group to gasp. The amber liquid ran into the middle of the table. Her face burned red as she dabbed napkins on the spill.

Another team member, ignoring the spill said, "Duh, there were photos all over Twitter of him at Tivoli. I hope I run into him—he is so my type."

"Your problem is you actually think you have a chance with him," retorted another. The group laughed and picked up their phones to scroll through their social feeds, grabbing information to continue the conversation.

Kat did the best acting job she could muster to keep her face neutral. She thought it was funny that the source said he just got to Copenhagen since he'd been there for weeks—likely because he was only spotted this week. She had a twinge of guilt for outing him in the city.

"I heard he was gay," said another. "I mean, isn't everyone in Hollywood at least bi?" There were a lot of head nods, and they took some time to dissect all the people he had dated and guess which men and women he was secretly sleeping with. They became particularly giddy with this topic and Kat couldn't stomach such a private topic being casually discussed as if it were the weather. Kat searched her mind for something . . . anything . . . to change the subject.

"Hey, Kat," Poul said, jarring her out of her thoughts. "I heard he lives in New York. You ever run into him?"

"New York City is a big place," she said, avoiding the question. In her brain, she logged another reason why she wanted to keep her and Jake a secret: she would be outed as a liar to this entire team, not to mention change her reputation from leader to woman sleeping with a celebrity. She could only imagine the work gossip circles that would gleefully ignite with that information.

They spent the next ten minutes mapping where they thought the filming was taking place, where they might spot him, guessing what the movie was about, where he was staying, why he was at Tivoli, and generally any crumb of information that would put them in his orbit, even for just a minute.

Most of the chatter was harmless, but Kat cringed as she listened to the way they talked about him. He was an object, not a human. She knew it wasn't particular to him, but it was the same way she had heard friends, colleagues, and even herself talk about celebrities. Nothing was off-limits. In one minute, celebrated; in the next, torn down. It was hard to listen to, especially since the conversation was not about his work and his art, but his body and his face.

If the conversation continued to be about Jake, she feared the reactions on her face would give her away. She finally got them to change the subject to the Copenhagen RLFC, the local rugby team. Here, as in the US, celebrities and sports were the easiest conversation starters. She glanced at her watch. She didn't want to stay for long since it was a team celebration and, as a visitor—especially one from corporate—she knew better than to overstay her welcome.

She untangled herself from the booth and made her way out of the café. She mapped her way back to Jake's apartment and decided to walk in the cool September air. He was most likely still on set, and she enjoyed the time to herself as she meandered back home.

She climbed the stairs, and she heard her texts chimed. It was Emily texting her to connect via video chat. She was ready to discuss the current status of the launch. Things seemed to be back on track, but they connected daily.

Once they were on video, Emily walked her through other parts of the launch plan, including media. Kat took over the screen to share a TikTok influencer video the Denmark team had completed and recommended the US marketing team replicate the campaign. They fell into a familiar groove of optimizing the launch and adding improvements.

Kat was in their shared document, uploading links for the marketing team, and Emily was multitasking. They were silent as Kat finished. So silent that Jake, not realizing she was on video, plopped down next to her in full view.

"Oh hi!" Emily said with surprise in her voice, and Kat froze. "You must be mystery pronoun," she said, letting out a loud laugh.

Jake's entire face lit up in a smile. "And you must be the famous Emily. Hello, Famous Emily," he said with his usual charm. He bounded off the couch and moved out of view of the camera. He mouthed "sorry" at Kat, but his eyes were twinkling.

Kat hit the mute button. Despite her internal panic she kept her voice steady. "I didn't think you'd be here. I thought you were on set."

"I was and then we had a break. I'm heading back now. We're shooting a cluster of night scenes," he said. "You need anything?"

She shook her head no. Before she could protest, he leaned down, waved to Emily, and gave Kat a quick kiss on the cheek. "Text me if you need anything," he called as he walked out the door.

Once she heard the door close, she turned back to the call, took her laptop off mute, and saw Emily's stunned face. "Let's go through the marketing document one more time," she said, trying to pivot back to the task at hand.

"No way, Kat. I finally learned that mystery pronoun is a real person, and you want to talk launch logistics? We're discussing this," Emily said in a firm tone, but with a giggle. "Ohhhh . . . is he on the design team? I think I met him a few weeks ago . . . one of the new hires, right? No wonder you don't want to tell anyone about him!"

Kat felt a flash of anger. She would never date anyone within the company. In her position, that secret was worse. "Oh my God Emily, NO. You know I would never do that." Kat was surprised that Emily had even considered that a possibility. Did she know her at all?

"Why does he look so familiar? Have I met him?" Emily's questions hung in the air.

Kat was staring right into Emily's determined face, and she knew she had to share the truth. She felt relieved to talk to *someone* about it. Emily, although a colleague, was her closest friend. She didn't have much time for friends outside of work and at this moment she needed a friend. "You *have* probably seen him before. It's Jake, eh, Jake Laurent." She stopped talking and watched realization wash over Emily's face.

"WHAT?" Emily yelled. "Right. That *is* him. I just saw his movie, last Saturday to be exact. *Cloud Catcher*, I think it was called. God, he looked so hot in that movie." Emily put her hand over her mouth. "Ugh . . . sorry. I just called your boyfriend hot. He *is* your boyfriend, right? Wait, how is he your boyfriend?"

Kat felt the unspoken, "But he's so young, and you aren't . . . he's so hot, and you . . . aren't." It hung in the air like a half-deflated balloon. Emily didn't say those words, but Kat felt like the question was in her eyes.

"No, no," Kat said shaking her head. "It's not like that. You know Jill and Adrian, my next-door neighbors? They are Jill and Adrian Laurent, Jake's parents. I've lived next door to them for years, Emily. He's here and I'm here, so we're hanging out." Just to add extra emphasis, she continued, "I wouldn't call him my *boyfriend*."

Kat had spent countless hours with Emily, but even so, she kept high walls up around her life. Kat wanted to tear down those walls, but she just needed Emily to stick her finger in a crack and pull away the concrete.

"Kat," Emily started, "I don't know what you call it, but I heard him the other morning asking you about coffee, and I saw that kiss just now. When two acquaintances find themselves in the same city, they have a lunch or a drink, they don't stay in the same apartment for ten days."

And just like that, Kat's wall came crashing down as she put her hands over her eyes and the words tumbled out. "It's crazy, right?"

Emily let out a large laugh and a squeal. "I knew it. Oh my God, this is so great, Kat, really!" She paused. "So, you *are* together?"

Kat was not prepared to answer that question. Being unprepared destabilized her, and she felt panic rise in her throat. She searched for an answer that was truthful, sounded smart, and didn't come across like the confused, scattered human she became when trying to make sense of Jake. She opened her mouth to answer and couldn't get the right words out, instead stammering, "Honestly, it's annoyingly complicated, and I don't know how to explain what we are."

"Okay. Let's take a step back. But you *are* something?" Emily asked talking through this as if they were dissecting a work problem.

"I think so, but I don't know what I want out of this. Emily, his life is so out in the open and mine is so . . . not. Our lives don't fit together, and I can't imagine a day when they will." There. She finally said it. No matter what this was, it couldn't be more than a diversion. Anything more would be disastrous. When she envisioned their relationship a few months down the road, she couldn't find a scenario that worked in their favor.

"But does he make you happy?" Emily asked. "I'm guessing you didn't fly all the way there because you don't like being with him." She scoffed at her own statement.

"Remember, I flew all this way for *work*," Kat said in a tone that sounded overly adamant. "But yes, I do like being with him . . . he can be wonderful and infuriating in the same day. He's not easy, that's for sure." That was the most accurate way to describe her feelings for Jake. But he also made her feel like her life was more than a series of tasks to be managed. When she turned off her brain, she felt freer and happier than she had for a long time.

Emily shook her head. "Not everything can be simple, but it doesn't make it wrong."

"My life, even without him, is too complicated, Emily. I have Becca, and she can't have a mom who is unfocused. I have this job, which takes up all my time. And if there is *any* chance I'm still in the running for COO, life is only going to get exponentially harder to manage," she said. She couldn't even imagine how they would ever see each other.

"If?" Emily said. "It isn't an 'if.' Will submitted his recommendations yesterday, and he told me you're the top candidate. Did you think that had changed?"

"I don't know. The biggest thing I had going for me was this launch, and it got messy," she said. "Besides that, I'm young, I'm a woman, and I'm just now getting global experience. And even this is minimal. It makes me a weaker candidate, at least to the board."

"Don't forget that you have the best reputation for getting things done in this company," Emily said. "That counts for something."

"True," Kat started. "Emily, I'm trusting you. Please don't say anything about Jake. The last thing I need is for people to see me as anything other than a leader. I'm worried that if people know about us, it will be used against me." It was tough enough to be taken seriously as a female in technology without everyone thinking about who was sharing her bed.

"Of course," Emily replied.

"Let's talk about you for a sec, Emily. Regardless of what happens with me, you are ready for the next level. I am going to recommend you get promoted to the president level in the product or sales organization. I worked on your write-up during my plane ride. It's the right next step for you."

Their yearly planning cycle was taking place, and Emily was at the top of Kat's list for a key leadership position. They had both worked toward this moment—Emily through learning and hard work, and Kat through attention and mentorship. She could feel herself beaming through the screen.

"Thank-you. I appreciate your vote of confidence, but now it's my turn to be honest, " Emily started. She paused before continuing, "I don't think I want it . . . actually, I *know* I don't want it."

Kat looked at her, stunned. She saw Emily as a mini-Kat, someone who was so much like her. She swallowed hard and stammered, "Wow. Really? Why not?"

"I've been thinking about this a lot," Emily started. "I watch Will, who's excited to finally spend some time with his wife and children. His children who are *grown*, Kat. He missed their entire childhood," Emily hesitated. "And I watch you. You live for this, night and day. Case in point, you're in Copenhagen—with Jake Laurent, of all people—and all I've seen you do is work." She paused, and Kat fought the urge to jump in. She physically put her hand over her mouth to keep quiet. "I don't want to live like that, Kat. I want to live life and work on the side. Not the other way around."

"Emily," Kat started. "I didn't know you felt this way. Why didn't you tell me sooner?"

"I didn't want to disappoint you," she said. "You've been an amazing champion for me since I started, and I've learned so much from you. Not just about product logistics, but how to be a strong woman and get your voice heard, how to get others to work together by transparently aligning on goals. And most importantly, how to clearly communicate what you want . . . which is how I'm finally coming to this. So, thank you, but I don't want to be promoted."

Kat leaned in toward the screen, wishing she was there, in person, with Emily. "So, what *do* you want?"

Emily laughed at Kat's question. "I don't know! Don't get me wrong, I do love my job, but I also want to travel with my girlfriend. I want to see the Northern Lights. I want to move out of the city someday. There are so many things I want to do, and this place, this job, is just a part of who I am. I don't want it to be my *whole life*. It's already a lot; I just don't want it to be *more*. So, I just want to stay where I am, if that's okay."

Kat couldn't find the right words to respond. She felt exposed, and she replayed all their interactions in her mind. The weekend phone calls. The late-night emails. She hadn't shown Emily how to sustain a leadership role without it demanding your entire life. Actually, she didn't know how to be a leader without giving nearly every moment to PathMobile. *I've failed her as a leader. I've failed myself*, played on repeat in her mind. For the first time, she thought about what her life could be without the demands of her job taking priority. She let her mind wander to lazy weekends with Becca and Jake without work taking up permanent residence in her mind. That fantasy filled her with a happy feeling.

"Oh no, do you hate me? I'm sorry to drop this on you . . . it seemed like the right time," Emily said, breaking Kat out of her fantasy world.

"Of course, I don't hate you. I *admire* you, Emily," Kat said. "You know what you want out of life, and you're refusing to compromise. That takes a lot of courage. I always knew you were smart. But it's more than that. You are very wise."

Emily laughed. "Kat, since you think I'm so wise, can I give *you* one piece of advice about Jake?"

"Yes, please," answered Kat.

"Being loved and loving someone back is rare and special. Don't reject it because it's complicated. Some of the best things that happen in life don't make any sense."

Once they hung up, Kat sat with Emily's statement for a minute. She was envious of Emily's conviction and her willingness to step aside and let her career take a back seat to her life. If only she could've done the same earlier in her career or before she became responsible for another human.

Her texts chimed. It was Jake. He'd been gone less than an hour. She smiled at her impulsive Jake, already reconnecting them after only a short time of being apart.

J: Hey, want to come to set? I will be late tonight. A long schedule of night shots.

J: I miss you.

She immediately typed her response.

K: I can't. I have work to catch up on.

As soon as she hit "send," she felt a knot in her stomach. Her conversation with Emily played over and over in her head. Yes, Jake was complicated, but he was also exciting, and she missed him too. Before she could convince herself otherwise, she tapped out a follow-up reply.

K: Yes. I want to come. Is nine too late?

J: 9 works. I'll send a car. Someone will meet you.

Kat marked his last text with a thumbs-up.

chapter fourteen

Just after nine, Kat received the notification telling her a car had arrived. She ran downstairs to the waiting car, opened the door, and did a double take when she spied someone sitting in the back seat. She glanced down at her phone to check if it was the right car, until the person spoke.

"Hi! I'm Savannah, Jake's PA on set. I think I met you, kinda, earlier." She flashed her pass and a warm smile. "He wanted to make sure you got on the set okay. Security is tight, especially at night." She motioned for Kat to get in.

She slid in the car and shook Savannah's hand. "Hi, Savannah, I'm Kat, nice to officially meet you," she said, returning the smile. She felt her cheeks redden, recalling their earlier meeting when Savannah had come to get Jake outside of his trailer. Kat looked out the window as the car maneuvered through the twinkling city lights.

After a few minutes, she turned from the window to face Savannah. "How long have you been a PA?" She knew so little about the people who surrounded Jake on a daily basis and wanted to know the business better. She didn't understand his life and was curious about the life he lived on set.

"A few years. This is my third job with Jake," she replied.

Kat hadn't realized he had consistent PAs, but it made sense that he would want people around who understood how he worked. Savannah was Jake's Famous Emily. The thought made her laugh. "Wow, I didn't know you'd done three films with him," Kat replied. "You travel with him to each shoot?"

"Yes, he's the best," she gushed. "I work off and on for a lot of actors, and I can honestly say, he's the easiest."

"How so?" She had never heard anyone describe Jake as easy.

"I don't want to go into it—privacy and all," she said. "All I will say is that he comes on set to work, and I help make his day go as smooth as possible—get him coffee, help him with his schedule, escort him to different parts of the set, charge and monitor his phone when he's actively shooting, all that stuff. When I get a chance, I help with the actual production. But he never asks for anything weird or becomes difficult or mean." Glancing down at her phone, she continued, "I've had some crazy requests before, but Jake isn't like that. He's serious, and he respects me. That means everything in this business."

It was fascinating to hear the perspective of someone else who was close to him. She was reminded that film sets were where Jake felt most at home. Kat appreciated how Savannah kept Jake's privacy intact. She took a mental note that he was respectful to the people who worked with him.

She watched Savannah rapid-fire type on her phone and could only imagine the amount of activity that went on during a film production. When her furious typing slowed, Kat asked her next question.

"Okay, but can you just tell me *one* crazy thing a celeb has asked you for?" Kat pried. "I don't even want to know who, nothing identifiable, just tell me what they asked."

Savannah looked up, her face brightened, and said, "One person asked me to FaceTime their dog. Like, two or three times a day. And not like, for a second. Like full ten-minute conversations to make sure their dog didn't get lonely." She looked thoughtful for a moment. "Come to think of it, I was going through a breakup at the time. Talking to that dog was pretty cathartic."

They both laughed, and Kat tried to imagine canine dating advice.

The car pulled up to the gates, an intimidating security guard came out, looking like he expected an argument. He leaned into the open window on the driver's side and when he saw Savannah, his demeanor changed and a smile spread across his face. He waved them in and returned to his post. She realized why Jake had sent Savannah to escort her. She pictured herself, alone with a driver, at 9:30 p.m., trying to convince the guard that Jake had really asked for her come to set. It would've sounded like every woman's fan fiction, as he laughed her right back to the city center.

Savannah walked her to Jake's trailer to drop off her bag before heading to where they were shooting scenes that evening. "I'll need your phone," she said as they walked out of his trailer. "No phones allowed anywhere we're actively filming."

Kat hesitated. Of course, she couldn't use her phone while watching them shoot, but she also didn't want to miss anything important from work, again.

Noticing her hesitation, Savannah jumped in. "Oh, Jake told me that you need to be reachable. I monitor his phone and let him know if anyone is texting or calling him. I'll do the same for you. I'll be back at his trailer but will come get you if I see anything."

Kat surrendered her phone and watched as Savannah silenced it and dropped it into a pouch at her hip, presumably alongside Jake's phone. She wondered how many text messages she had sent to Jake that Savannah had read—or even replied to.

She slipped a badge over Kat's head and spoke into her walkie-talkie to determine where they were filming with Jake. "Okay," she said as she started walking. "We're heading over; it'll be a small walk. Be very quiet as we approach, and I'll find you a spot to sit between takes."

Kat nodded and took it all in. There was constant motion—people bustling everywhere. Every person seemed to know where they were going, but to the uninitiated, it seemed like well-choreographed chaos. Her eyes darted around, and she tried to immortalize every image into her memory as they walked.

"Have you ever seen him work on a scene before?" Savannah whispered as they walked through the set, toward the areas that were lit up as bright as daytime.

Kat shook her head and whispered, "I've run lines with him. But I've never seen him on an actual set."

Savannah beamed. "You're in for a treat. He's amazing to watch." The pride on Savannah's face matched the pride in her voice.

When they got closer, Savannah slowed down and motioned for her to wait while they finished the active scene. Once they heard "Cut and reset," Savannah started walking faster, and Kat nearly had to jog to stay behind her. Savannah pulled her to the side of where the crew was working and grabbed her a chair to ensure Kat would be out of the way. Without hesitation, she took her seat so she wouldn't disrupt any of the intense activity swirling around her.

From her vantage point, she had full line of sight to Jake. He was in deep discussion with Garren Christiansen, and she felt her excitement grow as she realized she would get the privilege of watching an award-winning director command a scene.

With all the commotion around her, Kat couldn't hear what they were saying. She could only see Garren's hand motions indicating how the camera would move during the scene and what he expected. Jake took a few steps and demonstrated his body movement, and Garren nodded his approval as he practiced the motion. She didn't know if Jake had realized she'd arrived, and part of her didn't want him to. She was content to watch him from afar and observe him in his element. Even with hundreds of crew members milling around, his presence was palpable.

Kat glanced around to see if there were other actors that she recognized. He'd mentioned that the other principal actors had just arrived, but she'd failed to ask him about the rest of the cast. To her left was a man in costume. She'd seen him before in something, but she couldn't place his name. Next to him was Sloan Stevens. It would be impossible not to recognize her—she was gorgeous. Kat thought she might have seen that *People* magazine named her the most talented actress under twenty-five. She tried not to stare, focusing on watching Jake.

Garren called Sloan over to the scene and went over the same blocking with her. Jake and Sloan rehearsed a few times, and then nodded that they were ready. They went to different marks and waited for the director's cue. Once he shouted action, they ran toward each other as if they were being chased, fell into each other's arms, nearly fell to the ground, and then started running again.

As they ran toward each other, Kat could see the fear on their faces shift to relief when they fell into each other's arms, but their expressions once again turned into fear when they realized they were still not safe. It was perfectly choreographed with every step, every glance, and every emotion directed and timed out. They were flawless each time, both hitting their marks and emotions at the right moments. Garren walked over and gave them direction before resetting to shoot the scene again. They did the take six more times. It was a meticulous process, and Kat focused on watching the precise way the scene was executed each time it was shot.

On the seventh take, Garren said, "We got it, set up for the kiss, scene ninety-seven." Jake looked over to the crew, and his eyes landed on Kat. She gave him a little wave. His face broke out in a grin, and he jogged over to where she was sitting.

"You're here," he said, extending his hand to pull her up out of her chair. He gave her a quick but soft kiss on the lips and wrapped his arms around her. "I missed you," he whispered.

"I'm here," she whispered back and relaxed into his embrace. They hadn't seen each other for a year, but he missed her after just a few hours—her brain and body tingled as she squeezed him tighter. Kat was apprehensive about the crew milling around, but she trusted him in his environment.

As they broke apart from their embrace, Savannah rushed over with a bottle of water for Jake, and another crew member appeared with a makeup pallet to give him a touch-up before the next scene. Savannah thrust an iPad in Kat's hands and said, "Electronic NDA, everyone on set signs one. Sorry, I forgot to bring it with me in the car. Don't tell anyone, I should have had you do it right when we got here. Normal non-disclosure stuff, nothing out of the ordinary."

Kat, having signed many NDAs, scrolled through it once and then signed with the stylus. She handed it back to Savannah and said, "Your secret is safe with me." Savannah nodded and submitted the document. She took the water bottle back from Jake, asked him if he needed anything and, when he shook his head, she took a call and set off in the opposite direction.

Once makeup was finished with the touch-ups, they were finally alone—relatively alone, since there were still over a hundred people standing in the vicinity.

"I am afraid to touch you and mess up your wardrobe and makeup," Kat said reaching over and hooking her index finger in his.

"Wardrobe and makeup can be fixed," he said winking at her. "We have entire departments for that." He threaded his fingers through hers and kissed her hand. "Hey, I should tell you. The next scene—"

"It's a kissing scene," she interrupted. "I heard. It's okay. Do your job."

Before he could reply, Garren called out, "Jake, we're ready."

He squeezed her hand, turned around, and jogged back to his place. She was struck by the joy in his face and the energy she could feel radiating off him. He was right. This was where he fit in the world.

The assistant director announced that the next scene was set and ready. Jake had told her before that shooting a love scene was about as unsexy as it could be, and she watched firsthand how boring an on-screen kiss is to film. The first thing she noticed is how the crew micromanaged every second of the scene. As a viewer, she believed there was some passion between the actors kissing, even just for a moment. *They had to enjoy it a little bit, right?*

Watching Jake and Sloan's kiss being filmed confirmed how unpassionate the act really is when performed on camera. Viewing it right in front of her, without swelling music or sweeping camera angles, she was watching two paid actors following predetermined blocking, kissing methodically and silently, while bored crew members checked their watches, eager to be done for the night. It wasn't just unsexy—it was a remarkable mix of boring and awkward.

She watched them execute the kiss about five times while they filmed it from different angles and tried slightly different blocking. Sloan and Jake made a gorgeous couple, and she could imagine their beauty and chemistry were heightened by the camera lens. She crossed her arms and tried to ignore the twinge of jealousy seeping into her chest. She was no stranger to seeing Jake kiss actresses on screen . . . *or on Instagram*, she thought wryly. Jake would never fully be hers, her mind mused. She would always share him with costars, his adoring fans, the press, his team, and everyone else who wanted a piece of him. She asked herself if she was a strong enough person to share him so completely. She didn't know if she was.

It was just after 1:00 a.m. when they finished both the scheduled scenes, and Jake's extra reshoots. When Garren announced they were wrapped for the night, Savannah scurried over to Jake with some wipes to clean off his makeup, chatting as they walked toward Kat. She handed him another cloth, taking his dirty one. "I imagine you'll want to get out of here quickly. Your call time is 9:00 a.m.," she said. "I'm going to walk you both over to wardrobe so Jake can change, and I'll grab your bag and bring it to you. I'll meet you at the gate—a car is already waiting."

Kat admired her efficiency and in a different world, she would've hired her. She knew why Jake took her to each shoot. The three of them walked to wardrobe, and Jake was quiet. He intertwined his fingers with hers, and for a brief moment leaned his head on Kat's shoulder and snuggled into her neck. She reached up and brushed her fingers through his hair.

"Savannah," he started. "You haven't told Kat stories about me, have you? My ridiculous demands and the overall monster that I am?" he teased.

"I'll never tell, sir," she said with a wink.

This was their schtick, and Kat could feel the camaraderie between them. When they arrived at wardrobe, Savannah disappeared in the maze of trailers.

Kat waited outside while Jake changed in record time. He jumped down the two steps from the wardrobe trailers and threw his arms around her, his lips on hers before she could react. Warmth spread though her body as their lips moved against each other. She met his tongue with hers, and his hand trailed up her back causing shivers down her spine. She felt lost in his kiss until he pulled back.

"I've been waiting all night to do that," he said. "Let's go, I'm damn tired."

"Okay, I knew you were tired, but if you're *damn* tired, that is a state of emergency," said Kat, linking her hand with his again and matching his brisk walk to the gate.

When they walked into the apartment, it was after 2:00 a.m. Kat's eyes were heavy, and she couldn't wait to lie down. She could only imagine how Jake felt. He looked like he would be asleep as soon as he hit the bed. She did the math in her head. He had less than seven hours before he was required to be back on set. They were trying to get the production on schedule, and she was getting a sense of how grueling it would be to get back on track.

"Did you have fun?" he asked, yawning as he walked into the bathroom where Kat was brushing her teeth. He brushed his teeth next to her and playfully bumped her hip. She bumped him back and spit into the sink.

Kat wiped her mouth and nodded. "I loved watching you work, Jake. Thanks for asking me to come," she said, walking into the bedroom with him and pulling back the covers. "It was so much more technical than I expected." Climbing into bed, feeling the weight of the blanket envelop her body, she was delighted to know that sleep was imminent. As he climbed into bed next to her, she continued, "Of course, I didn't love seeing you kiss Sloan Stevens. God, she is so damn gorgeous. Wow. I mean, I practically wanted to kiss her," Kat teased.

He laughed, his voice sounding hoarse. "Well, she *is* a witch, so I didn't like kissing Sloan Stevens." And with that, he pulled her close to him, curled his arms around her, and she fell asleep.

chapter fifteen

The pinging was incessant. Jake looked around to see a game show all around him. In order to win, he had to act out a scene from a random movie in fifteen seconds or less. An annoying tone would sound every time the scene changed. He felt an inescapable panic and could not control the game. *The Godfather* . . . ping . . . *Karate Kid* . . . ping . . . *Pulp Fiction* . . . ping . . . The audience was cheering, but he just wanted it to stop. How could he make it stop? Why wouldn't it fucking stop?

"Jake!" His eyes flew open to see Kat sitting up in bed. "Who's texting you?" she asked, reaching over him to pull his phone off the nightstand. She thrust it into his hand before flopping back down on her pillow.

He shook the dream out of his head and swiped open his phone. Putting on his glasses, he looked at the time: 6:30 a.m. He had a dozen texts, most of them from Cindy.

C: Hey, call me when you're awake, doesn't matter the time.

C: There are a few things surfacing. I want to know what you want to do.

C: There are two different reports.

C: One is that you're filming in Copenhagen. No shit, right?

C: One is a leak from the set that you had a woman with you last night and you both seemed very "close."

C: Assuming that's Kat but let me know if there's someone new I need to know about.

C: Good news: The exposure is limited for now.

C: Bad news: it's only a matter of time . . .

C: We should get ahead of this . . . please.

"Shit," he said and let out an audible sigh as he rang Cindy. He put her on speaker. Kat was giving him a questioning look, and he motioned for her to slide next to him.

"Hey," Cindy answered on the second ring.

"How bad is it?" Jake asked her, blowing past any normal pleasantries.

"Hold on, I'll send you a screenshot."

His phone pinged with a picture of the tweet.

Exit25Tea

Good authority says that Jake Laurent has been seen on the set of Zero Code kissing a mystery woman. Is he finally off the market?

He rested his free hand on Kat's thigh. He knew, no matter how little this was, it would upset her. He heard her take a sharp breath.

"This seems harmless," Jake said, giving Kat a reassuring look. He had seen more salacious tweets connecting him to women he wasn't actually sleeping with, which made this speculation seem innocuous.

Cindy continued, "This is a Danish gossip blogger. The tweet has limited retweets, but once a US fan retweets it—which will happen—it will get a lot more visibility."

"How much visibility? Like thousands or millions?" Kat asked Jake.

Cindy chimed in. "Oh, Kat is there with you? Good," she said. "It's tough to tell. The last dating rumor was retweeted sixty-two thousand times. Views were probably in the single millions, but he has a much bigger fan base now."

Jake felt Kat push his hand off her as she pulled her knees up to her chest. He threw his arm around her and pulled her closer. He wasn't going to let her retreat. Not because of one hundred and forty characters of gossip. This was nothing, and he doubted it would go further than the normal rumor cycle of the internet, which had a shelf life of a few days, max. Once she'd arrived, he'd expected this to happen. He was surprised it took this long.

"This seems pretty normal. Is there anything we should do, Cindy?" Jake asked, turning his attention back to the phone.

"No, we'll monitor it and let you know if it escalates or if anything comes out that starts to confirm your relationship or identify Kat. Honestly, I don't foresee it lasting long—a flurry of retweets, some speculation, and in thirty-six hours everyone has moved on. Exposure is never bad for you Jake, so this should be just fine." Cindy continued, "Jake, what I want to talk about . . . we discussed this . . . if you're together, which it sounds like you are, it's only a matter of time before something does come out. I wish you would let us get ahead of this, control it."

Kat's eyes widened, and Jake went to protest, but Kat jumped in first. "What does that mean?" she asked Cindy.

"Well, Kat, everything Jake does is of interest to his fans, whether it's friends, relationships . . . you name it, they want to know. I guarantee you, there *will* be a point where something gets out, and we'll need to navigate the fan interest in your relationship. I suggested to Jake that we just do a well-timed social post or leak to an entertainment site—control the narrative so it doesn't get twisted. You two have a really intriguing story between his emerging stardom, your past . . . it reads like a goddamn novel. It would be great for Jake. It'd make him seem a little more serious," she said. "For you, the connection to Jake would make you semi-famous, and who doesn't want that?"

"Me," Kat said. "I don't want that. And I can't have that, especially right now." Jake could hear the edge in her voice. "And I want some control, some say in this," she looked at Jake. "Jake and I don't even know if we're—"

Cindy interrupted. "Yes, and I wish we all had a say in what's picked up by the press and social media," Cindy said with her usual brashness, "but it doesn't matter *what* you are. We live in a society where perception trumps reality. Kat, you shouldn't even be there if you're so worried."

Jake knew he needed to end the call before Cindy tried to push Kat any further. Cindy could be a lot to take, and although Jake was used to her brashness, Kat was visibly bristling.

"It's only a matter of time, Kat. You seem smart. Surely you know this," Cindy said.

"Yes. I'm not an idiot. But now is not the time," Kat stated with a firm voice.

"Cindy, we talked about this, and we're not doing anything that will identify Kat. This will blow over, as you said, so we'll just lay low until it does." With that, Jake hit end, and he threw his phone to the end of the bed.

He put both arms around her and let out his breath when she leaned into him. "I'm sorry," he said quietly. "I should have been more careful on set yesterday." He tightened his hold on her, waiting for her to pull away.

"We knew this could happen," she said without emotion. "I thought it was a closed set, NDAs and all. I'm surprised this happened so fast."

"True, this shouldn't happen, but it does. And it does happen this fast," he said. He needed her to understand how he lived. He didn't disagree with Cindy's idea to get ahead of the narrative. He would talk to Kat about it in time. It was inevitable, and the worst thing they could do was let others speculate—it made the swirl last even longer.

"This is my fault. There were almost one hundred crew members on set." He let that hang in the air for a second. He should've known that at least one of them would text a friend, wanting the immediate glory of a celebrity scoop, and in this age of technology, information traveled at light speed.

She was so quiet it unnerved him. He couldn't read her face or emotions. "Kat, talk to me, what's going on in your head?"

She didn't reply right away. "Well," she started and then hesitated, "I certainly shouldn't come to set again."

Jake didn't agree, but he wasn't going to argue with her. He felt her shrug off his embrace and lift her head off his shoulder. She turned so they were face-to-face.

"I think I should go back to New York or at least stay in a hotel," she said.

It was like she dropped a bomb right into his brain. He reached out and grabbed her hand. He needed to quell his own panic by physically connecting himself to her so she wouldn't just evaporate before his eyes.

"No Kat, come on, don't do this," he said, his voice nearly pleading. "This is nothing, it'll be over in a day, and no one will figure out who you are." He was frustrated that something this small would make her retreat.

"And what do we do when it *is* something?" she challenged. "Cindy is right about one thing: I shouldn't be here right now, with everything at stake." She paused and took a deep breath. "I'm not going to be here much longer anyway. You seem fine now, and this is just a distraction."

Jake clenched his jaw and breathed through the hurt and frustration he felt bubbling up to the surface. He blew out a breath, reached over, and pushed her chin up and made her look in his eyes. "Do you honestly believe this is just a distraction?" he said, and he could feel the tightness in his throat. "Because if you do, you *should* leave," he said.

When she didn't reply, he continued, "This is not just a distraction to me." This was him, bringing forward all his complicated, messy life, just asking her to take a chance. He didn't know if she would, or if it was even fair of him to ask. All he knew was that he needed her, starting in those early days of the pandemic, when the only place that had felt right was wherever she was.

It seemed like forever before she spoke. It came out so quiet, he would have missed it if they weren't the words he desperately wanted to hear. "This is more than a distraction," she said, putting her forehead against his. "But I don't know how to do this."

He brought his hands up to the sides of her face and kissed her. "My sweet Kat, you don't need to *do* anything." He sighed. "I'll protect you, if you'll just give it a chance, give *me* a chance."

"But I don't see a way that I—and Becca—won't be in the public eye," she said, "and it scares me more than you know. I fear that it will be the thing that tears us apart, and I don't want to lose you."

Jake knew this moment was crucial, because safety and protection were the only things Kat craved in this world, and his life was the ultimate risk. But he couldn't change what his life had become and the realities of being with him.

"I'll be honest: I won't be able to keep you secret, nor do I want to," he said. "I've come to learn the difference between secret and private. They're not the same, especially to me." He looked at her and made sure he was making sense. "I can keep us private. I have a whole team of people I can use to keep you and Becca protected from the circus."

She looked at him and he could see the skepticism on her

face. "How, Jake? This all seems uncontrollable. We were on set together for only a few hours and then. . . ."

Jake didn't have a plan, but he did know the resources he could use to give her the level of protection she wanted. He couldn't make her anonymous, but he did believe he could bring her into his life without compromising hers or Becca's safety.

"Kat, I've had to figure out how to navigate the world differently. And, because of that, I have a lot of resources at my disposal—"

"How?" she interrupted.

He was reminded that she lived in specificity and didn't exist in the gray. "Kat, it's about creating my—*our*—own bubble. I'm learning how and when I need it. Think about it this way: if there's anything we need to do, I'll hire someone to do it. If something gets out and you're worried about Becca's safety, she'll have security. I can and will do anything you need."

Kat nodded and he could see her trying to process the world he was proposing. He was only asking her to try. That was all he really wanted—a chance for them to be more than a distraction or an escape from life. He wanted to try to be something more to her, to be something to Becca. But most of all, he just didn't want her to keep running away from him. He couldn't chase her forever. But he knew he had to be honest with her and himself about the realities of living a life in public.

"But why can't I just be with you *and* stay anonymous?" Kat asked him as she rested her forehead on his shoulder. Jake heard and felt her sigh. "It was so much easier when we could be a secret."

"Kat, please don't run away because this is no longer easy," he said, taking her hand, almost as if holding on to her would keep her from running. "Given the importance of the public side of my life, even if we are private, I can't keep you anonymous. Our relationship, and you, *will* come into the spotlight."

There. He said it. The big elephant they were always dancing around. He pulled it out of the tent and plopped it right down in the middle of the apartment.

She didn't respond, but she also didn't pull away. He continued, "And even if we could, I don't *want* us to be a secret. I want to be able to be more than some neighbor to Becca. I want to be on a set and look up and see you there. Last night was one of my best nights because you were there. I don't believe that a secret will ever result in anything more than stolen moments. I want *all* the moments."

He caught her eyes and put his hand on the side of her face, rubbing her temple with his thumb. He wanted to believe that he could protect her, and that they could find a common ground between his public life and her private nature. He was pushing her toward a risk he didn't know if she'd be willing to take.

"All the moments," she whispered, repeating his words. "You're killing me, Jake."

He wasn't sure how to interpret her statement, but when she moved into his lap and brought her lips to his, he felt her answer. As he leaned back against the headboard, melting into their kiss, he stopped thinking.

chapter sixteen

Kat was in the middle of her own reconnaissance of the morning's situation—as well as gathering some intel about Cindy—when Jake walked into the living room, showered and ready to go back to set for the day. She watched him. He looked the same, but something was different. He methodically packed his backpack as he sang to himself with an unusual air of calm.

She, on the other hand, was anything but calm. He had her on edge and was pushing hard. Pushing her toward a life full of exposure, risks, and uncontrolled elements. She felt more alive with him than she had in years, but she didn't know if she had enough of herself left to be the kind of woman Jake wanted in his vibrant and open life.

When Jake walked up behind her, she minimized her screen, hoping he didn't see. She didn't want to discuss the tweet any longer and just hoped that Cindy was right—it would be short-lived and inconsequential.

"Going into the office today?" Jake asked, opening each kitchen cabinet and drawer, leaving them open as he searched.

"Yes, in an hour." She was looking forward to going into the office, bringing her back into a world that was built on process and rational thoughts. "What are you looking for?" she asked.

"Coffee cup with a lid," he said. "I have to leave in five, and I'm not properly caffeinated."

Kat got up, opened the cabinet under the sink, grabbed a stainless-steel mug and handed it to him. She walked behind him and started closing all the doors he'd left open.

"Cindy . . . she seems intense," Kat said.

She saw Jake's shoulders tense, so she didn't dare say anything further. He was busy making coffee and she wasn't sure if he would even reply. The apartment was silent except for the sound of coffee flowing into Jake's coffee cup.

When the cup was full, he finally spoke, "She can be. She's good at what she does. She's cleaned up more than one PR mess I've dropped in her lap."

"How did you choose her?" Kat asked.

"I didn't really," he replied. "Roger did. Back when I got my first role. She's been with me from the beginning, so I'm pretty loyal to her, even though I don't think she likes me much. I frustrate her." He snapped the lid on his cup and took a long sip. "I keep telling her I'm only human. I can't be perfect all the time, but she keeps telling me I need to play a part, a character, in my public life. I don't want to do that. Public image is one thing, but being someone else entirely. . . ."

Kat studied him for a second as he set his coffee down to put on his shoes. She took a deep breath and tried to choose her words carefully. "She isn't wrong. Your personal image has taken a hit for most of this year," she mused. "It's fascinating to me. You're a business, Jake. I never thought about you that way, but you are. You're in the business of *you* . . . or at least, the version of you they can sell to the public."

"That's one way to look at it," Jake said and shrugged. "Seems kinda bleak. I want to focus on playing meaningful roles and letting other people take care of everything else. I don't like to think about the business side. That's why I have a team."

Kat continued, "But do you have a team that respects who *you* want to be, not just who *they* want you to be? And can those ever be the same thing?" It was his life and his career, and she didn't know enough to have a clear opinion, but she wondered. She'd just begun to realize he was a product. That's what he was to everyone who made a living off Jake's work and image. The concept intrigued her as a businessperson; as a human, it made her sad.

He stood up and checked his phone. "Good question. Not sure. Can we work on my business plan later?" he asked, winking at her. "Car is here. I gotta go." He gave her a quick kiss and bounded out the door.

As she walked into the Path offices, Kat finally exhaled. This was her safe space, and she needed to spend a few hours in a world she knew how to navigate. She could no longer deny that she wanted to be with Jake, and that would mean stepping out of her overly controlled world. Every time she thought about it, her mouth went dry, and her heart raced, but it also made her feel more like herself than she had in years.

She'd sat down in the office when her phone chimed.

J: Hey, Garren's hosting a cast dinner tonight, please come.

K: Are you sure? Right now? That sounds like a bad idea.

K: Hard pass.

After a small outing on a closed set had made it to Twitter, she wanted to stay in their safe, secret bubble. At least for the next few days.

J: It's a private dinner, only eight of us. It'll be okay.

J: Private, not secret, remember?

J: All the moments. ;)

Ugh. Against her better judgment, Kat agreed. He certainly had ways to make her say yes.

K: Fine. Text me the address. I'll meet you there. We can come and go separately.

J: Great. I'll send a car.

She busied herself with meetings and her endless to-do list but found herself watching the clock. Despite her reservations she couldn't stop smiling when she thought of him. She opened her calendar to see if she could run over to the apartment to change clothes before dinner. One glance at her overloaded calendar gave her an answer. She and Emily were knee-deep in reviewing regional launch plans when she received a text letting her know the car Jake had sent was five minutes away.

"Emily, are we good? I have to leave for dinner," she said, hitting share on the document they were working on. She glanced down at her jeans and black sweater and wished she had worn something more interesting. Her hair was pulled back into a low knot at the base of her neck—a quick hairstyle done earlier this morning, in the haze of minimal sleep. She stared at her own reflection on the video screen and sighed. When she'd dressed for the day, her itinerary did not include a dinner full of famous people.

"Yes," Emily replied. "Happy hour with the team again?"

"No, with Jake," she said, packing up her bag. It was nice to be honest with someone, and she trusted Emily to keep her relationship with Jake secret, or at least private. She tried on Jake's language, and it made sense in her mind. The normalcy of heading to dinner after a day at work made her almost forgot she was in Copenhagen, without Becca, living a temporary life. She indulged herself, leaning into a brief, alternative reality, where she'd made different choices living a different life.

Emily smiled at her. "Oh, good for you. You aren't ever coming home, are you?" she asked, her voice light and teasing.

"I'll be back in a few days," Kat replied, her voice flat as her mind shifted from her alternative reality to the present day.

"Right. That was a fast trip. We're good here. You should take your last few days with Jake." Kat went to protest, but Emily jumped in and spoke over her. "Kat seriously, I'll text you if we need you. Just keep your phone on *and* charged."

Kat knew Emily was teasing. She rolled her eyes. "I'll consider it."

She didn't want to count the number of days before she left. More than that, she didn't want to plan every second. She just wanted to be. Be with Jake.

Once Kat entered the restaurant, the host wasted no time, escorting her to a door marked PRIVATE. The door opened to a room bursting with wild energy, a decibel that sounded like a thousand voices chattering at once. A waiter held a tray in front of her and she grabbed a glass of red. She assessed at least twenty people in the room, a far cry from the eight Jake had promised. She reminded herself that Jake was trying, but he was nothing if not inexact.

She scanned the room until her eyes landed on Jake. He was holding court with a group of people, some of whom she recognized. His face was dancing as his arm gestured wildly. She hung back and observed him in his element, so at ease, so effortlessly charming, that he quite literally lit up the entire room. Up until this trip, she'd only thought of him as scattered, funny, emotional Jake. She was seeing him in a new light for the smart, dynamic, magnetic man that he was. She couldn't take her eyes off him.

As he hit the crescendo of his story, the group erupted in laughter. His eyes moved past his audience, and a smile lit up his entire face. He gestured for her to come over, and all of a sudden everyone's eyes were on her. Her hands shook ever so slightly as she took a sip of wine and walked over. He stepped toward her, grabbed her hand, and gave her a kiss on the lips.

He put an arm around her waist and brought her physically into their circle. He rubbed her hip with his thumb and gazed at her as she met all his fellow cast members. Her hands stopped shaking as he drew her closer to him, but she still felt jittery. She couldn't decipher her feelings. In her day-to-day life, Kat often felt needed—by Becca, by her job, even by Jake. But the way he was looking at her made her feel wanted. Desired and special. Having a man want her—especially a man as passionate as Jake—stirred up emotions she had long since buried.

She vaguely recognized his other cast members. The conversation turned to the social media chatter. There was a flurry of apologies, but all were dismissive of its longevity. Each person launched into a story of their own of a private moment gone public. The more she listened she became innately curious: why they would choose this life at all? One devoid of privacy and full of scrutiny. She posed the question to the group and received different versions of the same answer. It wasn't a choice:

"*It was the only thing I was ever called to do.*"

"*I don't know how to be anything else.*"

"*It's the only way I feel alive.*"

"*I have to create.*"

"*If I hadn't found acting, I think I'd be dead by now.*"

They all agreed that the celebrity side of fame was the hardest part, but the art was inside their soul. It was who they were as humans, and separating themselves from their craft was an impossible task. She watched Jake as they were speaking. He remained silent but nodded along. She was beginning to understand the intense struggle she often felt radiating from Jake. Acting, living with your heart on the outside, would give him a sense of being human, while simultaneously trapping him in a life of public scrutiny.

Jake leaned over and whispered that he wanted to introduce her to Garren, who had just finished a conversation with his partner and the waitstaff. He pulled her out of the circle toward the back of the room. As they approached, she once again felt her hands start to shake. She was officially intimidated by the formidable man in front of her. He towered over her, his shocking blond hair falling over his forehead. His eyes fixed on her as if there were no one else in the room. His role and relationship to everyone in the room was palpable. There was no question he was their leader.

"Great to meet you, Kat, officially," said Garren, shaking her hand. She cringed inside, realizing he would remember anyone that visited his set, especially one that created a flurry of gossip. It wasn't the best first impression. Jake tightened his arm around her waist, and she let out a breath as she felt his protection.

"I'm sure you hear this all the time, but your movie, *Ticket*, just broke me . . . in a good way. I cried for an hour after I left the theater. Come to think of it, *Numb* did that to me, too. I'm rambling, but I just wanted to say that I love your movies. I'm hoping *Ticket* and *Numb* are part of a trilogy . . . sorry, I'll stop now."

Kat couldn't keep herself from gushing over the Oscar-winning director. It wasn't like her to be scattered—she sounded more like Jake than herself. She spied Jake smirking, and she imperceptibly elbowed him. Kat was nervous, and she could tell it amused him.

Garren smiled and bowed his head for a moment. "That's very gracious, Kat, thank-you. And a trilogy just might be in the works, perhaps next year." He gave her a wink. "Jake says you're the head of product for PathMobile. What a great company. I love the new 4.6P. It's been a game changer. I can stream dailies right to my device," he said, holding up his mobile phone.

This was a topic she knew well, which allowed her heart to stop racing and her brain to settle down. She became markedly less awkward talking about mobile devices than movies. "Then you'll love our virtual assistant coming out over the holidays. I'll send you one. We just launched the pre-orders here in Denmark, and I have my hands on a few. It'll have all the power of the 4.6, but with a much larger display and increased voice technology."

Garren clasped his hands together. "Wonderful!"

A wave of relief rolled through her. She really wanted to change her first impression. She knew how important Garren was to Jake. She pulled out her phone and typed a quick note to remind her to get one of the PVAs to Garren.

"So, Kat, what brought you to Copenhagen?" Garren asked.

She didn't really know how much to reveal, so she went with the truth. "We have a regional office here, so I came for work," she paused. "Oh, and this guy." She motioned to Jake, who grinned and nudged her shoulder.

"Well," Garren started, "this guy is killing it. Really Jake, you're giving us a brilliant performance. I was watching the footage from this morning, and it's exactly what I was looking for."

Kat beamed at Jake. When she'd arrived, she'd found a man with his confidence shaken, deep in a hole dug by his own fear and anger. She'd watched Jake pull himself out and now, judging by what she was hearing from Garren, he'd found his way back.

Jake said a quiet thank-you to his director, and to her surprise he elaborated. "Actually, Kat has been instrumental in helping me find the characterization and physicality of Tom. You know I struggled for a while, but she was key to helping me work through it."

She could feel heat rising to her face.

Garren raised his glass as if to toast, locked eyes with Kat, and simply said, "Thank-you."

Kat shook her head and protested. “Not true at all. He’s giving me too much credit. He—” She was interrupted by Garren’s partner’s booming voice asking everyone to take their seats.

They moved toward the tables and Jake grasped her arm, pulling her away from the group meandering to their seats. He leaned over and whispered in her ear. “Hey, why’d you do that? Don’t sell yourself short. You *did* help me find the character,” he said, and she could hear the earnestness in his voice.

But Kat needed him to understand that it was inside him all along. She put her hand on his cheek for a moment and looked at him intently. She felt so much love for the creative soul in front of her. “Jake, I didn’t help you find a character. I’ve been helping you find *you*.”

He closed his eyes for a moment before he covered her hand with his and took a breath. When he opened his eyes, he took her hand off his cheek and kissed it. “Let’s sit,” he said, gesturing to the table.

They found their name cards and sat down in the center of the long table. Kat introduced herself to Garren’s partner, seated to her left. She spied the name card across from her: Sloan Stevens. She smoothed her hair and tugged at the hem of her shirt, wishing she hadn’t come straight from work. Kat wasn’t used to a world built on physical beauty. Up until now, she prided herself on favoring practical efficiency over anything extra. And Sloan Stevens was all kinds of extra. Looking around the table, she tried to be casual, but honestly, she was starstruck.

Sloan sat down with a flourish, her attention focusing only on Jake. “Hey, here, in case you need it,” she said, and tossed a package on the table. It slid toward them, dangerously close to knocking over Kat’s wine glass.

He didn’t pick it up. Kat looked at him, eyebrows raised. Jake ignored Sloan and turned his body toward Kat. “It’s an edible. It takes the edge off. It’s the oldest actor trick in the books.

We're all anxious and hungry as hell all the time." He laughed and gestured around the table. "I bet half this room is high on something."

She rolled her eyes. "Jake, I know what an edible is. I don't live under a rock. I wondered whether you wanted one because being in this room, I might." She could hold her own with some of the best minds in technology and the most powerful business leaders, but she was out of her element in *this* room. "God, I'm nervous as hell in here."

"Don't be nervous," he said, sliding his arm around her chair and leaning over until his lips were millimeters from her ear. He nuzzled her for a split second before whispering, "I think you're the most impressive person in this entire room." He picked up the orange package with his free hand and tossed it back to Sloan. Still whispering in Kat's ear, Jake said, "No, I don't want any. At least not right now. A very wise person told me to not cloud my mind." He gave her a quick, soft kiss before leaning back.

His eyes sparkled and he gazed at her as if she was the only person in the room. Kat fought against the heaviness creeping into this moment. She only had days left and her brain would not reconcile with her heart. The brevity of this moment put her on edge, and all she wanted to do was kiss him right there at the table. Instead, she resigned herself to putting her chin in her hands and running her eyes across his face in an attempt to burn the image of this moment in her mind. He brought his hand up to caress the back of her neck and shivers ran down her back.

Jake moved his arm to the back of her chair, and Kat took a sip of wine. She rested her hand on his leg and relaxed into the moment. As if he could read her mind, he leaned over and repeated her own words back to her: "Stop thinking, just feel." Finally, she allowed herself to lean into Jake.

⋙ ⋘

Jake watched Kat relax into the moment as she leaned her body against his. It was the most at ease he'd ever seen her. She didn't need to control, manage, or drive this moment and for the first time, he watched Kat just be. Kat was deep in conversation with Garren's partner, and he caught snippets of their conversation as they discussed the best movies developed since the pandemic. He didn't join the conversation, but instead found comfort in observing. He was used to being the absolute center of attention, but tonight he only wanted to lean back and take it all in. *I want to be in the moment. Not be the moment*, he thought. It was a unique freedom he hadn't realized he'd lost.

He was jolted out of his thoughts by Sloan. It was an unwelcome intrusion. He didn't enjoy her company, having worked with her on his last film. It hadn't taken long to realize that although the camera liked them together, they didn't work well together. During the press tour, they acted like close friends, maybe more, but only to drive further PR for the film. Fans shipped them like crazy, but the reality was very different. Jake could not stand how Sloan seemed to revel in making people's lives difficult just to show her power. Despite her physical beauty, he found her ugly. He almost grabbed a drink—or an edible—just to make the evening with her tolerable.

He looked at her with a weary face. In *Zero Code*, they were playing lovers, so they needed to get along, but he didn't have to like her when the cameras weren't rolling.

"Jake, we didn't get a chance to chat earlier. How are you doing?" Sloan lowered her voice and leaned across the table. "Like, really doing?"

"Great, Sloan, never better," Jake said with a forced smile, giving her nothing. He'd learned the hard way that Sloan always had an angle.

"I'm glad to hear that," she said, her smile a little too big. "I heard there were some bumps early on. You okay?"

Jake paused and searched his brain for a response. "It was fine. I'm fine, Sloan," he said. He knew better than to give her a centimeter of information.

He pushed the chair back and let Kat know he was going to the bar. He might need that drink after all. At least leaving the table would get him away from Sloan. He was unsettled to hear that she knew anything about the first few weeks of production. He'd put his terrible performance and the cost to the studio out of his mind. He breathed out slowly and stepped up to the bar inside their private room. He thought better of alcohol and ordered a club soda with lime. He took a long drink to calm his nerves and delay his return to the table. When he turned around, Sloan was right behind him.

"Jake, stop avoiding me. I thought *at least* we were friends, after, you know . . ." Sloan said, standing too close.

He hated himself for ever sleeping with Sloan. It had been a weak moment, after their last film wrapped. He had been basking in the euphoria of the end-of-shooting wrap party. It was the wildest party in his career with a cast and crew that knew no limits. Sloan and Jake had done cocaine together with the cinematographer—his one and only time doing hard drugs. Said drugs, fueled by expensive whiskey and chased with champagne, resulted in waking up in Sloan's hotel room. He had never felt so physically wrecked and emotionally charged with regret. Thinking back, the last year, the person he'd been, throwing himself into a self-created black hole of destruction, felt distant to him now.

"I can't see us ever being friends," he said refusing to hide the bitterness in his voice. Sloan had been angry when Jake went to leave and had called him a shitty actor and a bad fuck. Later, she'd posted a blurry Instagram post of his shirt on her hotel room floor. She refused to take it down. It had the fans chattering across every social platform for days. They didn't need to be officially together for her to use him to boost her own public profile. Like everyone else, she cared very little about him unless he could help her stardom.

She let out a dramatic laugh, and Jake turned away from her. He glanced over at Kat, who hadn't noticed. She was busy debating the artistic merit of the entire rom-com genre. Jake watched the scene unfold as Garren tried to argue against Kat's well-thought-out and systematic reasons as to why rom-coms brought the world joy, and therefore did indeed have artistic merit.

He listened to her deliver a thoughtful counterpoint at every turn, making the entire table scream with laughter. They were delighting in the sport of watching her take their *serious* director to task on the subject of rom-coms, of all things. The conspiratorial glances between Garren and Kat told him they were both enjoying this debate, and each other. Jake smirked to himself. He'd been in debates with Kat before, and Garren had clearly underestimated her.

Sloan looked from Kat to Jake. "How long has this been going on?" she asked, dripping with fake sincerity. "Older woman. And a normie too. I'm surprised. How did you two get together?"

Jake gave her a long, hard look. He shook his head, conveying that he would give her nothing. "Sloan, I know it was you who leaked the rumor." Honestly, he didn't know, but it seemed plausible. What he didn't know was why.

"I can't believe you think it was me," she said, feigning innocence, but her smug face told him he'd guessed right.

Discontinuing the conversation, he picked up his drink and walked back to the table. When he sat down, Kat did not look over from her conversation, but she slid her hand onto Jake's leg and rubbed her thumb up and down his knee. It was a small gesture, but the feeling of her hand on him and the comfort of her touch sent waves of calm through his entire body. He leaned over and gave her a quick kiss on the cheek and joined the conversation. Out of the corner of his eye, he saw Sloan lean against the bar, preoccupied with her phone. He didn't know what she was up to, but he didn't trust her.

It seemed impossible, but the dinner conversation got louder and rowdier as the evening went on, and Jake found himself getting hoarse from laughter. He leaned back and took it all in. This was his life, and he loved it. This environment filled with extroverted artists and boisterous personalities gave him energy, gave him life. *Kat may not recognize it, but she fits into this life. My life.* He couldn't stop watching how easy it was for her to slip into this tough, loud group. She kept up beautifully with the conversation, and much of the table was enamored with her wit and ability to match even the quickest banter. What he saw was a woman who'd once told him she was broken, but out of her cracks glowed a confidence that drew people to her.

Kat turned to him, her eyes bright and her cheeks pink. He was reminded of their first kiss, and he felt as if his entire body was tingling. Like that night, he wanted to hold her face in his hands and kiss her like nothing else mattered, but unlike that night, he didn't want to escape. He wanted to be in the present, with her.

She nuzzled the side of his face and whispered in his ear, "Thank-you . . . this is amazing . . . you are amazing . . . really . . . God, I don't know how you are so fucking amazing."

She was giggling, and he could tell from the drawl in her voice, she was sloppy from too much wine. He loved it and in his heart, he knew he loved her. His heart had known before his mind, and he believed that was why, in one of his darkest moments, he'd called her. She was his lifeline, his safe place, his soft landing.

He needed to get out of that room and just be with her. As

much as he liked leaning back and observing, he admitted to himself that he wanted her attention. He also realized that, given how much wine, weed, and who knows what else was flowing, the evening was going to get messy.

It was a new feeling to be the most sober and focused person in the room. He was no stranger to the out-of-control dinners and knew the feeling of regret when it tipped over into a state of debauchery. Kat had a core of control and order, and he didn't want to completely challenge her in one evening. He leaned over and placed a kiss right behind her ear to get her attention. "Are you ready to get out of here?" he asked with a whisper. "I want you to myself."

She looked over, squeezed his knee, and nodded. He wasted no time in texting Savannah, who kept a car on standby for him, especially for nights like this.

J: Hey, we're ready. Can you send the driver and confirm when he's here?

S: Yes, just texted him. He's about five to seven minutes out.

Jake popped his phone on the table and stood up to signal they were leaving. There was a chorus of protests, but he waved them away. Kat and Garren were hugging goodbye when his phone rang. It was Savannah.

"Hey Savy, what's up? Something wrong with the car?" he asked, grabbing his coat.

"I just talked to the driver, and he spotted some paps near the front and back entrances of the restaurant. I'm sure someone tipped them off," she said in a rush. "Stay on the phone but walk through the kitchen. He'll pick you up in the alley."

Jake was always grateful for Savannah, but never more so than now. He whispered in Garren's ear about the paparazzi, said final goodbyes, and grabbed Kat's hand.

"Slight change in plans: we're going to go out through the kitchen," he whispered to her. He kept his voice calm.

"Why?" she giggled, her eyes widening. She steadied herself on his arm.

"Tell you in the car," he said, picking up their pace. He grasped her hand and pulled her through the kitchen. The photographers knew every trick, and he knew they'd need to be fast. The alley wasn't foolproof, but it was the best option.

They arrived at the kitchen door leading out the back, and he handed his coat to Kat. "This is what's going to happen: I'll open this door, and when I do, look down, put this over your head, and get straight in the car. Got it?" he asked. When she nodded, he pushed the door open. He kept his arm around her and guided her into the backseat before climbing in himself.

When they were successfully in the car, he turned his attention back to Savannah. "Thanks for the heads up, we're good," he said breathlessly into his phone. "Have I told you how much I appreciate you?"

"Yes, I think you did twice today already," she replied.

"Well, this is the third. Thank-you," Jake said, hitting end on the call.

He turned his attention to Kat, who was leaning against him, similarly breathless. "Was that to avoid the paparazzi?" she asked, her eyes closing, heavy from the never-ending glass of red wine.

"Yes. But our driver here noticed them, and Savannah figured out another exit," he said, pulling her a little closer. "This is what I mean. I can keep us private, I can." He was trying to convince himself as much as her.

He drew in a deep breath to slow his heart rate as he pulled her close, happy to have a minute to enjoy the quiet of just each other. Kat leaned over and pushed her lips into his. Her lips on his brought a stillness and calm back to his entire body. He no longer felt like the world was against him. He understood it now. He didn't need the world to be with him. He just needed her.

He groaned low and soft, trying to be quiet and not alert the driver. He was ready to get lost in the kiss . . . ready to get lost in *her*. He leaned his head back on the seat as she trailed kisses down his neck. She moved back up to his ear and mumbled, "I want you, Ben."

chapter seventeen

Kat's head pounded as the sun streamed straight from the skylight into her eyeballs. She could feel that it was late. When she grabbed her phone off the nightstand, it said 10:13 a.m. She fell back on the pillow, her mouth dry, as if she hadn't had water for days.

The apartment was eerily quiet, and she sensed the absence of Jake. She put her phone back on the nightstand and saw the Tylenol and Gatorade. He must have left them for her, knowing she would be feeling rough this morning. She wondered, *How many glasses of wine did I have?* It had never seemed to empty, so technically one? The thought made her laugh for a moment, which made her head throb even more. She lay back on the pillow and, all at once, everything came flooding back to her—including their cloak-and-dagger move to avoid the paparazzi.

And then it hit her. And she remembered. At least she thought she did. She hoped it was a dream, but she had a vague recollection of calling him Ben. She put her head in her hands as a few hot tears came fast. *Am I trying to fuck this up?* Maybe she was. She'd finally let go, just a little, and she'd detonated a bomb into the middle of the two of them. Thinking back to the car ride, she felt like puking. Oh wait, she *was* going to puke. She ran to the bathroom to be sick, her body trying to expel last night. If only she could expel it from her mind.

As she walked out, she heard her text chime. She ran to her phone.

J: Drink the Gatorade.

J: I am done at noon today.

J: Be downstairs at 12:30.

J: We need to talk.

Her heart started to pound at the curtness of his texts. She replied with a simple thumbs-up. She texted Emily to let her know she was going to take the day with Jake—she canceled their routine status meetings.

She was waiting downstairs when the car pulled up promptly at 12:30 p.m. She swung open the door, anxious to clear the air with Jake. He was on the phone, deep in conversation. He gave her a half nod of acknowledgment, but nothing else. From what she could hear from the one-sided conversation, he was talking to Roger. They were discussing the next shoot coming up in just under six weeks. Jake was frustrated at the timeline, and it didn't sound as if there was any movement in the schedule.

Kat could feel the iciness radiating from Jake, so she stared out the window. The day alternated between sun and hazy mist, a frenetic fall day that couldn't decide if it would cling to summer a little longer or let winter begin to take hold. She wished the weather would make up its mind. She wished she knew where the hell he was taking her.

Thirty minutes later, they turned into a parking lot, and Jake finally ended his call. "Stop the car. This is fine," he said to the driver.

Kat read the sign—SKJOLDUNGESTIEN LAND PARK—and she could see a beautiful forest, just beginning to turn with fall colors. They were coming to neutral ground, she realized. A place where neither of them had an upper hand.

"This is gorgeous. How did you find this place?" She asked, trying to get him to say something . . . anything.

"Google." He said in a clipped tone. He barely glanced in her direction before he opened his door, exited the car, and slammed it closed.

She took a pause before finally getting out of the car. As she stepped out of the car and looked around, she also realized that, due to the weekday and the misty, cool weather, it was an incredibly private place where she saw no other cars or people.

Jake pulled a backpack out of the trunk of the car, put two bottles of water in the side pockets and slipped it on. She stood there awkwardly, watching him. He didn't say a word.

"Have you brought me out to the woods to kill me, Mr. Soprano?" she tried to joke, knowing it would fall flat, but wanting nothing more than to return to the Jake and Kat of last night, before her stupid slipup. "I wouldn't blame you," she mumbled.

"Ha," he said without a hint of humor, "so you do remember?" He stared at her for a moment, and the hurt on his face nearly knocked her to her knees. He motioned toward a path to the right, turned, and started walking briskly, his body language challenging her to catch up to him.

They walked side by side for a minute. "I'm sorry," she said in a low voice. "I don't know what else to say."

She knew he was hurt, and it was her fault. Multiple times, he'd laid his heart at her feet, and she'd walked over it, seemingly without care. She glanced over as they were walking to see Jake looking deep in thought, his face blank, showing her nothing. She was aware that he had the ability to control the outward expression of his emotion and that, more than anything, scared her.

"Please say something," she said, putting her hand on his arm as they walked together under the trees. He moved his arm away from her touch.

He remained quiet and pensive, and Kat thought he might never speak. He drew in a deep breath through his nose. "Kat, I just need to know, is this why you keep pushing me away? Do you know how much it sucks to try to convince someone to be in your life? God. Even saying it makes me sound pathetic. Is it him? Do I just not measure up . . . to him? I think what we have . . . I don't know . . . it could be something, but I can't—I won't—compete with a ghost."

Kat fought back tears as she both longed for the past and was frightened for the future he wanted and pushed her toward. She didn't look at Jake in the same light as Ben. Ben would forever be canonized as an amazing and tragic person; she hadn't known him long enough to be aware of and accept all his flaws. Death, especially young death, takes broken pieces and smooths them together over time, making them beautiful, flawless objects. It was easy to think of Ben as perfect, someone to long for and put up on a pedestal. It would be impossible for anyone to measure up to his memory. Jake was right. No one should compete with the dead.

She considered her words carefully. "This city . . . this city is complicated for me. I haven't been honest with you . . . but I didn't mean to be dishonest . . . I just didn't say anything. . . ." Now it was her turn to ramble. She finally blurted it out. "I've been here before, with Ben," she said, speaking fast. "I didn't say anything because it didn't come up. You called and then I came here. I feel like I should have told you. But I didn't know how to bring it up. Also, it was so many years ago, I didn't think I would see him so vividly once I got here. So yes, he is on my *mind*, especially here—but no, you are not competing with him inside my *heart*."

"Shit, Kat," he finally said, his frustration palpable. He scratched his head and ran his hands through his hair, growing damp from the misty weather. "I wish I'd known. And I'm pissed that you didn't tell me. I can't ask you *everything*, you need to just tell me some things. I want to know them." He looked over at her. "I can only imagine how hard it's been to be here."

Kat paused before answering. "It's been hard. But, it hasn't been as hard as I thought it might be. Jake, please understand, it's been over five years since he died. I've lived a lot of life in five years. I've lived more years *after* him than I had *with* him," she mused.

He had only been in her life for three years. *What kind of messed up universe is that?* She had only known Ben for 11.1 percent of her entire life. Her fucked-up brain kept doing that math each year, and the percentage of time kept going down the longer she lived without him.

"Five years . . . enough time that he lives in my brain and my heart, but I no longer hope to wake from some bad dream and see him around every corner." She paused to make sure he really understood that she had come here for him, not to live out a memory of Ben. "I would be lying though, if I didn't admit that I feel, at times, forever broken."

She took a breath and told him what had held her back this entire time. "Jake, I don't know if I have anything left," she started. "I think sometimes that I've just lost too many people. My heart is so used to losing and grieving that I don't actually know how to live in the present. I wonder if I even know how to love."

There, she'd said it. She was letting him see her darkest fear. The fear that she was incapable of letting herself go enough to love someone completely—especially someone like Jake, who wouldn't accept anything less than unbridled, authentic love. A tear fell and she brushed it away and turned her head, hoping he wouldn't see.

"Kat, I haven't been fair to you," he said as they walked. "I'm selfish," he said, his voice tight.

Kat opened her mouth to contradict him, but he put up his hand and continued. "Listen, I am. I know that. I live a life focused on myself, literally," he said, letting out a dry laugh. "I've been unfair to you. I asked you to come here just because I was having a hard time, which is the epitome of self-centeredness.

"And I disregarded the parts of your life that don't center around me. To me, you only live in my mind from the moment we became friends, lovers . . . you exist from the moment you meant something to *me*. You had a life before me. God, I never think about that. Like, when I think about the time I learned you'd moved in next door, I conveniently only think about you and Becca, not even the time before, when Ben was alive. How fucked-up is that?"

He shook his head and continued. "I used to get updates in emails from my mom almost daily about the neighbor with cancer, his wife, and their newborn daughter. It feels surreal to me that I was so close and so far from your life at that time. I don't connect that family to you. *You* are in my mind, only as you, and you with *me*. You're *my* safe place to land. I've asked you to jump into this with me, all the while ignoring your past, and that's not fair."

She appreciated his recognition of the differences in their lives, but she didn't agree that it was selfish to disconnect her from his minimal knowledge of her life with Ben. It was one of the many reasons she existed so well in his orbit. His awareness of that time in her life was through others, but he hadn't witnessed the horror of watching a family disintegrate. She wasn't another man's widow in his mind. She existed in a space between tragedy and the remaking of her life post-Ben, and Jake allowed her to be present only among the living.

"That's not selfish," she said, as she couldn't help but reassure him. "I love that you see me, but as I am *right now*. It's hard to have people think they know you . . . define you . . . by something that's only part of you, but not the whole you."

"Tell me about it," he said, the sarcasm clear in his voice.

Kat realized that he did indeed understand the feeling of living in an alternate reality, locked into your own private prison of others' seemingly intimate views of your life. They had a common understanding of a life before and a life after.

They walked in silence and Jake was the first to speak. "I want to know all of you," he started. "You only let me see the controlled, perfect, safe you. I saw the messy, sloppy you last night, and I also want to know the profoundly sad you. I don't want a version of you. I want *you*."

He looked over at her as they navigated the trees and rocks. The rain started to drizzle around them. They were sheltered by the thick canopy of trees, but it added a somber quality to their conversation. Kat couldn't speak. When talking about herself, the words never came easy. She didn't know if she could ever let him see all of her. She didn't know if she even understood all of herself.

He broke the silence as they walked. "I met him once, Ben. I'd been home from a shoot in Vancouver, stopping off in New York for the weekend. I met him in the elevator. I'd known who he was and that he was fighting for his life, but all I managed was a stupid 'hi.'" He cleared his throat. "Um, I will say, even sick, that man looked like he could snap me like a twig." He let out a small laugh, and Kat looked over at him and smiled. "Kat, tell me about him. I want to know who he was, about your life together. . . ."

She hesitated. "Jake, why do you want to know? It's in the past," she said, her words tentative. She didn't want to have this conversation. She hadn't talked to anyone about Ben since his death. She liked keeping him in the past. It was easier.

"Ben, and what happened to him, has everything to do with who you are today," he said. "If I want to know you, really know you, I *need* to know," he replied. His voice was firm and tinged with kindness.

His ask was fair, even if it wasn't easy. He had been open with her about all the parts of him—the good, the messy, the selfish—and she owed him some honesty. She took a deep breath and began the narrative of the best and worst years of her life.

"Before he got sick, he was a firefighter," she started. "I met him when I was still at NYU. It was the last year of my MBA."

Kat had been a resident adviser and there was a small fire—a smoking bag of popcorn left too long in a microwave. It wasn't a real fire, but enough to set off the smoke detector and make a jumpy freshman pull the fire alarm. The entire dorm had evacuated and stood outside in their pajamas on a cold February night. A fire engine arrived, and a rookie fireman was sent to investigate the "non-fire" fire. Part of her duty as the RA was to be the leader/spokesperson whenever any potentially dangerous situation arose.

The rookie fireman was Ben. Even though it had been a very straightforward non-fire fire, he was thorough in his investigation. He interviewed six different people in the dorm. Kat accompanied him for every interview, each time reminding him that they *knew* it was Casey Nova that left the popcorn in the microwave. He'd lectured the entire dorm on fire safety and asked that appropriate cook times be posted in the kitchen.

Later that night, Kat emailed Ben all her notes from every single interview in case he'd needed them, along with her version of the event. He'd emailed her back five minutes later. Her notes were so detailed, he'd no longer needed to write the report. His shift ended at 10:00 p.m. As a thank-you, he'd offered to buy her a drink. She'd said yes.

Jake murmured, almost to himself, "He was a firefighter, wow. Badass."

"He was, but also more sensitive and introverted than he appeared." She smiled, remembering the dichotomy between his appearance and his personality.

Ben's thick head of brown hair, beard, and host of tattoos made people believe he was intimidating, but he'd been the most calm and gentle person Kat had ever met. Ben had had an intense, internal need to take care of people. She'd been instantly smitten.

Their relationship happened fast. On their third date, she'd found herself crammed in an Irish pub on 11th Street. They had been out with the off-duty members of his precinct. It had been hot and loud, with cheap beer flowing freely. He had wrapped his arms around her, shielding her from the boisterous crowd. The entire bar had vibrated with energy, and she'd felt so protected in his arms.

His hair had been wet with sweat, and his eyes heavy from too much beer. He'd whispered in her ear, "I'm going to marry you. Just you wait." She'd chalked it up to his drunken state. But six months later, after she'd graduated, they were married.

Kat paused before saying any more, and before Jake could comment, she said, "Yes, I know it's not like me, marrying him so quickly, not overthinking everything and creating long timelines." She laughed at herself. That person, the Kat with Ben, felt foreign to her now.

Jake shook his head. "It makes perfect sense to me, actually, for a person who wanted an umbrella of safety. Firefighter. Solid choice."

"Right?" she asked, choking back tears. Jake saw her so clearly. Of course, he would understand why she chose Ben. "You know, I was a different person then, and he liked things to be simple. He balanced me in a way that I just didn't have to . . . I don't know how to explain it . . . didn't have to try so hard at life."

She knew Ben would be disappointed in her now—so precise, so rational, tightly controlling every aspect of her and Becca's life. He had given her the safe space she'd needed. Until he'd gotten sick.

They started walking again, up an incline that made them both breathe a little heavier. The rocks in front of them looked wet and glistening. Jake took the lead, and once he'd hiked up the rocks, he turned and held out his hand to steady her. Once they were both at the top of the hill, Jake continued to keep their hands connected. She was silent, unable to continue. She was wary of arriving at the horrible end of their love story.

Jake spoke, breaking the silence. "When did he get sick?"

Kat knew he wasn't going to let up until she found it inside her to tell him the complete story. "It wasn't long after we got married. I'd found out I was pregnant. Honestly, Becca was a bit of an 'oops.' I'd wanted to wait a few years, but I think the universe knew that we needed to live fast. Ben had been thrilled. Being a firefighter and a dad had been the two biggest dreams of his life, and within a few years, he'd achieved both."

Kat had never in her life felt more cherished. During the first trimester, she'd been very sick, and every single thing had made her ill. Ben had also consistently been not feeling well and often had stomach issues. He used to call it "sympathy puking." As she'd gotten into the second trimester, she'd felt better, but Ben had not. She'd finally convinced him to get checked out. They were going to have a baby, and she'd needed him.

"Stomach cancer," she said. "Stage four. Out of fucking nowhere. Honestly, I thought he hadn't felt well from eating all that shitty firehouse food. I had no idea he'd been really sick." She laughed a laugh that did not hold a hint of humor. "He was twenty-eight. What twenty-eight-year-old just gets stomach cancer?"

She was quiet for a time. "It was aggressive. He didn't even tell me how much until it got really bad. He'd been determined to fight and said the 'I'm going to beat it' bullshit. But I believe he knew. He'd asked his parents for money to get us a good apartment and created a village around me, because he knew he wouldn't be there." She knew he'd been trying to take care of her, even in the face of death.

She didn't know how much more she wanted to—or could—relive. She rarely talked about Ben's illness. It was easier to compartmentalize and not think about it, and she'd gotten really good at pretending her life with Ben was nothing more than a bad dream.

"So, long story short, we moved next door to your parents when I was seven months pregnant, and Ben was in the thick of chemo. Did I ever tell you how amazing your family was to us, especially once Becca was born? Did you know your dad used to accompany Ben to chemo every Wednesday?" The cancer center was no place for a baby, and Kat wouldn't leave Becca when she was only weeks old. "Your dad organized poker games during the infusions. He and Ben became very close." She thought back to how Ben came to find a way to enjoy Wednesdays.

"And your mom. I couldn't have survived it all without her. One day, she must have heard Becca wailing all morning and knocked on my door. I thought she was annoyed from the noise, but she just took Becca in her arms. She had a magical ability to calm her. She took her over to their apartment and put her down for a nap. After I took a shower and checked on Ben, I went next door. God, I felt like an inadequate mom who couldn't even care for her own baby. Your mom . . . well, she just held me. She just let me cry it out that day—ugly, messy crying. I think I cried more that day than at Ben's funeral. After that, she took Becca nearly every afternoon, not only giving me a break, but also giving Ben and me time together."

Jake gave her a smile. "No, I hadn't heard all this, but I did know about the afternoons with Becca. Those I heard about in detail. I never knew how it had started, but I knew my mom loved it. Loves her."

Kat gave him a weary smile before finishing her story. "Jake, it was horrible to watch someone so strong just wither away. He died right before Becca's first birthday. I used to be so pissed that he didn't make it to her birthday. It was a milestone I kept in my head, but the only purpose it served was to disappoint me. Life is cruel and unpredictable. He promised to protect me, and then I had to watch him die. I was mad at him, at the universe, at everything. For a long time." She paused. "I still am," she said whispered under her breath.

The one person who had promised to keep her safe had died right before her eyes, and in many ways, she would never get over it. That undercurrent of disappointment clouded her ability to feel joy, and that, more than anything, made her angry.

They walked along the trail for a bit longer. The mist stopped, and sunshine peeked out from behind the clouds, mocking their morose conversation.

Jake cut through the silence. "I remember my mom saying he put up a strong fight, Kat. I'm sure he did everything he could to stay with you, to protect you."

His statement broke her. The tears came rushing from her eyes, and she finally let them out without shoving them back in. The dam had burst, and the darkness was flowing out. She saw him look over at her with concern on his face, but he didn't speak. Instead, he stopped and pulled her into a tight embrace. Kat felt the cover of his body cocooning her into the web of his arms. He asked for all the parts of her, and she desperately wanted him to see her, really see her, for the first time. She didn't let *anyone* see how fractured she was inside; only inches into that calm exterior was the messiest of humans.

"I've never told anyone, but. . . ." she paused, considering whether to continue. She decided he needed to know the truth. "At the end, I wanted him to die." And with that, she buried her face in his chest and let the tears flow. "It was unexplainably hard. He was so sick and getting worse, and I had a newborn who was so needy. I was suffocating inside my own life. He felt like a burden to us and decided to end chemo early," she took a shuddered breath, "and I let him. I could have worked harder to keep him with us longer . . . he could have made it to her birthday. I should have tried to keep him with Becca longer, but I just gave up."

She saw Jake open his mouth to speak, but she didn't want him to make her feel better. She cut him off before he spoke. "I never give up on anything. But I gave up on him," she said. She pushed against his chest and pulled away, taking a few steps forward. "There, you wanted to know me. That's me. Hope you don't get sick one day, because I'll just let you die."

Jake caught up to her grabbing her arm. "Kat," he started, as he pulled her to face him, "you know that's not true. You were facing an impossible time, and nothing you could have done would've changed the outcome."

She tried to pull herself out of his grasp. She didn't want his kindness, she wanted to punish herself and live in the guilt of that decision. It was easier to live with the power of anger than allow the waves of sadness to crash in on her, but Jake held tight and pulled her closer to him, using his physical dominance over her. She buried her head in his shoulder so he couldn't see her cry. She felt him step back and move his hands to her face, forcing her to look at him.

"Don't fight grief with shame," he said. "It's an impossible way to live." He cupped her face in his hands and kissed her tears. With each one, he showered her with love. "You are good. You are strong. You are beautiful. You deserve to be happy."

She tried to look away. He held her face firmly, not allowing her to break away.

"I love you."

She questioned for a moment if he'd really spoken those words or if it was simply wind blowing in the canopy of trees above them. She tilted her face up to him to meet his lips. His kiss was gentle, bringing her back to the present.

chapter eighteen

Jake awoke to the ping of rain on the skylight. He rolled over and slid his arm around Kat, drawing her back to the embrace they'd been in before falling asleep. When they'd finally made it back to the apartment, they'd been wet and exhausted. Kat seemed so drained she barely spoke to him. They did nothing more than shed their wet clothes and lie down in the safe cocoon of his bedroom. They held on to each other as though one of them might float away into the night. The light of the moon shone brightly through the window above, but he could feel morning approaching.

He propped himself up on one elbow and pressed his lips to each one of her closed eyes. She looked peaceful, bathed in the moonlight of the impending morning. He brushed her hair away from her face, his hand lingering on her cheek. Kat opened her eyes, lifted her face to his, and mirrored him, her lips softly brushing each of his eyes. He kept them closed, then kissed her as if they were merging into one being. The power of the moment rendered him speechless. They lingered delightfully as they re-mapped each other's bodies with tongues, fingers, and lips until the near twilight of morning. Jake kissed her as if he could command time.

Once his lips had touched the entire surface of her body, he needed to be inside her. He took control and moved his body on top of hers. He reached over to the bedside drawer for a condom, and Kat pulled his arm back, as if refusing to separate from him for even a minute.

"Jake, no," she said, breathless. "I want nothing between us."

His heart lurched and he searched her face. "Are you sure? Kat, is that okay?"

"Yes, yes it's . . . safe," she said, answering his unspoken question.

Of course it would be, Jake thought, *Kat doesn't take risks.* He realized that she was offering her whole self to him in the most intimate way possible. After all the times she'd pushed him away, she was bringing them together without barriers between them, emotional or physical. He dropped his head and sucked in his breath, his throat tight. She ran her fingers through his hair, tilted his head toward her, and he felt her lips meet his. Their faces were wet, and Jake couldn't discern which tears were whose.

Kat rolled her hips slightly to better align their bodies and Jake pushed into her. Electricity seemed to flow through his body as he felt a virginal reawakening. A guttural moan escaped his lips. He stilled himself inside her—he wanted to stay in the moment. He didn't want to escape, no longer chasing a quick release.

Jake pulled his lips from hers and pushed up on his elbows locking their eyes together. He moved in a slow rhythm allowing him to feel every second, imprinting this moment into his brain. He'd never felt this connected to another human and every movement pulled him further out of his own murky water. He came inside her and was overwhelmed by the realization that a physical part of him had joined her body. Despite human evolution, his primal response was to physically claim her as his. She was giving it all to him, and he wanted to be enough.

He slowed his breathing while they rested, still intertwined, unable to be in the same space and not physically connect.

She spoke, saying the words he was longing to hear: "Jake, I've been in love with you for a long time."

In the empty café, barely open for the day, Kat fixed her eyes on Jake as gray light began to peek through the front window. She unequivocally loved this man. She loved all parts of him—the way he looked at the world with emotion and intellect intertwined, the way his desire for brilliance overwhelmed him but did not deter him, even the way he was drinking his coffee like it was the finest champagne. The last observation made her laugh. Jake didn't just live life. He attacked life, felt it with his whole being, and was uncompromising in his passion to never waste a second. All at once, she was feeling understood by him and changed by him.

He looked up at her and cocked his head. "What?" he asked, a tiny smile forming on his lips, showing his awareness that she'd been watching him.

Kat took a sip of her coffee and said, "I'm just happy, that's all." She couldn't stop smiling. In that moment, she wasn't thinking ahead to all the things that could go wrong. She wasn't fast- forwarding to the day she would leave, mapping the challenges they would face in navigating a life together. She wanted to figure it all out for a chance to have a life with Jake, even with its complications.

He leaned forward, reached for her hand, laced his fingers through hers, and rested his chin on their intertwined hands. In her burgeoning fluency of his physical language, she understood this meant more than any words could say. Kat could feel his love radiating off him. Gone were his manic vibrations, now replaced with a kinetic affection. He kissed her hand before setting it down, and she reflexively looked around.

"It's 5:37 in the morning Kat, the city is barely awake," he said, gesturing to the empty café in front of them and waterfront out the window. "You don't need to worry."

"I know, I know," she said. "Is it bad that I just want to walk back to your apartment where I can kiss you whenever I want?" She didn't want to worry about every touch, every glance, every kiss. Her emotions were unsteady as they crashed down around her. She felt exposed and jittery and needed to retreat with him to a place where she felt protected. It was her idea to walk to the café, but she realized now it was her way to retreat from the intimacy of the morning. Now she wanted nothing more than to go back.

He jumped up and went to the counter and grabbed a take-away bag for the pastries they had ordered. She giggled at his haste to leave. Without sitting down, he bagged them up and offered his hand to Kat.

She relaxed into him as they walked along the canal. An overcast, misty day greeted them once again. Yesterday, the weather had cast a somber tone, but today, it felt like shelter, allowing them to slip into the fog, seen only by each other. To Kat it seemed like they were the only two people in the entire city.

Jake's curls glistened from the light mist, and she reached up to tousle his hair, causing tiny water droplets to fly everywhere. He shook his head, laughed, and pulled her to him under a store awning. For the first time, Kat did not look around as their lips met. She pulled back only to look at his beautiful face. She felt his hand on the side of hers, thumb caressing her jaw, but she could feel his hesitation, too.

"Talk to me, Jake."

"We *are* going to do this, right? Like, we're going to try?" he asked, his eyes earnest and hopeful.

"Yes," she said, bringing her hand up to his face, mirroring his gesture to show that they were in this together. She wanted him to know that she was all in. She'd had a list of reasons why they shouldn't be together, but now, none of them mattered.

"No more running?" he asked, more a statement than a question.

"No more running," she said. She didn't know what the future held for them, but she didn't want to run from him any longer.

And with that, they embraced, Kat's heart beating fast.

Walking back, she allowed herself the joy of just being two lovers, nothing more, enjoying the romance and beauty of the city. They were not Jake and Kat—two people with vastly different lives, stepping into something with more difficulties than they could yet imagine—they were Jake and Kat, two broken people who, in finding each other, had mended their broken pieces to become whole again.

chapter nineteen

"Got it. We can move on," Garren said, flashing Jake a thumbs-up.

Today everything flowed with ease, and they were flying through the shots. The entire cast was starting to gel, and Jake could even tolerate Sloan. He was optimistic—about this film, about his career, and about Kat. He was acutely aware of every passing hour and the countdown until the day Kat would leave. Two days. Twenty-four hours. He looked down at his watch. Twenty-three-and-a-half hours to be exact. Every ounce of his being wanted her to stay longer, but he knew she needed to get home to Becca. He reminded himself they were still together, even when physically apart, and it helped to tame his anxiety about their future. Kat insisted they needed some sort of a plan, and Jake had promised that this evening they would discuss the inevitable.

The crew took a short break, so Jake had a chance to look at his script and reorient himself with the next scene. He'd been off book for a while, but Garren liked to jump around, and it helped to re-read the scene before and after. He looked up to see Savannah walking fast toward him, her face tight. Before she could reach him, Garren announced they would start again and asked for anyone not in the next scene to step behind the cameras. The next two scenes would be shot back-to-back, with minimal breaks, so everyone was to leave the principal cast alone. He watched Savannah's face fall with a look of defeat. He gave her a curious look and shrug. He made a mental note to ask her when they were finished.

They made quick work of the next two scenes, or he thought as much. When Garren called the final "cut," he realized they'd been focused for the past two-and-a-half hours.

Savannah scurried up to him, and he felt her hand on his back push him forward. "I need to talk to you, right now. Walk with me." She started back toward his trailer. This was unlike her. Jake followed her and didn't ask questions.

He was trying to read her face, but she stared straight ahead, eyes fixed in front of them. She was silent until they got to the trailer, but once they closed the door, she shoved an iPad in his face. "Read this."

Jake looked down at the screen and saw what had prompted Savannah to get him away from the crew. He stared at his own face under a headline that read: TROUBLE ON SET: STUDIO LOSES $1 MILLION WHILE JAKE LAURENT HAS A MELTDOWN.

His ears started to ring, and stress rose in his throat. "What the fuck?" he said, his voice rising with anger.

He tried to keep calm as the fury surfaced, but every anxiety he had about never being good enough rushed back into his brain, firing multiple synapses at once. He opened his mouth to speak, but he couldn't even form a sentence. He yanked open a cabinet and pulled out a bottle of bourbon. He slammed a glass on the table and poured himself a shot. He gestured to Savannah to ask if she wanted one.

She shook her head no. He tipped his head back, and the alcohol burned his throat and the fumes flew through his nose. For a second, the feeling was a welcome distraction from the panic he was fighting. He poured another, but merely sipped this round.

"I didn't have a goddamn meltdown," he said, mostly to himself.

"I know, Jake," Savannah said. "It's stupid clickbait. If you read the article, it's all speculation and hearsay anyway."

Her pocket buzzed and she handed him his phone. He scrolled rapid-fire through his mounting text messages. He counted no less than fifteen texts from Cindy and five from Roger. He hadn't gotten anything more than a good luck text from Kat all day. He presumed that she hadn't read it yet. He checked the posting time—roughly three hours ago. He threw his head back and laughed silently. So that's why Garren hadn't allowed them any breaks. He'd known this would derail the entire day. He saw Savannah had replied to Cindy and Roger, letting them know he was in the middle of shooting a scene.

"Savannah, who do you think is the leak on set?" he asked. He was trying to focus on anything other than the fucked-up situation in front of him.

"Sloan. I guarantee it," she said, her voice confident.

"Why?" he asked. "I know she thinks I'm an asshole, but that's not a reason to try to destroy someone."

"Because she's a horrible person. Does she need more of a reason?" Savannah said, scrolling on her phone and taking screenshots. She stopped scrolling and looked up. "Listen, I heard this all thirdhand, and you know I'm allergic to gossip. . . ."

"Spit it out," he said, the irritation clear in his voice.

"She's having an affair with Jude Yarly," she announced.

He gave her a look and raised his hands indicating that he didn't understand. This was no time to be cryptic.

"He's one of the executive producers," she explained. "His wife has late-stage dementia, so if it got out that he and Sloan were together, enter the cavalry of cancel culture. The entire crew has been talking about the affair since she got here, which is why she leaked the story about you and Kat. It would make Garren clamp down on any more rumors getting out."

This was the most Jake had ever heard her break down the culture of the set. He reminded himself to ask her for information more often. "Why leak this?" he asked, resigned. He didn't need to know, but it was calming him down to focus on the why, not just what had happened.

"No idea, but certainly sleeping with a producer would give her inside information on the production schedule and studio budgets. My bet is on her, that diva bitch."

Jake sat back and just stared at the article, contemplating what to do, but also stalling a bit before his brain would bring him back to the nightmare in front of him.

"Jake," Savannah said, "Cindy and Roger are waiting. You need to call them. You want to FaceTime or just use your phone?"

He gestured to the iPad and scrolled through the contacts for Cindy's number. He hesitated before dialing, his hands shaking. Talking to both of them made it real, and in his gut, he knew it was bad.

"I'll leave you," Savannah said, putting her hand on the door. "Jake, what I can do? What do you need?"

Jake tossed his phone to her. "Can you call Kat? Let her know what's going on? I don't think she's seen it." While he made a game plan with his team, he wanted to make sure she knew. He wanted . . . no, needed her near, as she was the one person who calmed him.

Savannah nodded and let herself out of the trailer to give him privacy.

Cindy answered on the first ring. "I'm here with Roger," she said in a curt tone.

"Cindy, how bad is it?" he asked, his heart starting to race. He was hopeful this could be squashed or at least minimized.

"Well, it's bad," she said. "Unfortunately, it's a slow news day, so this is spreading like wildfire. Everyone is picking it up."

Roger jumped in. "Jake, I'm going to be honest with you, I already received a call from your upcoming production, and they're concerned. They aren't dropping you—*yet*—but they needed reassurance that you'll deliver. Also, we're still in contract negotiations with Ink Studios, which might get derailed."

Jake spoke directly to Roger, "Wow, that's my next project. This could fuck up my entire year. Are you kidding me?" He finished his second glass of bourbon and winced.

"It could," he said. "And you will probably have to move from 'offer only' back to auditions. Studios don't like to lose money, and this will make all of them think twice about hiring you."

Jake could hear the disappointment in Roger's voice, which cut him far worse than if Roger were angry. He felt ashamed, as if he were disappointing his own father. Jake ran his fingers through his hair. "Why the fuck is this happening to me?" It was a rhetorical question, but Cindy jumped in to answer it.

"People love idols, people they can put on pedestals, and then knock them down. It's almost a sport, especially in this business. You've been the 'it' boy for quite a while, so I'm not surprised this is getting so much traction."

Roger jumped in. "We have to make sure you don't get painted as an unstable actor. If you lose fans or have a reputation that impacts how potential moviegoers see you, you'll become less bankable, no matter how good you are. Remember Billy Castle? His cocaine overdose changed his bankability by 50 percent for at least three years."

"You're comparing me to a drug addict," he said, raising his voice. This was unfair. He'd only had a few bad weeks. It was burnout, not a meltdown, and he'd pulled it together. He couldn't believe a few weeks could derail the last nine years he had been building his career.

"There is one bright spot," Roger said looking down at his phone. "I've been texting with Garren, and he's going to personally call Art Savou, one of the producers of your next project, so that will help. At least a little bit."

"Okay. That should help a lot, right? Not just a bit. It's all speculation and rumor, so couldn't it just die down?" Jake asked. He was grasping at straws, but this was worse than he'd imagined.

Both Cindy and Roger were completely silent.

Roger spoke first. "There's more. And this is worse. Are you alone?" When Jake nodded, he continued. "There's a leaked email from Garren to the studio, about you."

"Fuck!" Jake said. "What did it say?" His ears started to ring as the panic set in again.

"The good news is that it hasn't been published yet. The bad news is that it details the number of scenes that Garren would need to reshoot, the number of days they were behind schedule, and an estimated cost to the studio." He went on, "Jake, it's bad. It details a plan to replace you if needed."

Jake felt bile rise up into his throat. This would absolutely destroy his future projects with any major, or even minor, studio. He wasn't at the level of fame to survive this hit to his reputation, nor was he financially in a place where he could fund his own projects. But even more than that, he was ashamed that it was true. He'd put them behind schedule; he'd not delivered for the first time in his career. It was easier when he could focus on unsubstantiated rumors and a blip in the production schedule. But the reality of the situation was that he had set them back millions and was nearly replaced. It was a tough pill to swallow. He had to face his own shortfall.

"What do we do?" he asked, resigned.

Cindy put on her glasses. "Let's start with what's out there. To combat the rumors, we'll get a quote from Garren about how great your performance is and hype up the film. We might convince the studio to release some behind-the-scenes footage."

"And he'll do that?" Jake asked, unsure of whether Garren would ultimately stand behind him. They were working well together now, but there was a time when Garren was planning to replace him.

"Yes. It's not good for the box office to be surrounded by this kind of drama," she said. "The data shows that negativity never translates to good numbers."

Roger jumped in. "Jake, he already texted me that he's preparing a statement with the studio on the power of your performance and your brilliance on set. He's in your corner."

Of course he is, Jake thought. *We still have a lot of movie left to shoot, and he needs me.* The realization reminded him of the transactional nature of relationships in the entertainment business: if I need something from you and you need something from me, we have a relationship. As soon as that dynamic changes, people disappear. He expected Garren to retreat from this situation immediately.

"Okay, that all sounds workable, but what about the email?" he asked. He ran his hands through his hair.

Cindy answered, "We know TMZ has the email, and my sources tell me they're the only ones. There are a lot of people focused on figuring out how to keep this quiet. The studio does not want their documents, especially itemized budgets, in the press. There's an entire machine built around this film, and it's going to work on this."

"Do you think it will get squashed?" he asked. He opened a drawer on the left and pulled out his cannabis. He'd been taking great care to stay off all substances in order to get his head together, but right now, he needed to tamp down this nightmare. After years on the road, where a quick fix was all that was tolerated, this was the best way he knew how.

"Honestly?" Cindy asked.

"Yes, honestly," he said, not hiding the exasperation in his voice.

"Plan A is that the studio will try to keep it from being published. For TMZ not to release it, they will need something equally as good. Breaking this scandal will drive a lot of traffic, and therefore advertising revenue. It will take a lot to give them something as beneficial as this scandal. The studio is trying to offer up exclusive access to multiple projects under the studio umbrella," she outlined.

"Do you think that will work? Plan A?" Jake asked.

Cindy took off her glasses and shook her head. "I don't. I think it's going to be a big 'meh' to TMZ. They're going to use this email as a negotiation to get access to something just as valuable to them. It's all about what will make them more money. Behind-the-scenes footage isn't going to do it. Plan A, to me, is a necessary step to let the studios try, but it's not going to work."

"So, what's Plan B?" he asked. He wanted to hear the answer, but he was also getting a bad feeling in the pit of his stomach.

She finally spoke after what felt like a full minute. "Jake, just don't say no. . . . Don't say anything yet. But you are sitting on the perfect story that I know, one thousand percent, if given an exclusive, TMZ would make a trade."

He didn't answer, taking a minute to think while loading his cannabis vaporizer. He put the vape pen to his lips and started to shake his head. He knew where she was going, but it wasn't a route he wanted to take.

This time Roger spoke. "Jake, she's right. This is a good idea. Don't react. Just listen."

Jake trusted Roger more than Cindy, so if Roger thought it was worth listening to, he would listen. He didn't have to like it, but he would listen.

"Go on," he said, lowering his voice.

"Plan B," Cindy started, "is that we leak the story of you and Kat. Not just a leak, but a narrative of your new love helping you through some mental burnout—a young widow and her daughter. 'Love after Tragedy' . . . A celebrity with a new secret love affair? One that helped him through mental burnout? Who wouldn't relate to, and more importantly, *love* this story? It's positive, explains the rumors, and reframes your supposed meltdown as mental health. Mental health is very on trend right now."

She continued, "We give an exclusive to TMZ in exchange for not publishing the email. This is a goldmine for them. The story will not only get a lot of direct traffic and social media shares, but it will also be redistributed by every major news outlet. The current story of your meltdown will get traction, but it's negative and frankly, old news because it already leaked. Breaking a story about your love life will have at least twice the longevity. Whether you like it or not, your love life is a big topic, and whoever breaks *that* story is going to benefit in a big way."

Jake was trying to process what Cindy outlined. "Kat will never go for it."

"We can do it without her," Cindy replied. "I have everything I need. She doesn't need to know, and if you don't confirm or deny the story, you're not culpable either. We'll release the minimum we need to get them to bite. I'll make sure that TMZ reports it as anonymous, not coming from us. So, you don't need to say yes, just don't say no. You say no, and we have nothing to leverage to stop this email. You know I'm right. This will be hard to come back from, if you even can. Say nothing and we'll only use it if the studio is unsuccessful. I won't consult with you on the story or the details, and I won't even show you the pictures. You won't know anything so you can't be at fault."

"Where would you have gotten pictures?" Jake asked, his voice almost a yell. "Pictures of what?" Jake wondered if Cindy was behind the paparazzi that had started following him in Denmark. He knew she was good at her job and knew how to use the media to her advantage, but this seemed overboard.

"Jake, I have them. You two haven't been as careful as you think," she said. "I would rather not show them to you in order to keep you clean from all of this. Trust me. I will only use them if I have to. I will try to give them as little as I can."

"Cindy, I don't know if we'll still have a relationship after this," Jake said, his tone resigned. He longed to talk to Kat, to get her thoughts, but she was unbending and rigid, and he knew she wouldn't even try to understand this option. If her reaction to an anonymous, blind tweet was to run away, he couldn't imagine telling her this plan. And if she said no, he was out of options and his career was over.

It's better this way, he told himself. *They're just leaking it early, before someone else does.* He was trying to convince himself that this decision would be okay.

He was caught between two impossible choices. The first was to let everything he'd built over nine years go down the drain: the endless days, working into the wee hours of the morning at every director's whim, just to put art into the world. He'd missed holidays with his family and endured a life with zero privacy. None of his sacrifices would mean anything. Acting was who he was, he didn't know what he would be . . . who he would be without it. He pictured himself retreating back into community theater or worse, commercials, and his head began to throb.

But the second choice was no easier. Kat would feel betrayed, at least at first, and navigating her felt impossible. He did agree with Cindy on one thing: their relationship would not have stayed secret, and they should be the ones to control how and when it went public—not the paparazzi. Would navigating this option with Kat be tougher than losing his entire sense of identity and livelihood? He didn't know if it was.

Cindy broke into his thoughts. "I know this isn't what you wanted, but it will be good for you, for both of you. Once Kat gets over the initial shock, she'll come around. Someone was going to break the story eventually, so why shouldn't it be you? You can use it to your advantage. Your story is so heartwarming, people are going to root for you both. I'll make you the most loved couple in entertainment."

He didn't reply. He stared into his glass of brown liquid. Tapping his finger on the side, he contemplated a decision that would have lasting ramifications on his life, no matter which path he chose. Roger and Cindy were quiet, waiting for his decision.

Finally, he spoke. "Minimal information. Nothing about Becca. Keep Ben out of it. The narrative needs to focus on me and my issues. Do very little on Kat. *Minimal,* Cindy. I mean it."

"You're making a smart decision," she said. "I will give them as little as I can to make this go away. A year from now, we'll all be sitting around laughing about it."

He couldn't listen any longer, so he jammed his finger on "end call," put his head in his hands, and let the tears flow.

Kat stood with her arms crossed by the entry doors to the apartment building, waiting for Jake to arrive. She looked at her watch for the fifth time and tapped her foot. She could barely contain herself. She needed to physically lay eyes on him to stop the feeling of impending dread. She'd feel better once she could talk to him and help him gain some control of the situation.

She'd been at the Path offices, sequestered in a conference room, writing her section for this quarter's board meeting. Once she'd finished, she'd FaceTimed Becca, realizing with all the intensity of yesterday that she hadn't called her. She couldn't remember a time when she went a day without hearing Becca's voice. She couldn't believe calling Becca had slipped her mind—her *child* had slipped her mind. She'd been beating herself up internally for the better part of the day.

When she apologized to Linda, she'd replied, "You must be

having fun. Good for you," which made her cringe. Yesterday had been emotional, sexy, and exhilarating, more so than she wanted to admit. She felt disconnected from home, as if she were on a vacation from her real life.

When she first saw Jake's call come in, she hit ignore to finish her call with Becca. Becca was relaying, in detail, her day with the neighbor's new puppy. She would have to call him back, because she wouldn't cut Becca short.

A text had come next.

J: Hey Kat, it's Savannah. Can you talk?

Her heart began to race. Something was wrong.

K: Yes, give me a minute. What happened?

Three dots flashed and showed that Savannah was typing.

Her screen had filled with screenshots of articles reporting on how Jake had become unreliable, cost the studio money, and one UK website even speculated that he had a cocaine problem. Kat hid her shock as she finished her call with Becca and Linda. Reading the articles, anger flooded her mind. *How could speculation and rumors spread this quickly without a fact checker in sight*, she'd wondered.

She'd dialed Jake's number, her fingers trembling.

"Hey," Savannah had answered after the first ring.

"How is he?" Kat had asked.

"As you can imagine, not great. He's talking with Roger and Cindy now. As soon as they're done, I need to get him off set. Are you staying at his apartment? Can you be there?" she'd asked with her typical air of efficiency.

"Yes, but I'm at work. I'll head back now and wait for him," she'd said, gathering her things and rushing out.

Now, while she waited at the door, she scrolled through all the news she could find on the story. She had to admit, it was terrible. She'd seen this unfold before in her own company. A hit to your reputation, especially regarding your ability to deliver, was derailing, if not devastating. She felt a twist of emotions in her gut as the car pulled up. She felt relief, but also an anticipatory feeling akin to the moment between a lightning flash and the first clap of thunder. She was holding her breath, waiting for thunder to crash around her.

She took a few steps toward the car, and Savannah opened the door and jumped out. She peered into the SUV and saw Jake sliding toward the exit. His eyes were red and glassy, and he still had makeup on from the shoot earlier. He was in an altered state, and she could smell the booze on him as he stumbled out. Peering in his eyes, she could see he was high as well. Before he could speak, she wrapped her arms around him, just for a minute. She nodded at Savannah and watched as she retreated back into the vehicle.

"I'm sorry," he whispered, his voice trembling. Gone was the overconfident, wise beyond-his-years Jake, replaced by a twenty-five-year-old thrust into public life, who sounded hesitant, nervous, and utterly defeated.

She guided him into the building. "It's okay. It's all going to be okay," she reassured him as they climbed the stairs.

"No, Kat. It's not. I fucked up. You don't even know the half of it," he rambled.

She'd forgotten this side of him—the manic, dramatic Jake who could slide into a black hole and struggle for air. She could see him drowning in his own self-loathing. They were two floors up when Jake spun around and sat down on the stairs.

Kat tried to get him to stand up and keep moving, but he was determined to stay right there. She plopped down next to him on the step.

"Kat," he started, "promise me, no matter what happens, you won't hate me? At least not forever." His voice slurred. He lowered his head and started to shake it slowly. "I know it. You're going to hate me," he rambled and pressed the heels of his hands against his eyes.

"Why would I hate you, Jake? It doesn't matter to me. The fame, the notoriety, any of it. *You* matter to me. And I know you'll get through this—*we* will get through this." She hoped her words would help him understand that she really believed he would come out on top. Even if it became a bump in his career, it wouldn't ruin him. Maybe less famous, but would that be a bad thing? Kat didn't think so. *I'd prefer it if he was out of the spotlight,* she thought.

Jake didn't reply. He just looked at her in a way that instantly brought back the feeling of dread she was trying to control. It was a look of resignation, shame, and sorrow. She wished she could open up his brain and see what he was thinking, because the look on his face absolutely scared her.

After what seemed like over a half hour, she coaxed him upstairs and into the apartment. She took him straight to the bedroom, took off his shoes, and once Jake lay down, he either fell asleep or passed out. Kat wasn't sure which. She was just happy that he looked a bit more peaceful.

She went out into the living room and sat down on the couch. She tipped her head toward the ceiling and drew in a deep breath. She needed to find a way to help him. Her mind raced . . . she had to find a way to fix this . . . the couch vibrated and she jumped at the feeling—she'd forgotten she'd slipped Jake's phone into her pocket when Savannah had passed it over to her. It was his mom calling for the third time that hour. She hesitated, but after taking another long breath, she hit accept.

"Hi Jill, it's Kat."

"Hi, Kat. Is Jake alright? I've seen the press. He has to be devastated. Is he there? Can I talk to him?" she asked, and Kat could hear the concern in her voice.

Kat was curious that Jill didn't seem at all surprised when she'd answered Jake's phone. "He's pretty upset. He's not in any shape to come to the phone. He's sleeping, maybe passed out. I've never seen him this rough," she confessed.

"I can only imagine. I was shocked when I saw the rumor of a meltdown. I talked to him yesterday, and he was so happy," she started. "He told me about you, his new projects, and he was in a good headspace."

She had a surge of pride realizing Jake had taken steps to reconnect with his mom after their conversation. "He was. I mean, he is. He hit a rough patch a few weeks ago, but really nothing more than burnout. He pushed himself so hard, he was literally breaking apart," said Kat, happy to confide in someone.

She shook her head, remembering the Jake she'd first encountered in Copenhagen. He'd been broken, unsure, and disconnected from everything and everyone. A sensitive soul, lost in the expectations of others and the unrelenting chase of fame. She'd witnessed Jake claw himself out of the darkness, and now, she was watching him fall back right back into that murky black hole.

"That's Jake. He's all or nothing. He'll practically destroy himself to get something he wants. He's always been that way," she said. "When he was a kid, it was hard to watch the intensity with which he navigated life."

Kat could only imagine, as a parent, the challenges they faced to raise this creative and complicated human. Opening up to the one person who understood, she said, "I love him, but he scares me."

"Me too," his mom said with an audible sigh. "Kat, I was thrilled when he told me about the two of you. I had my suspicions once, but I had no idea you were together now." She paused, "Given what's happening, I feel better knowing you're there with him."

They chatted a little while longer, and Kat hung up the phone. Before she could walk to the bedroom to set his phone on the nightstand, her eyes caught a text alert.

C: *It's done.*

C: *You can thank me later.*

What's done? she pondered as she set the phone down. She had a sinking feeling there was a lot about Jake's situation that she didn't know. What really happened—and what had they done?

chapter twenty

Jake opened his eyes and quickly shut them again. His head was pounding and felt heavy. He sat up, rubbed his eyes, and felt like he was going to be sick. Blowing out a breath, he realized that he *was* going to be sick, so he ran to the bathroom as all his bad decisions came violently out of him. *It's fitting*, he thought, *I deserve all this and more*. He sat on the floor, knees up to his chest.

Kat knocked and opened the door. She came walking toward him as if he was some sort of wounded animal. "Hey," she whispered, "you okay?"

He couldn't take the pity he saw in her eyes. He nodded but remained silent. Just then, he was sick again. He felt Kat's gentle hand rubbing his back.

"Just leave me," he said, sounding terser than he meant to. His stomach threatened to lurch again, and he could feel the back of his neck tighten. He didn't want her to see him like this. "I just need to lie down a bit longer." He stood up, shuffled over to the sink, brushed his teeth, and brushed past her to the bedroom where he flopped down on the bed.

"Jake, we should—"

"I don't want to talk about it . . . Not yet. Let me sleep," he said, his face turned toward the wall. He heard the door shut as she left the bedroom.

He felt relief. He couldn't be around her. He'd felt many

things in his life, but complete failure was a new feeling. It destabilized him as he felt every emotion coursing through his body and mind. Every thought reminding him that he was broken. The emotional victor was guilt. The guilt of not saying no. Not saying no to Cindy had said everything. Functionally, it allowed her to move on to Plan B, but it also showed he wasn't strong enough to put Kat before his own fame. And for that, he hated himself.

Knowing Kat was on the other side of the door, Jake sat up again and checked his phone. He saw the text from Cindy letting him know she'd taken care of the email. He threw his phone across the bed in frustration. It would only be a matter of time before the story broke, and he couldn't picture a scenario that didn't include Kat hating him. The anticipatory dread consumed him. He hugged his knees to his chest and closed his eyes, hopeful that he would somehow sleep through this daytime nightmare.

He was barely asleep when his phone rang. He grabbed it off the nightstand, trying not to alert Kat. It was Garren.

"Hey," he answered, sitting up in bed.

"Jake, this is all so out of hand. I'm sorry this is happening," Garren spoke.

"Thanks. Why are you calling?" Jake asked keeping his voice flat.

"Jake, I needed you to know I wasn't planning to replace you. The studio just wanted to know my backup plan should I *need* to. I always believed you'd be a great lead in the film, even when it wasn't going so well," he said. "I am issuing a statement, alongside the studio, about the health of the film."

"Thanks. I appreciate it. I feel like I'm giving you what you want now. I just had a rough start," Jake said quietly. He felt the weight of his initial struggle and was hoping for reassurance that he was not a failure.

"Yes, Jake, you are doing an amazing job. You are a gifted actor," Garren said with an uncharacteristic softness in his voice.

"Can I ask what was blocking you? You don't have to tell me, but I wonder if I could have directed you differently in the beginning."

"A lot of things," Jake paused and took a moment to collect his thoughts. He'd thought about this a lot over the last few days. "I'm finally learning that, between roles, I need time to find myself again before I can turn around and transform into another person. Transforming too many times in rapid succession, at least for me, is dangerous. I mean, mentally. I only had a few weeks in between projects, and it was too little."

Jake paused as he walked back to the bathroom and pulled a bottle of Tylenol out of the cabinet. He downed the pills quickly.

"And, Garren," Jake started. "You're one of the best directors I've worked with. So no, there was nothing you should have done differently. Not letting me get away with a bad performance and giving me a few days off—telling me to get my shit together—was the gift I needed." He meant every word. Garren could have just replaced him as soon as there had been a problem, but he hadn't. He'd given Jake a wakeup call and a second chance.

"Thanks, but I'll think twice before forcing any of my principals to start a project before they're ready," Garren said. "If you'd told me, we could've tried to adjust the schedule. Jake—a word of advice. You have a long career ahead of you, and you've got to ask for things you need to do your best work."

He focused his brain and listened to the advice of a man whose career length he envied. At the end of the call, Garren gave him the next morning off, and they agreed to put it behind them and start fresh. They hung up, and Jake leaned back on the pillows. For a moment, he felt at peace as he reflected on Garren's advice. His body and his ego still ached, but at least his headache was beginning to subside.

For the tenth time, he refreshed his social feeds to see if the story had broken. It wasn't there, giving him momentary relief. *Maybe Cindy was able to bury it without releasing anything*, he hoped. He typed in the web address for TMZ and as soon as the website loaded, he saw it, splashed right on the home page. Plan B. It had broken fifteen minutes ago. He closed his eyes for a moment, took a deep breath, and started to scan the post. He expected a quick news alert or half-page gossip post, but when his eyes scanned the screen, what he found was not minimal. He saw a near feature-length article, complete with photos—photos of them together in the rain, kissing the morning they had agreed to stop running from each other. It was their entire story, complete with Kat's past, Ben, Becca, and her reasons for being in Copenhagen, which identified her as a key leader at Path. All of it. Right there for everyone to read. Jake's heart raced and stress brought bile into his throat. He pulled his knees to his forehead, closed his eyes, and waited for his world to crash around him.

It was all Kat could do to leave him alone. Every instinct she had told her to march back in the room, make him feel better, control the situation, and solve it all. It went against everything in her nature to give him the space he requested, but ultimately, she didn't know how to fix this situation. She only knew how to love him through it, and she was going to do just that. Once he got some rest and sobered up, she was going to make sure he understood she loved him with or without fame. She believed he would land on his feet, even if it meant he stopped being the *it boy* of the moment. *It would actually be easier for both of us if he wasn't famous*, she told herself.

While he slept, she calmed her mind by working on the revised forecast for holiday production cycle. She could do these forecasts in her sleep, so it was a welcome diversion from the situation with Jake. As she was double-checking her calculations, her phone chimed in rapid succession, pulling her attention away from her spreadsheet. She picked up her phone.

E: OMG. *Wow!*

E: *Those pics are so beautiful.*

E: *Did you know??*

Kat cocked her head and wondered if Emily was texting the wrong person. She was typing a reply when a text from Linda flashed on the screen.

L: *Call me when you get a minute . . .*

Below Linda's text was a link, and she immediately clicked. Her mouth fell open. She let out an audible gasp at the headline in front of her.

A NEW LOVE AND NEW START FOR JAKE LAURENT. And there it was. All of it. She scrolled through the article and read through it as fast as she could. It was the first site to deliver breaking news of Jake's new relationship with a woman named Kat, a young widow of a New York firefighter and single mother of an adorable and precocious child. The details were all there: they had been family friends for years; she was currently with him in Copenhagen and had helped him through a mental crisis brought on by stress; it explained the rumors of his meltdown on set and every detail in between. She gritted her teeth as she forced herself to read every word.

She put her hand over her mouth when her eyes landed on the gallery of photos. There were three photos, capturing them the morning in the fog after they'd committed to try to bring their lives together. They were shots of them kissing under the store awning, Jake's lips on hers, their hair damp from the mist. It even included one with her hand on his cheek at the exact moment they'd decided to stop running. The pictures were stunning and looked like they could've been part of an actual photoshoot. It was their most intimate moment, and now the entire world could see it. *How could this have happened?* The photos. The details in the article.

"It's done" reverberated in her mind. Kat felt sick to her stomach.

She slid off her chair and walked the few feet into the bedroom. She walked slow, knowing once she opened that door, if Jake had authorized the article, there was no going back. She turned the knob and silently pushed open the door to the bedroom. She looked at Jake sitting on the bed, knees raised to his chest, phone in his hand, eyes red, and she knew. She stood in the doorway and held up her phone, the article filled the screen.

"What did you do?" she whispered. "Why?"

"I didn't know. . . ." he said, and she could hear the panic in his voice.

She shook her head back and forth as her disappointment began to transform to anger. It flooded in fast, making her ears buzz. "It's not possible you didn't know. The details they have . . . the timing. . . ." she said, her voice rising. She was hoping he wouldn't lie to her.

"I didn't know it was going to be . . . this," he said, his voice resigned.

"You didn't know what they would leak? Are you *kidding* me? They work for *you*, Jake," she yelled, her tears burning her eyes. "They shouldn't do anything you don't approve first. I saw Cindy's text. 'It's done.' I'm not a fool."

His hesitation told her everything she needed to know.

She stormed into the bedroom, yanked her suitcase out of his closet, and began shoving clothes into her suitcase. She wanted to get out of there as quickly as possible. For a second, she thought about just running right out the door, leaving all her stuff and Jake's entire world behind.

She paused for a moment to look at him. He hadn't moved an inch and just watched her, seemingly paralyzed.

"So that morning under the awning was staged? Two lovers, in the mist, on the stone streets—you must have known those would be gorgeous photos." She stopped to wipe her tears. "Good job, Jake, they're fucking cinematic. I'd think they were beautiful if they didn't make me sick."

His eyes flashed with anger. "No!" he hissed. "Do you think so little of me that you'd believe I would stage those photos? *That* morning, of all mornings?" His voice was angry, and he clenched his jaw tight. "That morning, after we . . . That you would even think for a minute—"

"But you knew they had photos," she said, cutting him off, "and they were going to release them?"

He looked resigned and nodded, so imperceptible she almost missed it, but Kat already knew the answer. She just wanted to see if he would be honest with her.

"There was an email. From Garren to the studio about replacing me. It was the kind of thing that would *destroy* my reputation. Cindy traded the story so they wouldn't release the email. Honestly, I didn't know they had pictures of that morning. It was the last resort, and even Roger said it was the only leverage we had to keep the email from going public. I thought she was going to release minimal information.

"I have to trust them. They know this industry better than I do and have always taken care of me. Kat, I believe she did it for us. If she hadn't changed the narrative, my career would tank at twenty-five. Where would that leave me, leave us?" He was rambling, and instead of having its usual charming effect, it grated on her.

"Tell me this: did you give Cindy all those details? Did you know how deep the article was going to go? They mentioned Becca. And Ben, for fuck's sake. He has a family. How do you think that is going to affect them? This isn't just about us now!" She was yelling now, but she didn't care.

"No! Kat, I swear. Cindy told me she had information and photos, and I trusted her to do the minimum to bury the email. I didn't see it before it broke. I really thought this would be a quick alert, a paragraph or two at most. I know Cindy didn't mean to do anything to hurt you, to hurt us." He tried to move closer to her, but she moved to the other side of the room.

She was reminded, again, of how young and naive he was. Starting his career as a teenager, he had developed a blind trust of those who played parental figures during those formative years. He'd yet to grasp the business behind his art and was easily manipulated. It would make her sad if she wasn't so angry.

"Jake, grow up. Your entire team exists to make money selling a product. And their product is *you*. Don't kid yourself. You're their golden ticket, and they would destroy us—destroy *me*—in a second if it meant keeping you in the spotlight."

He had his head in his hands. He rubbed his hands over his face and looked up. "Kat, at some point, we would've been a story. At least now we're controlling it. Using it to our advantage. It'll blow over, be a blip in the news, and then everyone will move on. We can get through this. I know we can."

"Advantage? Blow over? Maybe for you. Maybe for me, too, if I'd had some warning and could've prepared, even a little bit. Did you ever think 'controlling the story' would mean *I* would also have at least some say? Have you seen the social comments?" She thrust her phone in his face and waited for him to respond.

"You know I don't read that stuff, and I'm not going to start now," he said, and she could hear the irritation and hesitation in his voice.

"Let me read them to you. It's been live for, let's see . . . sixty-one minutes. Hmm . . . where should we start? Instagram. Yes, let's start there. I have twenty-two DMs, each one worse than the next: 'You're too ugly for a man as fine as Jake.' 'Why did he ever choose you? I bet you're a bitch.' 'I wish you would die.' Who the fuck are these people?

"And look at this, someone posted a picture of Becca already, on a fan account with over twenty-two thousand people. Twenty-two thousand strangers have a picture of my child. You cannot begin to understand how frightening that is. Okay, let's go to Twitter. People don't DM there, they just outwardly call me horrible things—"

She went to go on, but he interrupted. "I'm sure it's not all negative Kat, you're just focusing on the bad. Ignore the trolls. They'll go away," he said. "Cindy believes that this will trend positively for both of us."

She almost threw her phone at him. "Fuck that woman. And you know what? This isn't some story; this is real life. And in real life, these things have consequences." She went on, "I'm not done. Did you know that #SwitchDaBitch is trending? Some psycho created a hashtag telling people to switch your mobile device from Path to anything else. Why? Why would someone do this? Oh, God. I've created a situation that has people boycotting our devices. Jake, I could lose my job over this."

Kat noticed the tears on Jake's face that matched her own. *Good*, she thought, *he needs to feel the weight of how bad this is.* She wasn't just angry about the story. He didn't trust her enough to tell her about the email. The mixture of hurt and anger waged a war inside her.

"Fuck. There has to be a way to fix this, I'll get a team on it. I will do whatever I can to make this go away," he started, and she put her hand up, motioning for him to stop.

"Yes, do anything you can, but I know this stuff never really disappears. I need to get to Becca, back to real life and away from this circus. Away from you. I trusted you, Jake! I was so stupid. God, what was I thinking?" And with that, she grabbed her backpack and roller bag and began toward the door.

Jake darted out of the room and stood between her and front door. He put his hand on her arm. "Come on, Kat. Don't do this," he pleaded. "Your flight is in two days. Stay until we figure this out, get it under control. I'll make this right. I love you . . . doesn't that matter?"

"Get the fuck out of my way," she said, her voice shaking. She pushed his hand off her.

He bowed his head and stepped to the side. "I thought you said you wouldn't run," he said, and she could hear the challenge in his voice.

"I thought you said you would protect me," she replied, knowing the phrase to cut him the most. "I guess we both lied."

chapter twenty-one

Kat's heart rate began to slow when she pulled up to Ben's parents' house, and Becca came running out. She needed to hold her to quell the panic she'd had her entire journey back to New York. She'd scrambled to take an overnight flight back to New York, landing in the wee hours of the morning.

The conversation she'd had with Linda was on replay in her mind, but she couldn't decipher Linda's reaction to the article. She only knew Linda was surprised to see Ben's name in the press, and that she'd been in Copenhagen for more than work. She was overwhelmed by the guilt of hurting the people who had done the most for her. The entire flight, she'd resigned herself to the realization that she'd taken a vacation from her life, her *real* life. She berated herself for getting so wrapped up in Jake that she separated her two lives. At some point, they were going to come crashing together, and once again her instincts were right. It never would've worked.

Once she'd left Jake, she attacked the problem as systematically as a work project. First, she'd shut down all her social media to keep Becca's pictures from getting more traction. The one circulated was from four years ago, and that chubby toddler barely resembled the girl she was now. Once her social media was gone, she didn't have to deal with strangers giving her their opinions about her relationship.

Second, there were the myriad of phone calls from various press outlets, but those were ignored and deleted. Third, she'd spoken to the Path corporate communications team. They were actively involved with press inquiries and working overtime to protect the company from any negative impact. They were not worried about her well-being, only that her actions didn't impact sales. It had been a tense and transactional discussion.

But none of that mattered now that she had Becca in her arms. She squeezed Becca so tight she exclaimed, "Mommy you are squashing me." It amazed her how her daughter's presence melted away the hurt and anxiety she was feeling. Kat loosened her grip but didn't let go. "We're watching Little Mermaid . . . Ariel just got legs . . . can I go inside now?" Becca protested. Kat let go and Becca ran back inside.

She slipped on her backpack to follow. Linda grabbed Kat's suitcase before she could protest. Once inside, she couldn't hold back her emotion any longer. It was more than what happened in Copenhagen.

Her emotions felt out of control as the loss of Ben and the loss of her family simultaneously twisted her gut, head, and heart. The barriers she'd put around herself had kept her from recognizing how lost she really was. Jake had broken down those walls and without them—without *him*—she felt exposed and raw. She no longer knew her way forward.

Linda dropped her bag in the hall and when she walked back in, Kat choked out, "I am so sorry. After everything you've done for me."

Linda closed the distance between them and wrapped her arms around Kat. She let herself relax into Linda's arms. It was a mother's touch she'd been missing for so long. Linda released her and motioned for her to sit down. Kat sat down obediently but couldn't bring herself to speak. She didn't know what to say. Linda brought Kat a glass of water and sat down across from her.

"Kat, please talk to me. Are you okay?" she asked, and Kat didn't hear anything other than love. It sprung tears to her eyes. This time, she put her hands over her eyes. She hated crying, especially in front of anyone, but it's all she'd done in the past twenty-four hours. She shook her head. She was not okay. She didn't know what to say to fix the situation, so like a broken record, she started, "I'm. . . ."

"I know," Linda said with a light chuckle. "Kat, *why* are you sorry?"

"I didn't know about the article, and if I had, I never would've allowed them to use Ben's or Becca's names. I'm sure you have people asking you questions, and I couldn't even give you a warning. I'm being hounded by the press, by people I don't even know. The company I work for is angry. This is messy, and I dragged you into it."

"Meh. This article is just words. On the internet. You kids make so much of things that are in the ether. We're fine. Just surprised and a little caught off guard. The only people contacting me are my friends. You've made me a bit of a celebrity among the over-sixty crowd." She winked. "Becca? You two can stay here—no one knows you're here. She doesn't go to school for another few days, and we'll see if it's still a thing by then. I can only imagine how hard it is for you. But you've been through worse, and you'll get through this," she said in her matter-of-fact tone. "So, tell me, why are you *really* saying you're sorry?"

"It's complicated. I feel . . . feel . . ." she said, her voice dropping down to a whisper, "like I cheated on Ben . . . his memory . . . or, well. . . . you . . ." Her words caught in her throat, so she just stopped talking. She watched Linda suck in a deep breath.

"Kat, I watch you. You are so focused on doing everything right, all the time, that I often wonder, who takes care of you? Are you happy?"

Kat looked up at her, her eyes filling with tears once again.

She slowly shook her head. Before Copenhagen, she couldn't remember a time when she'd been genuinely happy. Sitting there with Linda, she was ready to admit the truth. She wanted to be the woman who held everything together, but her cracks had finally broken wide open.

Linda started, "Honey, you have to let go of all this. I see you working so hard at life. You can't control every little thing to keep bad things from happening. Bad stuff happens. Unfair things happen. People die before they should. Life is the ultimate mess and if you try staying clean, you lose the joy of that mess.

"I look at Becca," she mused, "and she approaches everything with anticipatory joy. She finds every little nugget of happiness that can be extracted out of the day. She is so much like Ben. You know, people thought he was fearless because he was a firefighter, but I saw that he was fearless in how he lived his whole life. He pursued joy with abandon and never thought twice about taking a risk, whether physical or emotional. Look at the two of you. He met you and married you after a few months. He didn't think about if it made sense."

"Look where it got him," Kat quipped.

"It got him a wife who adored him and made sure his final days were filled with love. It gave him a daughter, and he got to experience the joy of seeing her take her first breath. Kat, Ben's fate was sealed when the cancer took hold of his body, and that would have happened with or without you in his life. Yes, we thought he was nuts when he said you two were getting married, but if you hadn't, think of what his life would have been. He would've died without meeting the love of his life and seeing the birth of his child. He would have died only a son. Instead, he died as a husband and a father."

"It just isn't fair that he died," Kat said. Kat felt a lightness take over her body. *It feels good to say it*, she thought. "It kills me that he isn't here to watch Becca grow up." Kat stopped talking as her voice broke. She couldn't choke out the thoughts coursing through her mind. *He would've loved dragons and fairy forks. He'd be better at this than me.*

"It isn't fair," Linda said, breaking into Kat's thoughts. They were silent, and Linda let out an audible sigh. "We've never talked about Ben's death, but I want to share with you what he told me when he stopped chemo. I wouldn't recognize it then, but our time with him was measured in days, not weeks.

"He said to me, 'Mom, I'm sad I'm dying. I'm not afraid, but I'm sad. But I'm not sad about the life I've had.'" And with that, Linda's voice broke. "Kat, he wanted Becca to know the day she was born was the single best day of his life. He wanted us to know her and love her the way that he couldn't. He asked us to tell her stories about him so she could feel connected to her dad. I think we've tried to do that." Linda paused and Kat nodded.

"You're wonderful with Becca," Kat started. "Ben would be very happy."

Kat watched Linda fight back tears. Linda took a drink of water and continued. "Kat, he also told me something else. I remember the exact phrase," she said, her voice breaking once again. "'Don't let Kat hold on to me for too long. She's nothing if not determined.'"

Despite herself, Kat choked out a laugh. She could hear his voice in her head, and he was right.

Linda continued, "Ben wanted you to have a happy life. He told me life was too short to live with the dead, and he was afraid you'd do just that."

Kat couldn't get any words out. It was just like Ben to know she'd hold on so hard that she'd stop living the day he died. Although technically still breathing, the person she was died that day, too.

"Now it's *my* turn to apologize. I'm sorry I never told you," said Linda. "I saw you struggling and thought if I just supported when you asked, I was doing enough. But I realize now, he was telling me there would be a day when you would want permission to love again. Kat, of course you don't *need* permission, but if you're feeling any guilt and shame about falling in love with someone new, don't. You've always had permission to love again and to fully live your life."

Kat wiped the tears from her eyes. She was surprised she had any tears left. "Thank-you for telling me," she said. She realized she had been holding her breath ever since Ben had taken his last. She hadn't known it, but she *did* need permission to live after Ben. She'd stopped living that day, focused only on the passage of time through the lens of Becca. Her happiness no longer part of her equation.

At least until Jake. He'd made her feel again. And then he'd broken her.

Linda reached over to take her hand. "Frankly, once I got over the surprise, I couldn't stop smiling. Running off to Copenhagen for a secret love affair? Ben, always the romantic, would've loved that. You're more like him than you think."

Kat gave her a half-hearted laugh. "Well, it's over. So, it's not quite the fairy tale, it might seem."

Linda sighed. "I'm sure you had your reasons, and you don't have to explain them to me. But looking at those pictures, it's clear there was love and there was joy. And that's never a waste."

chapter twenty-two

Kat sipped her second cup of coffee as she got Becca ready for the day. The extra caffeine was clearing the fog of jet lag from her brain. After a few days upstate, in the cocoon of Ben's parents, Kat was ready to face the office today. She'd heard from Emily that the rumor mill was in full force. People were having a lot of fun at her expense. Her hands shook as she buttoned Becca's shirt. Concentrating on each button to focus her mind, she took a deep breath and blew it out slowly. *You can do this. You've handled far worse*, she told herself.

Once dressed, Becca ran down the hallway toward the kitchen. Kat followed behind and called out, "I have a surprise breakfast for you. This is your last Monday of preschool! Next week, kindergarten!"

Becca beamed and scrambled into her chair where Kat had placed a white bag at Becca's spot—a breakfast Kat had ordered to be delivered earlier that morning. It wasn't the usual Greek yogurt and berries, but something new.

"Momma, what's this? Can I open it?" she asked. Kat looked over her coffee cup, nodded and watched as Becca's small hands tore open the bag straight down the middle like she was ripping open the most exciting present. *That's one way to open it*, she thought, laughing to herself. Becca pulled out the foil-wrapped sandwich like a treasure and peeled back the layers to reveal a bagel with egg, cheese, and bacon. The cheese was dripping down the side, and as Becca took a bite, gooey cheese fell on her arm. She giggled. "Yum!" she said. "Momma, I love bacon. Why don't we have bacon every day?" she asked.

Kat started to explain why she didn't let Becca eat bacon every day, but she stopped herself and a smile came to her lips. "We should have bacon more often!"

Becca flashed her a grin and two thumbs-up, and Kat let out a laugh. She picked up the other half of the sandwich and took a bite. The sensory memory of sitting in the small kitchen of a temporary apartment in a foreign city hit her with such force she had to blink back tears. God, she missed Jake. She didn't want to *miss* him. She wanted to *hate* him. She struggled to reconcile the complex emotion of anger and longing.

When they arrived at Becca's preschool, Kat signed in at the front desk. Becca dashed in already chattering with her teacher.

"No run today?" asked the young girl at the front desk. Kat furrowed her brow, but then realized she was dressed for work instead of her usual run through the park.

"Oh, right. Yes, not today," Kat said muttered.

"Hey, I don't mean to be awkward, but I have to tell you, I'm a big fan. Of Jake, I mean, Jake Laurent. Sorry. But I would kick myself if I didn't say something to you . . ." she rambled. In the past seventy-two hours, Kat had been stopped more times than she'd ever imagined possible for interactions that were all versions of the same. Innocent but unnerving all the same.

Before she could respond, a woman approached her and held out her hand. "Hi Ms. Green, I'm Lena, the director. Do you have a minute to talk in my office?"

She nodded and stepped into a small office off to the side.

"Ms. Green, we are a very popular school for children of

public figures. We have the mayor's son, the governor's twins, and more celebrity children than we can count. We are discreet and, most importantly, secure," she recited.

Without wasting any time, Lena walked her through the security protocols they had in place. As Becca would transition from the preschool program to the kindergarten class next week, those protocols would stay in place.

"For situations like yours, with heightened interest, we need you to sign this authorization for discreet security on Becca, for at least the next two weeks. We have the end-of-year field trip to the Natural History Museum. I don't want you to worry, and we can't have our teachers distracted. You can sign right here," she said, handing Kat the document.

Kat read it over, including the incremental fees. "So, how does this work? Will you just add the cost to the tuition payments?" She winced at the price. The school was already very expensive, and this just added to the ever-growing list of costs.

Lena waved her hand. "Oh, I figured you knew. Mr. Laurent called this morning. He's taking care of it. We're recommending two weeks, but he authorized for it to continue as long as *you* want."

Kat stilled. The part of her brain that believed she had to do everything herself, almost said no out of spite. But, the truth was, she could use the help. She signed the papers and rushed out to make it to work.

Kat fell into her office chair and spun around to face the wall. She silently cursed the glass walls of her office. She rested her head on the back of the chair and took a shaky breath. The last hour had been the worst of her career. In the same boardroom where she had delivered on countless revenue-generating projects, she'd endured her corporate communications team dissecting the timeline and nature of her relationship with Jake.

She was no longer an executive leader at PathMobile; she was a girl who had dated Jake Laurent. Coming out of the meeting, she'd felt her reputation was forever changed.

There was a soft knock at her door. Kat turned around to see Emily standing in the doorway, holding two coffees. She waved her in.

"How bad was it?" Emily asked, sitting down as she slid a coffee across the desk.

"Well, it wasn't my favorite meeting," Kat deadpanned. She wasn't sure where to start.

"Why do they even care? It's nobody's business who you date, much less Path's," Emily said, lowering her voice.

"A few reasons," Kat started. "The article mentioned Path and has been viewed 8.2 million times. There're still a few lingering trolls using that stupid boycott hashtag. The comms teams has been fielding calls from industry and entertainment press for days. They've spent company resources on this situation . . . which is why they get to have an opinion.

"It wasn't just a meeting with comms. Will was there too. It looks like I was gallivanting around Copenhagen before the biggest launch Path has ever had in the US. The optics couldn't be worse. It was far from a vacation, as you know. I did work while I was there, and we *have* optimized our US launch based on the Denmark pre-launch, but it doesn't change what people want to believe. At least Will believed me . . . I think."

Kat was reminded that although she had given her nights and weekends to the company—essentially giving up her life for work—PathMobile owed her nothing. When it came down to it, Path would always protect itself over even its best employee.

"I'm sorry, Kat," Emily said, leaning back in her chair. "What does all this mean? What now?"

Kat hesitated before answering. "Well . . . I'm taking a leave of absence until this blows over." Emily tried to protest, but Kat cut her off. "I can't stand the way people are looking at me when I see them in the hallway. I feel like I'm just a distraction right now."

She was quiet for a moment before she spoke again. "I withdrew my name from the COO nomination." The shock was clear on Emily's face. After a pause, Kat continued. "I have been thinking a lot these past few days. I love this company, but I don't love this life. I need to take some time away from here to figure out what brings me joy. It's *not* working fourteen hours a day."

Hearing it out loud, she still surprised herself. It was true. Her life had revolved around PathMobile for years. Work had become an escape to avoid living her life. She'd been too busy to feel much of anything, too busy to feel the sadness of losing Ben—too busy to find the joy in raising her daughter.

She'd thought of nothing else since coming back from Copenhagen. Focusing on the next task at hand, solving the next problem, and chasing the next promotion had allowed her to convince herself she had everything under control, when in reality, she'd been avoiding her own grief and loneliness. She understood that now. She'd been holding on to Ben to protect herself. Ben had already left her, and if she never moved on from him, she wouldn't have another man she loved ever leave her again. Ben's prediction was right: she was living with the dead.

She was going to enter back into the land of the living—starting today. The idea made her heart race with excitement. *During the worst day in my career, I feel the most invigorated*, she mused.

It would be easy to paint her whole Copenhagen trip with a brush of anger because of how it'd ended. But her time with Jake *had* changed her. He showed her she wasn't just capable of love, she *wanted* to be loved. This time, she wouldn't let her brain override her heart. She wanted to be like Becca and live life with anticipatory joy. *And I am going to start paying attention . . . to Becca*

. . . *to life*, she thought. She couldn't do that if she spent every waking hour consumed with her job. It wasn't worth it.

"Wow, Kat. I haven't seen you take a full day off . . . ever. You really okay?" Emily asked.

"Yes. I'm going to take time to figure out my life. I owe it to Becca, and frankly to myself, to find a way to live life with work on the side and not the other way around," she said, repeating Emily's words back to her. Kat began to pack her bag to leave. She decided in that moment to spring Becca out of daycare in the middle of the day. An afternoon in the park was in their near future.

She stopped packing and looked at Emily. "A very smart person told me that once."

Emily smiled, stood up and gave Kat a hug. "Well, I'm proud of you. I have always admired you, Kat, but never more than now."

chapter twenty-three

Two Months Later

Jake checked the time on his phone as the plane touched down at JFK Airport. He stepped off the plane with a brisk walk. His body language made it clear—he didn't want to be interrupted. He made it through the airport with minimal notice. He was anxious to see her after all this time. He knew he should have called, but he wasn't sure until the last minute if the production schedule would allow him to get back to New York. After everything, he wouldn't disappoint her.

The city was quiet in the early morning, and he was thankful he didn't have a talkative driver. He gazed out the window as they crossed the Triborough Bridge and was treated to a sparkling view of the New York City skyline. He loved this city, with its combination of beauty and grit. He believed he was most at home on a movie set, but as he felt himself exhale, he realized this city also gave him life, a refuge for his soul.

Once the car pulled up to the apartment building, instead of going in, Jake jogged to the end of the block to a merchant on the corner. He picked up a bouquet filled with beautiful fall colors he knew she would love. He stalled at the street corner to breath a few deep breaths. He needed a minute before surprising her. He couldn't predict how she would react when she saw him standing at her door.

He finally entered, nodded at the doorman and slipped into the elevator. The ride to the twelfth floor felt atypically long, but eventually the door creaked open, and he stepped off. He walked the long hallway to apartment 12F and knocked on the door. He could hear laughing and commotion inside as the door burst open. The shocked smile on his mother's face was worth all the planning and the eight-hour flight back home.

"Jake!" she exclaimed. "I can't believe you're standing here! Get in here!" And with that, she pulled him into the apartment.

"Happy Thanksgiving, Mom," he said, kissing her on the cheek and handing her the flowers.

The apartment was still and quiet as Jake dried the last of the dishes. He and his mom fell into a comfortable silence as they worked side by side. Jake sank into the quiet after a day filled with boisterous family members, many of whom he hadn't seen for years. The fun and excitement of reconnecting, along with the overnight flight, had left him happy, but exhausted.

Jake set the last pot on the counter and flipped the towel over his shoulder. Instead of grabbing the pot to put it away, his mom touched his arm. He turned toward her, and she pulled him into a hug. It had been a long time since he'd been in the cocoon of her embrace. He lingered, resting his head on her shoulder. She ran her fingers through his hair, reminding him of the countless times he had come to her for comfort as a child. His mind cleared, and his shoulders lowered. He didn't pull away like he usually did, a man eager to be an adult. Instead, he allowed himself a minute of shelter and comfort.

"It's good to have you home, sweetheart," she whispered in his ear.

"I missed you, Mom. And I'm sorry . . . for everything," he whispered back. He felt her squeeze him tighter.

She was the first to pull away. She slid the towel off his shoulder and put it on the counter. "You look exhausted. Get some rest," she said.

He nodded, thankful for the understanding. Although they had a lot to discuss, what he needed at this moment was sleep. He walked down the hallway to his room, still a teenager's den, relatively untouched from when he first left. He lay down and fell into a dreamless sleep.

Jake's eyes opened and for a moment he didn't know what hotel he was in. His eyes landed the worn poster of *The Godfather*, held on his wall by yellowed tape, and he grinned. He stretched his arms until his shoulder popped and slipped on his glasses. The time on his phone said it was almost noon, and his eyes widened with surprise. *No wonder I feel rested*, he thought. He couldn't remember the last time he'd gotten fourteen hours of uninterrupted sleep.

He wandered into the kitchen to find his parents eating lunch. He looked over his dad's shoulder. "Try *audio*" he said pointing at the Wordle on his dad's iPad. His dad typed in the five letters and gave Jake a high five when audio was the daily answer. His mom put down the newspaper sale flyer she was reading and gave him a wink. Glancing at his phone, he was reminded it was Black Friday, and he was comforted by the sheer normalcy of the moment.

"Good afternoon, sleepyhead," his mom said, tossing his dad one of the flyers.

He smiled at her, opened the cabinet, and pulled out a glass. He filled it with water and sat down. "Hey, let me see," he said, grabbing a handful of papers. Flipping through the pages he looked at what his mom had circled. He made a mental note that she wanted a treadmill.

"What's your plan today?" his mom asked, handing him the remaining stack of papers.

"I have a meeting with Roger at 4:30 this afternoon. Besides that, I thought I would just hang with you today," he said. "So, I should ask you, what are *we* doing today?" He put his chin in his hand and flashed her a smile.

He watched a grin spread across her face. "You don't have to do that, Jake. I was going to brave Macy's, but I won't make you come."

He appreciated her foresight, but he just wanted to be a person that could accompany his mom to a store. Like before. It used to be a special kind of drudgery to go shopping with his mother, but right now, it was all he wanted to do.

"Mom, if that's what you want to do, I'm game," he said. He loved seeing how her entire face lit up—happy because her only son was spending a few hours with her. He felt a twinge of guilt he'd denied her this for years, all in the quest to show the world he needed no one.

His mom stood up to make him some lunch, and he waved her off and jumped up to take a shower.

The weather had turned cold, making it easier to disguise himself in bulky clothes, a stocking cap, and sunglasses. They started walking the fourteen blocks to Macy's on 34th. It was a long walk, but he loved being out on the city streets. He felt the energy of the people, the traffic, the noise—all of it. As they walked along, his mom made some uncharacteristic small talk.

"I am so happy you came," his mom said. "Everyone was so excited to see you yesterday."

"Mmm. It was nice to see everyone. I was shocked that Cousin Danny grew a full beard," Jake said with a laugh.

"Too bad Kat wasn't here this year."

His shoulders stiffened. He tried to act casual. "You told me last week she would be upstate, so I wasn't surprised."

"Would you've come if she had been here?"

Jake stayed silent. He needed to think about the answer. After a few moments he nodded. He was giving her space, that was true, but he wouldn't avoid her. It'd been over two months since Kat had left Copenhagen, and in that time, he'd tried to talk to her, but now he was resigned to just give her space.

He was giving her space physically, but she took up so much space in his mind, it was maddening. Everything in the last twenty-four hours made him think of her. He saw her apartment door every time they went in and out, toys for Becca were tucked away in the corner of his parents' living room, and even the egg-and-cheese bagel he bought from a food cart flooded his mind with memories.

His mom put her hand on his arm. He could feel that she was about to ask him a question, so he jumped in first. "How is she? Are she and Becca okay? She won't talk to me." The last sentence he said under his breath.

"She and Becca are fine, Jake," she said. "They spend a lot of time with Becca's grandparents, so I haven't seen them much, but when I have, they're doing well."

"Good," he said without elaborating. He was worried about the impact on Kat and Becca's life because of his actions. He'd been surprised by the backlash that had come after the article, especially against Kat. Of course, there'd been plenty of positive reactions, but as Kat had predicted, his young female fans tore her apart.

He'd not expected so much pointed criticism of her. She was either not pretty enough (and didn't deserve him) or too pretty (obsessed with her looks). They attacked her parenting (leaving her child to run off to a foreign city). She was too normal (professional working woman) or a total snob (New Yorker). No matter what, she wasn't good enough.

When he talked with Cindy about the negativity, she'd

shrugged and advised him to let it blow over. It didn't blow over, and all he could focus on were the negative comments and posts made about Kat. Reading each one felt like scratching a tender wound. He'd finally made his own statement, a simple message posted on Twitter and Instagram. "My ask of the world: be kind and don't hurt those I love." No interpretation needed. His ask was clear, and his fans responded by backing down and moving on. He wished he'd done it immediately.

His mom's voice brought him back to the present. "Honey," she started, "are *you* okay?"

They crossed the street and walked halfway down the block before he answered. "Yes and no," he said. "I will be. I think." He put his head down while they walked. "I love her, Mom. But I really messed it up."

"Yes. Yes, you did," his mom said.

"Thanks for the support," he deadpanned. She was right, but her brutal honesty was hard to take.

"Jake," she linked her arm with his, "you know I support you. You made the decision you believed you had to. I don't believe you were trying to hurt anyone. But you have to live with the consequences of that decision . . . and so does Kat," she said, with a matter-of-fact tone.

"I miss her," he said, looking toward the sky.

"Jake," she started with a slight nudge of his shoulder. "The universe has a way of working out just as it should. I'm not giving up on you two just yet."

He smiled at her. He didn't share her optimism, but in that moment, he wanted to believe she was right.

Bluestone Café was quiet when Jake arrived to meet Roger. While in New York, he'd requested a rare in-person meeting. There were things he needed to say, and he owed Roger a personal conversation. His mom offered to head home, but he wanted her there to support and understand his future.

He held open the door for his mom and stepped into the warm coffee shop. His eyes landed on Roger sitting in a back, private corner. As they reached his table, Roger stood up, gave Jake a hug and his mother a kiss on the cheek.

"It is so great to see you in the flesh, Jake," Roger said as they sat down. "You look good." Roger pulled out his phone and pushed it across the table. "Here's the latest gross of *Cloud Catcher*. It has officially surpassed the one hundred-million-dollar mark globally. Congrats." Roger's face outwardly beamed with pride.

Jake barely looked at the screen. He wasn't here to bask in his accomplishments. "Thanks . . . but let's—" Jake started, but Roger started speaking.

"I saw a few rough cuts for *Zero Code* from Garren. Jake, I'm telling you, it's going to be another hit. Man, you're really doing it," he said. "The number of calls and emails I get every day about you? It's astounding. I'm going to send a half dozen great projects you should consider over the next two years. . . ."

Jake leaned back in his chair, sighed, and waited for him to finish. He didn't try to hide the irritation was on his face. He was tired of being talked at and had things he needed to say. Once Roger was quiet, Jake began again. "We need to talk. I can't keep doing this." Jake felt his mom's hand rest on his arm, and he appreciated her silent show of support.

He watched the shock register on Roger's face before continuing. He let it linger to allow the seriousness of the conversation to sink in. Typically, Jake's thoughts were scattered, and he needed Roger to organize and drive business conversations, but today was different. He knew what he wanted and was focused on the direction his career would need to take. He needed a partner, not a father, and he wanted to see if Roger was willing to evolve their working relationship.

"Listen," he started, "I'm very grateful for everything you've done for me through the years. I wouldn't be anywhere without you." He took a deep breath. "I still want to work. And I *think* I still want to work with you, but a lot has to change. If it doesn't, this"—he gestured between himself and Roger—"isn't going to continue."

Roger was visibly relieved. "I'm listening. Go on."

Jake spent the next hour outlining everything he would need for them to continue their working relationship. First and foremost, he needed breaks between roles and would no longer be convinced to work on a timeline that didn't fit his life. He wanted a life that was boisterous, artistic, and even a little messy, but also grounded and mentally sustainable. He wouldn't sacrifice himself or the people he loved for his career.

Second, if Roger was right, he'd reached a point where he could pick his projects, and he wouldn't be pressured to take a role, no matter how lucrative. He was an artist and would take roles that interested him and refined his craft. He wouldn't chase fame, awards, or even the next job. It might mean less money in the short term, but if he was able to sustain his career through the years, the long-term payout was higher—for Jake *and* for Roger.

Third, he wanted to build his team. His team was built for him by Roger when he was just a teenager. That team, built to guide and protect a fifteen-year-old, wasn't the right team to help him navigate his adult life with this level of fame. He would listen to Roger's suggestions, but he wanted to decide on a new publicist, accountant, assistants, and every single person to make sure they were what he needed to build a life, not just play a role.

Gone was the frenetic teenager, blindly following an agent who promised to lead him to fame. Instead, they were two adults, discussing the business of Jake's career and what he needed to sustain a life doing what he loved.

chapter twenty-four

Six Months Later

After a morning of hopping on and off double-decker buses, Kat and Becca lounged in their Airbnb overlooking London's Regent's Park. Becca played on her iPad while Kat relaxed on the couch and scrolled through the news from MyLondon and the BBC.

They'd been in London for three days already and had settled into the foreign city with the comfort of seasoned travelers. Becca was most in love with the British sayings she heard during their trip. When they first saw Buckingham Palace, Becca shouted to her mom that she was "positively gobsmacked" and then doubled over with laughter. Kat was enamored with watching Becca absorb and react to foreign cities.

A headline caught her eye: JAKE LAURENT VISITS LONDON ON A PRESS TOUR FOR *ZERO CODE*. She didn't read the article, but the headline made her heart quicken. Her eyes wandered to the date and saw it was posted only yesterday. *Zero Code* had just been released, and the early buzz was phenomenal. She hadn't brought herself to see it, but the chatter surrounding the movie was about awards and accolades coming Jake's way. His prominence had skyrocketed, and he'd risen into the space that only a few actors ever reach. He'd truly done it. She swelled with a pride tinged with sadness.

She tossed her phone down and let out a loud sigh.

"What, Momma?" asked Becca, looking up from her iPad.

"I have a friend here also visiting London," she said. "Do you remember Jake from next door? He used to bring you orange Tootsie Pops?"

"Kinda," Becca said with the ambivalence of youth, and she went back to her device.

Kat smiled at the simple response. Before she could overthink it, she swiped opened her phone, pulled up her messaging app, and scrolled to Jake's contact information. She winced re-reading the final text chain between them. Jake had texted her daily to say he was sorry and tried to get her to talk to him.

She breathed out slowly as she read her response to his repeated apologies:

K: Jake. Please stop. Even if you weren't trying to hurt me, you did. If you loved me, you never would've used me. When we were an us, were you just playing a part? I know you'll have a great career. You're the best actor I know.

He didn't respond and at the time, Kat was relieved. Leveraging their relationship in the press was the largest betrayal he could have enacted, and Kat was in a panicked anger. Her anger was warranted, but her panic subsided as she realized that social cycles are indeed short.

Although embarrassing, the Twitter boycott of PathMobile devices was short-lived. In fact, sales eventually went up due to the extra exposure. More embarrassing were the endless memes circulated via company email and slack at her expense.

The most hateful was the vitriol she received on social media, but those accounts were easily shut down and that echo chamber could be ignored.

It turned out to be a frenzy that started fast but burned out just as quickly. She often wondered, if she had not been so afraid, if they could have managed it long-term. *Probably*, was her answer.

Months later, her anger had faded, and panic turned into perspective. She'd done a lot of thinking and breathing in the time away from PathMobile and from Jake. During that time, she'd begun to learn about who she was and how she wanted to navigate the world—not as a widow, not as a mom, or even a professional, but as Kat: a mixture of all and none of those labels.

Before she could convince herself not to, she hit send on a text:

K: Hi. It's me. Kat. In case you deleted me from your phone. I just saw on the news that you're in London. The universe works in funny ways, Becca and I are here right now. Just for fun.

J: . . .

J: Hi. It is good to hear from you.

J:. . .

J: Can I see you while you're in London? Both of you?

J: And for the record, I would never delete you.

Kat hesitated before responding. She needed to see him. Her life had changed course since those eight days in Copenhagen, but the transformation felt incomplete without gaining closure with Jake.

She waited for the sadness to creep in, but she only felt at peace. It felt good to no longer hate him as she understood her role in his betrayal. Her unbending nature had kept him from bringing her into the storm he was facing. She wished they could've figured it out together, all the while knowing she would've tried to unsuccessfully control an uncontrollable situation. She would've been fine with any outcome that pulled Jake out of the public eye, which would've stunted his art, and suffocated him in the end.

At the time, she wasn't strong enough to commit herself to him if it meant making any sacrifices for herself. *He must have felt so alone*, she thought. *He's a good person who made a tough decision.* Taking a deep breath, she responded:

K: Yes. We are staying across from Regent's Park. We could meet near the Marylebone Green playground.

J: Perfect, 4?

K: That works. I'll drop a pin. Text me if you get delayed.

J: I will be there on time. See you then.

Kat set down her phone and nudged Becca with her foot. "Hey, we're going to hang out with my friend this afternoon, at the park. Before then, do you want to go to The Wall Café to drink tea and eat lots of pastries?"

Kat's hands shook as she waited for Jake to arrive. Out of habit, she found an open patch of grass, devoid of people. She spied a playground down a path, but the field was isolated. Becca was climbing a nearby tree, her growing athleticism on full display.

At 3:58 p.m., she saw him jogging toward them, waving. Along with the prerequisite cap and sunglasses, he was wearing casual joggers and a nondescript sweatshirt. He had an orange backpack and, in his hand, a soccer ball still in the packaging.

Kat called for Becca to climb down, and they both walked toward him. She surprised herself with her inability to stop smiling as he approached. He looked good, healthy. She wondered for a second if she should hug him, or maybe shake his hand? *Surely not shake his hand!*

When they got close, Jake did neither of those things. He gave them both a wave and started to rip the ball out of the package.

"Hey, Kat," he said with tentative smile, turning his attention to Becca. "Hi, Becca, I'm Jake, in case you don't remember," he said, reaching down and shaking Becca's hand. She shook it hard, which made him laugh. He tossed the ball to her. "Your mom told me you play soccer, huh?" Jake said, leaning down to face her. "Want to kick around with me a bit? You can shoot, I'll be goalie."

Becca erupted with an enthusiastic "Yes!" and ran toward the open space. Jake ran after her, turning around to jog backward. "Kat, want to join? Although, I'm afraid to let you shoot soccer balls at my face."

She laughed and all of a sudden all the tension was lifted. She shook her head and motioned for him to go ahead without her. She sat down on the grass near a water fountain and watched the two of them play.

Jake set up two water bottles from his backpack to mark goal posts, and Becca was thrilled to try to score goals against Jake. At first, he was letting her kick past him and then he started to block her attempts. She protested and ran down the field kicking the ball. Kat was struck at how free Jake seemed, and she saw joy on his face as he ran after Becca. Kat, putting her face to the sun, soaked up the carefree laughter coming from the field. They chased each other until they were both breathing heavy, and they ran over to her.

"You are so fast," Jake said to Becca as he tossed a water bottle her way. She caught it with both hands.

She looked at him very seriously and said, "You are too . . . for an old person." Jake's eyes opened wide, he clutched his stomach and fell to the ground.

"You wound me with your words!"

Becca giggled in response and tossed the ball up in the air. "Momma, can I go to the playground?"

Kat nodded. "We'll be over here, honey." She gave Becca a kiss before she ran down the path toward the swings. Kat repositioned herself so she could see the play structure from where they were sitting. She thought about how, six months ago, the answer would have been "no," and certainly not where Kat was not within arm's reach of her. She'd come a long way in giving her daughter freedom and was rewarded by watching Becca's confidence soar.

Jake sat up and moved diagonally from her, so as not to block her view. His legs were crossed, knees almost touching hers. "Kat, I didn't think I would ever hear from you." He leaned forward and whispered, "Seeing your text . . . knowing I don't deserve to hear from you . . ." he paused. "Thank-you."

"I wanted to see you," she said. "You look good, Jake, really great . . . happy."

She looked straight in his eyes, clear and sparkly. She felt a surge of genuine affection for him, as everything else melted away. She'd found happiness and, in her quest to understand and heal herself, she'd had a persistent fear that Jake surfaced from their relationship more broken than ever. But she could feel a stillness and contentment radiating off him.

Defaulting to small talk, she asked, "How long are you in London?" He looked away, and she saw him stifle a smile.

"I was in London yesterday. I was in Paris when you texted me," he said, grinning.

Kat couldn't keep the stunned look off her face. "Jake, you didn't need to come back here just for this. We could have talked over the phone," she chided.

"Quick Eurostar ticket, and I'm here. I've missed you," he said. He turned to her and his face became serious. "Kat, you once traveled three thousand, eight hundred, sixty-four miles for me. I figured I could return the favor."

Kat laughed out loud and shook her head. She found herself still so enamored by the sweet, impulsive soul sitting on the grass in front of her. Out of habit, she deflected the moment, changing the subject. "*Zero Code* is getting great buzz. Things are going well for you?"

He nodded. "I have a whole new team, except Roger, and of course, Savannah. I've finally taken control of my career. I needed to grow up and take control of my life." He paused, looking as if he were about to elaborate, but he didn't. "Thanks . . . the movie finally . . . " he stopped speaking and shook his head.

He leaned back on his palms. "Kat, I didn't come all this way to sit here and talk about myself. I'm not going to run away from this . . . what I did . . . it wasn't fair to you . . . to us . . . I am sorry I wasn't strong enough, and I wish—"

She stopped him. "What you did," she said as tears started to burn her eyes, "after getting past my initial anger, I've come to realize it was the best thing that could've happened to us."

"I disagree," Jake said, and Kat could see his jaw tense as he sucked in a breath. His face was a mix of confusion and sadness.

Kat fought to blink back tears. "No, really. I think, no matter what would've happened, I was certainly not ready. We wouldn't have worked. I know that in my heart. Once I got back, I realized my time in Copenhagen was me taking a vacation from my life. I wasn't prepared to do the work to be with you. One of us would've blown up our relationship. You just beat me to it."

Jake looked up to the sky, and Kat could see him blinking back tears as well. "You are being too kind and too forgiving. I don't deserve it."

Kat reached out and rubbed his knee with her thumb. "Jake, what you did pushed me so far out of my perfect, controlled world. And you know what? I was okay. I survived. Until this, I was so afraid to let something happen out of my control that I stopped living. You reminded me that I don't need to be so afraid of life. Becca deserves a mom who is alive."

Jake nodded with a look of attention and understanding, communicating that he was fully processing her words. "Becca . . . she's one great kid," he said.

"She's incredible, and it's a privilege to guide her through part of her life. I love showing her the world. So, every chance we can, we hit the road and explore somewhere new. Over the holidays, we went to Austria to see the Christmas Markets, which I've wanted to do my whole life."

"That sounds amazing," Jake said. "But I have to admit I knew that. I was home this past December for the holidays. I was hoping to run into you, and I nearly broke down when my mom told me you weren't in New York." He gave her a weak smile. "I can't let you keep saying nice things to me, letting me off the hook without telling you I'm sorry. And if I could go back, I would do a lot of things differently."

"I quit my job," Kat blurted out. She registered the surprise on Jake's face.

"Please tell me you weren't forced because of me?" Jake asked, looking down. "I know things got weird for a while. I never meant to hurt your career."

"No, no," Kat said. "I did take a leave of absence right after, but taking that break made me realize I just wanted to stop—stop being in a job that was so all-consuming. God, that job ran my life. I wanted more flexibility to be with Becca. My time with her is short. This moment, when I'm the absolute center of her world, will be gone sooner than I want. In a blink, she'll be off living her own life and I didn't want her entire childhood to be with a mom that looked at her as a task to be completed."

Jake looked at her with a smile. "So what are you doing?"

"I found what I love. I love helping a business grow. I'm consulting with tech start-ups who need a solid business plan and financial projections but aren't ready for a full-time finance officer." She was proud of the financial stability she was able to create without the umbrella of an oppressive corporation. "Also, I balance the books for Ben's old precinct, in exchange for putting Becca and me on their health plan. It helps to keep a foot in that world, for her. I need to allow those who loved him to love her. It gives her a sense of her dad, and as she gets older, that's become even more important."

Jake took a breath. "I'm coming back home . . . at least to New York," he started, "and not just for a visit, but for the next six months. At least."

She raised her eyebrows. It was a surprising move. He'd often expounded that he didn't want to build his career in the US, as it centered around Los Angeles—a city he hated.

"Yeah, I even got my own place finally. I move in next week, but as you can imagine, there's not much to move," he chuckled. "My next project is *Joe Island,* a play by Tania Wells. It's a four-month run minimum and two months of rehearsal."

Kat was even more surprised to hear that his next project was live theater. It was an interesting sidestep for someone who had their pick of films.

He let out a sigh. "It just felt right. This past year, past eighteen months, haven't been easy. I got lost in this chase of fame." He took off his cap and ran his fingers through his hair. "I was so focused on it, I blew up the best thing in my life." He blew out a breath. "Kat, I called you and asked you to fix me, to clean up the mess I was making of my life, and then I shattered us, too. It will be the biggest regret of my life." Jake quickly wiped a tear from his eyes.

Kat reached over and placed her hand in his. She didn't say anything, but physically connected to him as a sign of understanding and forgiveness. He smiled at her tentatively. His thumb lightly caressed the back of her hand.

"Jake. We were both trying to fix each other. That's not a way to build a relationship." She was dangerously close to tears herself. She desperately wanted to focus on something other than their dramatic implosion. Taking a breath to beat back the tears, she said, "Talk to me. Are you excited to do theater again? Be back in New York?"

Jake's face brightened. "I really believe I need to be back in the theater, really hone my craft, get out of the rat race of movie productions. I'll figure it out after that. I told Roger no back-to-back projects. I'm playing the long game with my career."

Kat shot him a smile. She was taking in this new Jake, centered and focused. She looked away to gain sight of Becca. She spotted her on a swing, talking to another girl who looked to be her age.

Kat reached her hand up and waved at Becca for a few seconds and returned it to take Jake's hand once again. "I want to be angry about what happened, but I'm not." Her voice softened. "You called me, I came to you, and it changed my life."

Jake lifted her hand up to his lips and gave it a soft kiss. "You stole my line." He shot her a smile and just like that, she was transported back to a small apartment on the Nyhavn canal. Her mind lingered and indulged in the memories.

Kat felt the buzz of her watch bring her back to the present. She stood up and waved Becca over. "It's getting late, and we have theater tickets to see *Six* tonight."

"You'll love it," said Jake. Becca ran over and Jake threw her the soccer ball. "Hey, do you have room for this? It's for you."

Becca nodded and thanked him. Kat suddenly didn't know what to do with her hands. Jake took over when he high-fived Becca and then gave Kat a half hug and a sweet, quick kiss on the cheek.

"Bye, Jake," she said, and turned to walk away hand in hand with her favorite girl.

"Hey!" she heard him yell. She and Becca turned around to face him.

"When I'm back in New York, can I ask you out?" He was standing there, looking so earnest with a full smile. Kat saw a man who knew what he wanted, no longer an unsure human, searching for anything to escape himself.

Given all that they had experienced together, it was a ridiculous question, but a perfect question all at once.

It took all her resolve not to run back to him, feel his arms around her, and exist once again in his orbit. But she would play the long game too. They needed time to really know each other if there was a future for them. She knew that it wouldn't be simple—nothing ever was—and she couldn't predict what future they could find together. Exploring a future with Jake was a risk she was wanted to take.

"It's a date. Text me when you're back," she said, shooting him a big smile. "We'll figure it out."

epilogue

Four Years Later

Kat sat in her seat and could barely breathe. It might have been the SPANX she was wearing, but most likely, it was just her own nerves. Jake, on the other hand, seemed remarkably calm.

The lights went up for a moment. It was a commercial break. The crowd chatter rose a few decibels as this group of actors, on the night of their largest award show of the year, was never one to stay quiet.

She reached over and laced her fingers with his. "You ready? Your category is up next," she said, squeezing his hand.

"Yes," he said. "I'm just happy to be nominated . . . I'm just happy to be nominated." He repeated the mantra under his breath, gave her a wink, and laughed.

Kat smiled at his attempt to convince himself that he'd be happy either way. She knew he would be, but it was still okay to want to win. He was no stranger to this moment. It had been nearly three years since they'd been here, at this very same awards show, when Jake was nominated for the first time for *Zero Code*.

He hadn't won that night, but Kat remembered the evening as one of their best. It was their first significant public appearance since Copenhagen, and they went late into the night to every after-party, enjoying the experience and each other. They'd watched the sun come up, still in their fancy clothes, from the roof of their LA hotel. They were in a blissful state of new love. She laughed to herself. Honestly, they still were.

It didn't mean the last four years had been simple. They'd had to figure out how to bring their lives together. Despite their best efforts, the lack of privacy was the hardest for Kat to get used to. It was something they navigated together with the help of a PR team. She was no longer scared of the public scrutiny, mostly just annoyed. Jake was uncompromising with his direction regarding no coordinated press around Becca.

One of things Kat loved the most was watching Jake and Becca's relationship grow. Jake gave her space and time to let their relationship bloom organically. Over time, it had grown into a beautiful friendship and eventually one of paternal comfort for Becca.

In order to grow as an artist, Jake focused on theater work, which kept him in New York. He did films and animation voice work, focused more on the quality of the script than the size of the role. He often spent weeks, not months, on location. Although Kat wanted him to follow his heart and take any job he loved, Jake was always quick to say that, by sticking close to New York, he was indeed following his heart.

But when Garren had called him for a second film, there wasn't a question. Despite the required four months in Sweden, Kat had insisted he go. It was the only film in years where Jake accepted a lead role, but at Jake's request, the majority of his shooting schedule was aligned with Becca's school break. They all enjoyed a magical summer in Stockholm together while Jake put everything into his performance. Garren and Jake found a strong artistic collaboration, and it showed. Here he was, nominated for Best Actor.

With thirty seconds left of the commercial break, the lights started to fade. Kat saw Garren take his seat right behind Jake.

He reached up and squeezed Jake's shoulder from behind before the lights went dark.

As the announcers read the names for Best Actor, she found herself holding her breath along with Jake. It was a tough category and the predictions were not in Jake's favor. Kat tempered her excitement and prepared herself to remind him of his earlier mantra.

And then it happened. They opened the envelope and read his name. Everything moved in slow motion. She looked at Jake with tears in her eyes, and he sat back in his seat, stunned.

Garren leaned forward said, "you did it" as he shook both of Jake's shoulders.

Jake snapped out it, stood up, hugged Garren and turned to Kat. They embraced while everyone patted Jake on the back.

"Get up there, my love. Take your moment," she said in his ear. And he walked up and took the stage.

"Wow," he said, letting out a breath. "I didn't expect that to happen," he said, and the crowd laughed. Kat knew it was actually true. He hadn't even brought himself to write a speech, he was so sure he wouldn't win.

Jake thanked the Academy, his producers, and his family. He was talking fast, knowing he had under a minute.

He looked out into the audience. "Thank-you to Garren Christensen, the world's best director. Your vision, your drive, and your inability to allow any bullshit on your set"—the crowd laughed—"makes me bring my A game every single day. I just want to be the best for you. Any actors sitting out there . . . I guess there are a lot"—the crowd laughed again—"if you get a chance to work for this man, don't hesitate, always say yes.

"I also want to say thank-you to Kat. I have so much to say and so little time. You came to me when I lost myself. I wouldn't be standing here if not for you. You all may not believe this, but I can be a lot"—the crowd chuckled once more—"but this woman. . . ." His eyes began to tear up. "She sees me. And you have always made me better, Kat. We make each other better. There is no one I want to have all the moments with more than you."

Jake paused for a second and took a deep breath. Kat could see he was trying to focus his thoughts. He blew out his breath and a smile lit up his entire face. He looked straight into the camera and said, "And to my favorite girl out there . . ." He dug into his pocket and held up a small object. The camera zoomed in on an orange Tootsie Pop. "Thanks for sending me with a good luck charm . . . It worked! I love you, sweetheart."

The music started playing, and Jake walked off stage. Kat's face was wet with tears. Tears for the man she loved on his greatest night. Tears for her daughter who was growing up with so many people who loved her. And the tears for herself? Kat's tears were simply physical drops of joy.

acknowledgments

Bringing the story of Kat and Jake to life would not have happened without the support of many, many people. I had very early readers who encouraged me to keep going, despite missing entire character arcs (Suz M & Kristin H). Friends who, despite my inability to use punctuation, kept reading (Angie). I thank every early reader for the thoughtful feedback to make sure Kat came through as a complex, strong woman and their romance felt authentic (Suzanne, Dana, Penny, Kari, Hayley, Colette, Sarah x 2, Linda, Brianna and Emily).

The biggest acknowledgment is to my family. Scott, you were instrumental in bringing this to life. From procuring a laptop in under twenty-four hours, to putting up with late night typing, you continue to be unwavering in your support. To Savy, you were the inspiration to finish and my creative partner throughout the development of this story. Thank you for being you. I simply love being your mom.

I dedicate this entire novel to my mom, Carol. My biggest wish in life is that you were still on this earth. I can only imagine the Sunday phone calls we'd be having about this adventure. I came to understand that writing Kat's story was the outpouring of my own grief. Arm in arm, Mom.

discussion questions

1. If you were Kat, would you have made the same decision to go to Copenhagen? Why or Why not?

2. How did you feel about Kat and Jake's chemistry and compatibility? Was their romance believable to you? Why or why not?

3. Did you relate to the feeling of being "stuck" in life?

4. Do you think the setting (Copenhagen) added to the story?

5. Which character did you relate to the most?

6. How did the novel explore themes of love, trust, family and identity?

7. How do you feel social media has changed pop culture and/or celebrities?

8. What do you think happens to the main couple after the novel ends?

about the author

Shelby Saville resides in a suburb west of Chicago, but she grew up in a town of 2,000 people and is still a small-town girl at heart. Her first writing job was for the *Lacon Home Journal*, where she covered local news. But the city was calling, and when she got her dream job in the advertising industry, she moved to Chicago. She's spent the last twenty-five years at Publicis Media, where she's focused on media investment—how advertising space is bought and sold. When not at her computer, Shelby can be found in the cafes of Chicago and Elmhurst, IL, or hanging at home with her husband, Scott, teenage daughter, three dogs, and one mean cat.

Looking for your next great read?

We can help!

Visit www.shewritespress.com/next-read
or scan the QR code below for a list
of our recommended titles.

She Writes Press is an award-winning
independent publishing company founded to
serve women writers everywhere.